P9-BIW-448

GETTING MARRIED IN BUFFALO JUMP

Also by Susan Haley

A Nest of Singing Birds

Getting Married in Buffalo Jump

Susan Haley

Macmillan of Canada
A Division of Canada Publishing Corporation
Toronto, Ontario, Canada

Publisher's Note: This novel is a work of fiction. Names, characters, places, and incidents either are the product of the author's imagination or are used fictitiously, and any resemblance to actual persons, living or dead, events, or locales is entirely coincidental.

Macmillan of Canada
A Division of Canada Publishing Corporation
Toronto, Ontario, Canada

Canadian Cataloguing in Publication Data

Haley, Susan Charlotte, date.
Getting married in Buffalo Jump
ISBN 0-7715-9903-X
I. Title.
PS8565.A4334G48 1987 C813'.43 C86-093863-8
PR9199.3.H333G48 1987

Designed by Steven N. Stathakis

10 9 8 7 6 5 4 3 2 1

First Edition

GETTING MARRIED IN BUFFALO JUMP

1

Alexander Bresnyachuk

Sophie Ware, standing on the corner of the playground among the caterpillars, thinking, This has got to be a joke.

Last night, Alexander Bresnyachuk, leaning back in an orange plastic chair at the Buffalo Jump Café—they were there after the movie, a vampire movie at the Buffalo Jump Theatre. Leaning back, as I was saying, in an orange plastic chair, holding a coffee spoon—or, no, toying with a coffee spoon, which he held in longish masculine fingers, with a trace of hair on the backs of longish masculine fingers. Toying with a coffee spoon that he was inspecting closely with moody gray eyes, not leaning back in an orange plastic chair, but rather leaning forward over the Formica-topped table, Alexander Bresnyachuk . . .

The bell rang and Sophie gave it up.

It was undoubtedly a joke, and for this reason she was giving absolutely no thought to it, not even one hour of precious existence, although thirty-five more years of teaching kindergarten could hardly be regarded as . . .

Sophie Ware had met Alexander Bresynachuk again in her own farmyard after nearly fifteen years, on a Chinook weekend, the last in March. She was pitching dirty straw and manure into a wheelbarrow, and the western wind was blowing strongly down the back of her neck between one of her mother's headscarves and her father's old yard jacket.

She had already spotted Rudolph Bresnyachuk's long black car coming smoothly up the drive, and she began to mutter in the common parlance of the schoolyard:

"Rudi B. eats mice and frogs,
His mother cuts his fingernails . . ."

She was letting out her land to Rudolph, but he never did any of the dirty work.

"He uses his toes to pick his nose . . ."

continued Sophie, hearing the slam of the car door behind her. Rudolph had come to talk about this year's contract over a cozy cup of tea with Mother. She straightened up to stretch, and looked around, wondering about a second slam. Then she saw Alexander coming from the other side of the car.

"Whenever he takes his shoes off!"

Sophie thought to herself simply, Goodness gracious, that's Alexander Bresnyachuk! and continued to strain her shoulders back, hands on her hips, staring at him blankly.

"Hi, Sophie," said Rudi, pausing only briefly on his way to the back door. He looked bustling and preoccupied as usual, his full red lips pouted out through a couple of days' growth of beard. Sophie diverted herself momentarily with the suspicion that he had not bothered to get out of bed since Wednesday; she wondered whether he could see his feet over his stomach when he was lying down.

"Hi, Rudi," she said, then glanced again at Alexander. "Hi," she added shyly. He was standing with his back to the blowing, looking between the pitchfork and the full wheelbarrow.

"Comin' in?" said Rudi. He nodded at the kitchen door, his eyes gliding easily over the manure pile.

"I'll give you a hand," said Alexander to Sophie, and her surprised consciousness that she was looking at Rudi's prodigal younger brother disappeared before a full appreciation of his physical qualities. Not only was he taller and bigger and tougher and flatter than Rudi; he was nice, he was very good-looking.

With an effort she collected herself and beat him to the wheelbarrow.

"This is my reward," she said firmly, heaving up the handles. "You can do the next load if you want."

"Yeah, help her finish up," said Rudi bossily; but Alexander was already lifting the pitchfork, tidying up the pile. Sophie trundled off to the garden, realizing that she was in love.

It was not that there were not many men who would offer to help with a manure fork; it was that there were not many men. Sophie had begun to wonder whether there were any at all.

She began making some furtive adjustments to her clothing at once. Not that one could wish to be seen doing farmwork in a chiffon evening dress with ruffles at neck and wrists—or in a wheat-colored Italian knit two-piece—or even, Sophie comforted herself, in a pair of designer jeans with casual silk blouse and thin gold chain. She therefore merely removed the headscarf with scenes of Lethbridge, and also the woolen knitted gloves, and scraped as much of the muck off her cowboy boots as possible on the way back from the garden.

Alexander got the remainder of the manure into the wheelbarrow and picked up the handles.

"My turn, I guess," he said, as he wheeled it off.

Sophie hesitated, then ran after him.

"What are you doing here, Alexander?" she inquired, keeping up.

"Workin' for Rudi," said Alexander.

"So you've come back?" This struck her instantly as a silly question.

"Yeah," he replied agreeably. "Where should I put this down? Here?" He looked over the muddy garden, undug from last fall, a few pathetic-looking brussels sprouts standing out of the snow patches.

"Well—anywhere along here, yes," said Sophie, feeling sympathetic to the garden in its deshabille. He did not seem to approve of the way Rudi had left it. After he dumped the wheelbarrow he went over and jerked the tall stalks from their bed of snow.

"It's a mess, isn't it?" she remarked, still following.

"I hear your dad died," he said.

Sophie nodded, momentarily not trusting her voice to reply.

"So that's why you've got Rudi"—he looked around disgustedly—"doin' the work?"

"Well, I'm teaching, you see. And Mother—" Sophie paused. "We couldn't get anyone else," she said bluntly. It seemed an odd kind of thing to say to Rudi's brother, but he was certainly sharing her opinion of Rudi's treatment of the farm.

Alexander kicked thoughtfully with the heel of his workboot and dislodged a clump of grass.

He had been the star center forward of the soccer team when he was in grade twelve and Sophie was fourteen. He had long outgrown his beanstalk skinniness, but not that physical expression of perfect strength and coordination. He no longer looked like a runner, but he could have been a wrestler or a boxer. He had thick dark bushy hair, and red lips like Rudi, but Sophie saw as he looked down at her that his eyes were a distant cloudy gray.

"Well, I guess I'll be doin' it," he said. "This year."

And it was as a consequence of that assertion that Sophie, somewhat later, signed up Rudi Bresnyachuk on a contract for one more harvest. She did not even bother to subject him to the session of Maoist vilification she had been preparing for the occasion. Nothing, not even exile to a tractor factory in Outer Mongolia, or ten years hard in the Gulag, would have made any difference to Rudi. But Alexander drank tea without sugar and took his boots off outside the kitchen door.

As April turned to May, Sophie had no reason to regret this decision. Alexander worked very hard; he arrived in the morning before she got up, and usually came back after supper and worked on the machinery till long after dark. It was he who took off the storm windows and fixed the washing machine; he even looked after the horse and established an uneasy truce with the dog, who was kept in the basement during Rudi's infrequent visitations.

But as for her other hopes, nothing was coming of them, either when she accompanied him to Botvinnik's Seed and Feed, or when she drove him home in the truck after the long days of work in the fields and in the barn, or even later, when he took her to the cattle show in Calgary.

Not many men who invited you to a cattle show just took you to a cattle show, but there it was.

They went to see the Beefaloes.

Driving into Calgary, he had let fall a few meager pieces of information about himself.

"When I left here I never thought I'd come back," he said.

Sophie nodded. He had quit high school in the spring of his senior year. His sister Marfa was in her class. Marfa had been fifteen, a year older than Sophie.

"But when you been workin' a few years on the rigs up north, you start to think," he went on. "It isn't the cold and the loneliness—it's what're you doin' it for."

"I guess you might wonder that about any job," said Sophie. "I often wonder it about kindergarten."

"Do you?" he asked, turning his head to look at her briefly, inscrutably.

They didn't waste much time on the Beefaloes. Alexander spent half an hour talking to the owner of a Charolais bull while Sophie wandered about disconsolately. Then he stood her to a hot dog and they went home. Sophie drove on the way back, concentrating on the bucking steering mechanism of their old farm truck.

"That wasn't anything to write home about," remarked Alexander. He slumped in the seat beside her.

"It was all right."

"Yeah, but you wouldn't waste good land like yours on them buffaloes," he replied. "They're range cattle. What you need is a herd of purebreds—something fancy—maybe a couple of bulls."

"That's true," said Sophie, resigning herself to this conversation. "Dad was going to do something like that with horses. That's why we have Rocinante." Rocinante was her own horse, an Arab stallion. "We're going to sell, you know. Mother wants to move to the Coast," she added.

"The place is yours, isn't it?"

"Yes." This was the closest he had ever come to a personal question, and she decided to answer it thoroughly. "I can't keep it," she said. "I'd like to—for Dad's sake, if nothing else. But we can't go on letting it out. And then Mother really wants to go."

Alexander sat up and lit a cigarette.

"What about you?" he asked. "Where would you go?"

Sophie shrugged. "Maybe with Mother. I don't know. The trouble is that nobody wants to buy except the damn developers. And I won't sell to a developer!"

"Why don't you farm it yourself?" he asked. "It's real good land."

"I don't know anything about farming," said Sophie.

Alexander seemed to take this answer as definitive, for he lapsed into silence, finishing his cigarette.

Sophie drove on grimly through the darkness. Most men who invited you to a cattle show would eventually get around to proposing something else at some point during the evening—a sleazy motel, maybe; she would have settled for a field. It was a warm night. He appeared to have gone to sleep.

She turned off onto the section road leading to the uplands across by the Reserve, where he was boarding with his parents. Alexander woke up with a startled grunt as she crossed a pothole at the foot of his father's driveway.

"You're home," Sophie announced.

"Oh boy, I was sleepin'!" said Alexander, arching his back and stretching out his legs.

"So I noticed."

"Did I snore?"

"Not much," said Sophie nastily.

"Jesus, Sophia, I'm sorry," he said, as she drew up into the farmyard.

"All right," said Sophie, forgiving him because of his use of this form of her name. Nobody ever used it. She wanted to hear him say it again. "You didn't snore."

She stopped the truck neatly and reached for the ignition switch.

"See you tomorrow," said Alexander, smothering a yawn. He paused outside with the door open, appearing to notice Sophie's expression under the yard light. "Good night," he said, shutting it firmly.

It was an Armageddon year. It was the height of the caterpillar cycle. A volcano had erupted less than five hundred miles away, and there was a fine rain of ash in the air mixed with the dust of a dry spring.

"Keep your chin up, Sophie!" said Madeleine LeJeur in the staff room the next afternoon. "Only one more of those damn caterpillar inspections, and we're through for the day!"

They had been involved for several weeks in a death struggle with the children to keep caterpillars out of the school.

"How was the cattle show?" This was Robert Markovich, the principal of the elementary school. Their affair had terminated shortly before the death of her father, a year ago, but Robert pursued a campaign of casual espionage.

"Lots of cattle," Sophie parried.

"So you've decided not to sell out, then? Going to raise cattle?"

"No."

"No to which?" asked Robert smoothly. "You went with Alexander Bresnyachuk, I hear."

"I wanted to see a Beefalo," said Sophie.

Robert raised his eyebrows. "Don't you see him every day?"

"It's Friday night," said Alexander. "I thought maybe you'd be goin' out with somebody."

"No."

"Well, I got some things to do on the place, but could we go to the show afterwards? The nine-o'clock show in Buffalo Jump?"

"Okay." Sophie tried to keep her tone as indifferent as his.

"I don't know what it's goin' to be," he said doubtfully. "Probably some monster movie or something."

"That doesn't matter." Sophie had not been to a movie in this fashion since she was about eighteen. Remembering the cattle show, she determined to be more forthright this time. Perhaps he was just shy.

"I'm about finished seeding," said Alexander, accompanying her across the farmyard to the back door.

"That's wonderful," said Sophie, really meaning it.

"I'll get it finished up tomorrow for sure."

Several hours later they were in the Buffalo Jump Café. Alexander had tried commendably not to sleep through the movie (*Vampira Meets the Great Godzilla*). Otherwise this was turning out much like the cattle show, but with even less to talk about. Discontentedly, Sophie munched her limp and slightly dusty salad greens.

The only way it was paying off was in the horror it afforded her mother. The cattle show she had not regarded as a date. But when Sophie came downstairs at eight-thirty, wearing a yellow summer dress and with her hair freshly washed and dried, Mother demanded, "Where are you going, dear?"

"To a movie with Alexander."

"Sophie! He's our farmhand!"

"What difference does that make?"

"Oh, Sophie!" Mother wailed. "He's not educated! He's a Ukrainian! He doesn't even speak good English!"

Sophie was now wondering whether Alexander could talk at all.

"Boy!" he said at last, breaking a profound silence, and putting down his hamburger. "You'd never know this was beef-raisin' country!"

Sophie continued to munch unhappily. There was nothing to say to this. How to be forthright? He gave her no opening. Besides, he ought to remember what the food was like in the Buffalo Jump Café.

"I've got something to ask you, Sophia," he said suddenly, putting his elbows on the Formica-topped table.

Sophie glanced up, feeling no surge of hope. This was entirely too prosaic a beginning. The air was charged with lead, not with lightning. She noticed sadly how nice his hands were: large, long-fingered, and smoothly brown on the backs. But whatever he was going to ask her would have nothing to do with that.

"I want a place," he said. "I guess that's why I come back here."

"A place?" Sophie decided to give up on the salad.

"Yeah. A farm."

"Oh?" She wondered whether she was catching his drift. "Do you want to buy us—me—out?" she asked carefully.

"Not exactly." He was gazing at her seriously, and reluctantly she raised her eyes. A real-estate deal? In the Buffalo Jump Café? Stranger things had happened. When she was working in a carpet factory in East Pakistan around 1973, she had seen children sold on the street. But not in the Buffalo Jump Café! Not my farm!

"I'm not goin' to lie about this, Sophia. I've been thinkin' about it for a while. We both got something the other wants."

Well, you're right there, Sophie thought, and laughed nervously.

"You want to keep your place," he went on steadily. "And I want to farm it."

"So what are you proposing? A written agreement?" Sophie was becoming frightened. She wiped her palms on her napkin. "We've got one with Rudi."

"I'm proposing a marriage," said Alexander.

2

A Curious Proposal

"No, you're not!"

"We could have a long engagement. Till after harvest," he pointed out. "Then you could see—"

"See what?" cried Sophie.

"See that I can do it," he replied.

Sophie was temporarily speechless. She could not believe this was happening. She stared at him angrily.

"I can't put it to you any plainer," said Alexander patiently. "I'd be a good husband, and I think you'd make a pretty good wife."

"My God!"

The waitress slouched over to their table, understanding Sophie's cry to be a sign of some complaint against the food.

"All finished?" she asked, hardly bothering to put the requisite coaxing tone into her voice.

"Oh yes," muttered Sophie, pushing her plate away.

She stood up and walked to the large windows at the front of the restaurant, feeling a vacancy where her heart had earlier been full of birdsong.

He touched her arm, having apparently paid, and she followed him sullenly out of the café and back to the truck, parked in front of the theater.

They got in, Alexander taking the driver's side. He lit a cigarette.

"Did I insult you?" he asked presently.

"No," said Sophie. She had never been so insulted in her life. Unfortunately, she was still violently attracted to him. This added injury to insult.

"I know it's not much of a deal," he said, smoking quietly. "But you haven't seen what I could do with the place, Sophia. It makes sense if you really want to keep the place."

"When did you think of this?" she asked abruptly. "The other night, when I was telling you about trying to sell?"

"Nope. I already knew that. I've been thinking about it for quite a while."

"Since when?" she demanded. She recognized in herself the paranoia of the farmer: on the one side a tolerant government, listless in subsidy, unreasonably patient on the subject of irrigation; on the other side rapacious, intolerant ethnic minorities consuming the landscape like locusts. A march of invaders from the East, all mounted on huge green Mercedes-Benz reapers.

"Your mother told me to ask around about sellin' the horse last month," he said.

"Rocinante?"

"Yeah. He's eatin' up the hay crop."

"I won't sell Rocinante!" Sophie covered her face with her hands. Rocinante was the last of her father's projects. She could remember sitting on her father's hospital bed, making plans for Rocinante.

"Okay, but you can't board out a stallion, Sophia."

"Oh Christ!" said Sophie. She pulled herself together. "Well that's true," she said. "I'll have to sell him."

"Your mother said you wouldn't sell the place to nobody," Alexander went on reasonably. "Not just to them developers."

"It has to be the right person, that's all!"

"Don't cry, Sophia."

"I'm not crying!"

"You've got to think about it," said Alexander. "I know that." He started up the truck.

Sophie hunched her shoulders and rocked back and forth, trying to exchange tears for body English. She began to recover on the dark country road out of Buffalo Jump. The radio murmured country-and-western. Sophie reached out and snapped it off.

"Stop a minute," she said. They had turned up the section road on the western boundary of the Ware farm.

Alexander obediently switched off the ignition and let the truck drift to a halt on the long straight road. The moon was rising over a poplar windbreak ahead of them. Sophie recognized it as one of the rows of poplars planted by her father the year she was born.

"Don't you like me at all?" she asked, rather piteously.

"Sure," said Alexander. He laughed. "Think I'd ask you to marry me if I didn't?"

"But that isn't a reason to marry someone," said Sophie, puzzled. "You aren't in love with me. You can't be."

"Love is something else," he said. "I'm askin' you to marry me, Sophia."

"Couldn't we just go to bed together like reasonable adult human beings?" she asked, annoyed.

"That has nothing to do with this."

"People don't just get married!"

"Sure they do," said Alexander, looking at her attentively. "When they want to have something together."

"Yes—but—" Sophie gasped. "Have something together? Have my farm together? I already have that!"

"Yeah. But you're not doin' anything with it. And besides," he went on brutally, "you need a man. Don't you want to have a family, Sophia?"

"Are you suggesting that there's something wrong with me? I'm only twenty-eight!" said Sophie, outraged.

"I'm not suggesting anything," said Alexander. "I'll put it to you the other way around. I want that. I'm thirty-two. I want a woman and a family and a place."

"Yes, but the way you say it! It sounds as though just any old woman would do!"

"No," he said patiently. "But this is old-style, see? I haven't got anything, Sophia. So you've got to decide."

"Oh," she said, partly mollified.

"I know I could do something with that place of yours. I've been wastin' my life for fourteen years, but I know what I can do."

"Why don't you just buy it, then?" she asked.

"Because I want to have a wife," he answered. "A farmer's got to have a wife. I think you'd be real good at it."

"Are you kidding! The only thing I know about is horses!"

Alexander smiled into the moonlight. She saw this out of the corner of her eye.

There was a kind of tolerance, a condescension in this smile that she didn't like. But now he was looking straight at her again.

"Let's go home," said Sophie with finality. "The answer is no!"

"Sure," said Alexander. "You've got to think about it some more." He started up the truck.

Sophie had a lot of time to think about it all weekend.

They were planting the garden. Alexander harrowed the whole field, then turned over the home garden by hand. This absorbed most of his time on Saturday.

It did not escape Sophie's attention that he had failed

in his boast that he would have seeded all the fields by the weekend. She was supposed to be seeing whether he could do it, after all.

There seemed to be an unspoken agreement between Alexander and her mother that they were putting the home field into cabbage—a much larger crop than usual. Patiently, with rake and fertilizer pail, they constructed long rows of cabbage.

Sophie was not accustomed to this. Usually she put in the garden herself, a half-acre plot of mixed broccoli and carrots, dill and lettuce, spinach and sunflowers. It was something that she had always done, that she loved doing.

The cabbage plot was between Alexander and her mother. And it took up five acres at least, consuming the home garden entirely.

"Why so much cabbage?" Sophie asked her mother. They were having a tea break on Sunday morning. On Saturday night they had all been fatigued to the point of speechlessness, especially Alexander.

"I think it's too much cabbage," she said determinedly.

"They're gettin' thirty cents a pound at that Hutterite market by the Stampede Grounds," said Alexander, blowing on his tea.

"But—" Sophie was horrified. "Who's going to take cabbage to market! We're not Hutterites!"

"Well, dear." Her mother looked at her pacifically. "If they can get thirty cents—"

"Mother!" Sophie looked suspiciously from one to the other. This was so unlike her mother's usual attitude toward ethnic minorities that she could not possibly be the source of such an idea.

"Why, yes, dear," said her mother, surprised and evidently hurt.

They had to stretch caterpillar nets—long, hoop-strung structures to protect the young plants. Alexander was fond of the most prosaic order of vegetables, it seemed. The cabbage family predominated even in their own garden, with rutabagas and potatoes coming a close second. Sophie's newfangled ideas about mixed vegetables and flower and herb plantings were getting short shrift on the endless rows: draw a line with the rake handle, dribble the seed, back with the business end of the rake, then back again with the heavy irrigation pipes. Hoop, hoop, hoop—up and down, then string the net. There was no time for tetraploid dill, dark opal basil, or little clumps of marigolds.

"Put down the hose," said Alexander with a smile. "You're gettin' wet."

Sophie was standing in front of him by the pipes, winded and with her head down, holding out the dripping hose.

"What are we going to do with it all?" she moaned.

"Sell it, mostly."

"How? Why?" It was nearly dark and they weren't through yet.

"This reminds me of the old days, Alexander," said Mother, coming up with her rake, her straw hat hanging down her back. "You can make a fortune if you keep it up in a caterpillar year." She was sprightly in an old dress, cheerful, and hardly any the worse for the wear.

"This well's good," Sophie heard Alexander say as she turned and plodded down the row again. "It doesn't dry up, does it?"

"Never yet."

"Goin' to be a drought, they say."

"All the better," said Mother merrily.

Sophie was up early for school the following morning. She pulled an old short blue dress over her head and made her way, barefoot, to the kitchen.

"Hello, Sophia."

"Where are you going, dear? Breakfast is just—"

"I'll be right back."

She stared, stunned, out over the fields of net-protected cabbage. It was hard to believe.

Alexander joined her.

"Looks nice, doesn't it?" he said.

Sophie heard the pride and pleasure in his voice and turned her head to look at him coldly.

"I was goin' to ask you where you wanted to put the flowers," said Alexander. "I dug up a place around the side of the house." He led the way.

More startled than anything else by his sense of garden proprieties, Sophie planted the sunflower and zucchini seeds she had had in her pocket all weekend. Alexander weeded a hedge of currant bushes nearby.

"Sophie! Breakfast! School! You don't have much time!" Mother called.

"Coming!"

Watching him covertly, she encircled the zucchinis with parsley. When Alexander weeded, he did it on his hands and knees. He was nothing if not thorough.

"Can she bake a cherry pie,
Billy boy, Billy boy?
Can she bake a cherry pie,
charming Billy?"

hummed Sophie on her way to the staff room that day.

Robert Markovich appeared suddenly beside her. In the days of their affair he had often turned up unexpectedly like this; Sophie used to find it funny.

He began bustling her in the direction of the nurse's office. It was a place where they had taken refuge in the past. Sophie allowed herself to be pushed into the narrow room between the stretcher and the desk. Robert was always amusing, whatever else he was.

"Strong-arm stuff," he muttered, kicking the door shut behind him. "It's the only way."

He advanced on her and Sophie retreated, laughing but slightly alarmed, her arms out at full stretch to prevent him from getting too close. The nurse's swivel chair butted against the backs of her knees and she fell backwards into it, kicking him sharply and accidentally in the shin.

"Ow! My God, woman!"

"Sorry."

"Oh, not at all!" he said, hunching over his leg. "Your karate instructor would be proud."

"Did you want to say something to me?" asked Sophie innocently. She perceived that he had had some elaborate tease in mind. Kicking him was a satisfactory shortcut through the preliminaries, she felt.

Robert straightened up and limped over to the stretcher. He perched there, eyeing her severely.

"I have nothing against Ukrainians," he remarked. "I'm a Uke myself. Mostly a Uke," he added provisionally.

Sophie folded her arms. So this was his game. Robert loved to tease. It had been the basis of their whole relationship, if you could call it a basis—or, she reflected, if you could call it a relationship.

Robert leaned back on his arm, giving up on the pretense of nursing his wounded shin.

"You've been seen," he began, "with a Uke. On Friday night. In the theater, and then afterwards"—he raised his eyebrows—"in the Buffalo Jump Café."

"This is really none of your—"

He wasn't the slightest bit interested in her any longer; but the prospect of competition in any field excited Robert.

"Deny it not, darling! You were on your way to the No-Tell Motel with Alexander Bresnyachuk."

"What is it to you?" said Sophie, careless of the truth.

Robert loved women. The trouble was that he loved *all* women. Sophie no longer had time for this.

"I am here to warn you," he said coldly. "Watch it, Sophie! However he may have reveled in your—ahem!—that boy wants your farm."

"If that's all you wanted to tell me . . ." said Sophie, with a scornful toss of her head.

She knew that Robert wanted not so much to tell her

something as to have her tell him. Robert's major interest in life was explaining people to themselves. He was much too good at it for her to risk more time in his company. She rose to her feet and he watched her make for the door with an interested sparkle in his eyes.

She was in the hallway when he caught up with her.

"It's not that he's a Uke—I told you that already." He walked her down the corridor—slight, weedy, straw blond—somehow managing to *patter* at her side. "Nor is it that he's a creep. I'm a bit of a creep myself. And I don't think it's his coveting your—ahem! I covet it, too! But—"

He had been marking off these points on his fingers, like the grade-eight teacher he was. Now he stopped to emphasize his words, and Sophie strode on into the staff room, leaving him behind, his fourth finger still raised.

Sophie was just finishing up some paper chains after school. It had taken her quite a while to untangle the fussy things and then to hang them. Now she was depending stiff cardboard letters from the hanging loops.

Someone appeared behind her and Sophie glanced around. It was Madeleine LeJeur, the other kindergarten teacher. Madeleine looked at the paper chains with a professional eye and stretched out a long red fingernail to touch a swinging letter *M*.

"Like it?" said Sophie. She got along with Madeleine, even though rumor said she ate little boys.

"Looks like a lot of work. Tell me, are you intending to stay here till you finish this, Sophie?"

"Yes. Why?" Sophie began scrubbing away the glue on her hands preparatory to cutting out some more letters from bristol board.

"Well, then, I wonder whether you know that your, um, *suitor* is waiting for you in the parking lot."

"What?"

"It is causing a lot of talk in the staff room. Robert, in fact—"

"This is getting beyond a joke!" snarled Sophie, whirling past Madeleine and down the corridor.

"What are you doing here?" she demanded of Alexander a moment later, getting into the truck and slamming the door angrily. Her own car was gone from the parking lot.

"Waitin' for you," he replied. "I thought maybe it would be better if I waited outside."

"What? Where's my car?"

"Your mother took it," he said. "I brought her into town. She said she was goin' to do some shopping in the Grove."

"Oh."

Sophie now began to meditate on his assumption that she didn't want him to come into the school. He was right. How did he know?

Alexander started up the truck and pulled out onto the highway. Sophie opened her window and let the breeze blow over her face and through her hair. The whole matter was beginning to take on a decidedly threatening aspect.

"Alexander," she said. It might be a good idea to tell him this.

Instantly his attention was directed upon her. Sophie froze with terror.

He pulled off the highway onto the next section road and stopped the truck over a hummock beyond the railroad tracks.

"You been thinkin' about it?" he asked quietly.

"No. Yes. About what?"

"About gettin' married."

"Of course not," said Sophie.

Alexander lit a cigarette. He sat there, smoking, in three-quarter profile, while Sophie grappled with what she wanted to say.

"You're not in love with me," she said finally, gasping slightly.

"No." He smiled.

"Then *why*? What *is* this?" she cried.

"Like I said, I want to marry you."

"But you're not—if you don't—"

"I'm not hiding anything, Sophia," he said. "It's real simple. You want to keep the place. I want a place."

"Yes, but—people don't get married on that basis!"

"What basis *do* they get married on, then?"

She shrugged.

"Well . . . love, shared interests, things like that. You're making it sound like some kind of a *deal*."

"Yeah. That's what it is." He folded his arms, and the muscles bulged out under the sleeves of the T-shirt he was wearing. Sophie swallowed and looked away. Her fascination with this sort of detail was unhealthy under the circumstances.

"If we're going to be honest," she said, "I don't see what's in it for me at all."

"You'd have a working farm. And you'd be my wife."

"Well, I'm glad you included that little hitch in your description. I thought there was something like that in the fine print."

"This is the way they did it in the old country," he said.

"*Your* old country, maybe. Not mine."

"Sure. Yours too. If I just wanted a woman, I'd go down to the Buffalo Jump Bar and get one. Maybe you've done some things like that yourself. Love and all that other stuff's got nothing to do with gettin' married. You get married because you want to get married."

Sophie looked out the open window into the slough beyond the ditch. A couple of teals had set up housekeeping there, and were floating in circles on the tiny pond.

"I want to have kids, too," said Alexander.

She thought they were cinnamon teals, although one could hardly tell from looking at the colors of the female.

She was the usual dull duck brown. The male was exceedingly handsome. What he saw in the female she could not imagine.

"Let me just put it to you once more," he said seriously. "I've been around. I've been around too much and I'm tired of it. I want a place, and I want a wife, and I want to have kids. You're a real nice girl, Sophia. I think I'd make you a pretty good husband. So? What about it?"

"What if I said"—Sophie could feel herself blushing slightly—"that I'd want to sleep with you first?"

Was she bargaining with him?

"You could say that." He smiled.

It was now up to him to make a move. He was not making it. Sophie made a small hostile noise and looked at her knees.

"Is that what you're sayin'?" he inquired.

"No!"

"Well, personally, I think it'd just confuse the issue." He took a thoughtful drag on his cigarette. Sophie continued to regard her knees distantly, as though they were someone else's. "Of course, if you really wanted to . . ."

"Of *course,*" said Sophie sarcastically.

"You want to think this over some more, Sophia?" he asked kindly.

"What am I supposed to think about?"

"I gave you all my reasons. But maybe you've got to have some time to see it makes sense."

"Oh, it makes sense," she said. She sighed.

"Like I say, I can wait a long time," he said.

"No. It's okay. You don't have to," Sophie told him.

He looked at her in surprise.

"What do you mean?" he asked.

"I mean okay," she said sulkily. "But I warn you, I may change my mind."

"You're sayin' yes?" he asked, apparently incredulous.

"Maybe I am."

"Well." He let out a long breath. "Boy!" He stared

straight ahead for a moment, his arms on the wheel. Then he picked up one of her hands, stickily entwined in the folds of her skirt. He straightened out the gluey fingers carefully, looking down at it with serious attention.

"You have small hands," he observed.

"Thanks," said Sophie crossly.

"It's nice—small hands."

"Shall we go now?" she suggested. "I'm very thirsty."

"Yeah. It's hot," he agreed, letting go of her hand and starting up the truck again. They drove in silence through the brilliant white blaze of May, across the sections to the Ware land and up the driveway to the house.

Sophie got out slowly and paused momentarily by the door of the truck.

"I've got to go to work on the north field," he told her, getting out himself. "I'll just come in for a minute. Left my gloves in the kitchen."

Sophie preceded him up the porch steps, stopping as usual by the door to pat the dog, Argus, who gave Alexander a look of dislike and a perfunctory growl.

What she had just agreed to struck her more and more forcibly as she had a drink of water at the sink and rinsed the glue off her hands. Alexander lingered with his gloves in the middle of the floor.

Sophie turned around, saying, "Look, Alexander, I think I've already changed my—"

He took a step forward and, with perfect ease, slid his arms around her waist and bent to kiss her. Sophie closed her eyes and lifted her arms to his neck with a sinking feeling in her stomach, as of one taking a leap from a cliff with imperfect skydiving equipment. Alexander gave her a chaste kiss on the mouth, then set her firmly away from him.

"You're a hell of a girl, Sophia," he said. He stood still for a moment, two feet away, as Sophie opened her eyes in astonishment, and then he went out the back door with his gloves.

3

Mother

Mother came home from the Grove just as Alexander was returning from the field. Sophie had been reading a magazine in the front room for about an hour with an extreme absence of mind. Kneeling on the settee and peering out through the net curtains, she saw Alexander approach her mother and take over two grocery bags. They began to progress around the side of the house. Alexander was talking earnestly.

The back screen door slammed. "Sophie! So-phie!" called Mother in a high, agitated voice.

"Not right away," Alexander was saying. "She's got to finish up with school, and besides, it'll give her some time to get used to—"

"Sophie!"

"Mother?" said Sophie, emerging casually from the front room into the hall with a finger stuck in the magazine, keeping her place.

"Sophie! Is this true?"

Mother had just had her hair done. The tight ice-blue curls made her look matriarchal and severe, an Anglican, a member of the Imperial Order of Daughters of the Empire.

"Is what true?" asked Sophie, standing on one bare foot. She had taken off her school clothes and was wearing a pair of jeans.

"Alexander—Mr.—"

Sophie could see Alexander behind her, carefully putting down the grocery bags on the kitchen table.

"He says he's going to marry you!" Mrs. Ware had given up on the search for a suitable name.

"Oh yes. That," said Sophie facetiously.

"Is it true? Have you—? Oh my God!" said her mother.

"Sit down, Mother. It's too hot to talk about this out here in the hall." Sophie backed into the sitting room, fearful of what was coming.

"Just because I said I wanted to go to the Coast doesn't mean . . ." Her mother sat down histrionically on the sofa. "Have you thought about what you are doing? Sophie, your father—!"

"It's okay," said Sophie irritably. "I know what I'm doing."

Alexander was standing in the front-room door.

"It's all right, Mrs. Ware," he said calmly. "We're just gettin' married. It's not because of your plans." He went over and stood beside Sophie, who was twitching with annoyance.

"*Why* are you doing this? *Why?*" sobbed Mother. "You could have married anyone, but not a— Your father!"

"Leave him out of it!" shouted Sophie, losing her temper completely. "He would have thought it was all right, and anyway, I don't care!"

"But this is a farm laborer! What do you think you're doing with my daughter?" said Mrs. Ware fiercely to Alexander.

"Stop that, Mother. That's just snobbish, prejudiced—"

"A Ukrainian! Sophie, for heaven's sake!" Mrs. Ware turned away from the enraged face of her daughter and hissed at Alexander, "She's a teacher! An educated woman! She went to university. Why would she want to marry you?"

"Well, I'm a man," said Alexander, smiling at Sophie.

"You're not going to marry this—this man on the basis of some silly infatuation?" shrieked Mother, spinning out her tears. "That's no basis for a marriage at all."

Sophie began to laugh.

"It isn't an infatuation, Mother," she said.

"What is it, then? Why else would you marry a farm laborer?" Mrs. Ware was trying unsuccessfully to sustain her hysteria.

"People get married for all kinds of reasons," said Sophie, remembering this argument.

"Like I say," Alexander told Mother seriously, "we'll be givin' it a month or so before—"

"How long has this been going on?" Mrs. Ware blew her nose on a tiny handkerchief she withdrew from her purse.

"That's none of your business, Mother," said Sophie crossly. "I think I'll go do something about dinner."

She left the room, expecting one or the other of them to follow her, but to her surprise they remained in place, and as she unpacked the groceries she could hear them talking, quite calmly, it seemed, her mother's voice an octave and a half higher than the steady tones of Alexander.

After she finished putting away the groceries, she waited a few minutes, glancing at her magazine, an article entitled "What to Do About Your Self-Confidence." As they still continued to talk, she decided to do something about dinner. She could hardly do anything else after using this as an exit line. She was peeling an onion when Alexander came into the kitchen.

"Where's the sherry?" he asked.

Sophie pointed silently to a cupboard and got down a glass. Mother was temperance except at Christmas or when she had been crying.

"Just one glass?" he asked. "I thought we'd all have some."

"As a celebration?" she said sarcastically.

"Yeah." He got down two more glasses. "I'm a Russian, remember?"

"Has she been going on about that?" Sophie demanded indignantly. She put her hands on her hips, her eyes sparkling with anger.

"We've just been talkin'," said Alexander.

"I suppose she's been telling you about my college education."

"Well . . . yes." He smiled slowly. "And about this school principal who was chasin' you."

"Oh, for heaven's sake!" shouted Sophie.

"She's your mother, after all," he remarked, putting a glass of sherry in her hand.

"Yes, that's the trouble!"

"She's stubborn—like you. I like stubborn women," said Alexander.

Sophie now caught sight of her mother over his shoulder. Mrs. Ware had stopped in the doorway at these words, and was reaching back automatically to rearrange her hair.

"Give her a glass of sherry, then," Sophie said sharply, "and maybe we can get this toast over with."

"Oh yeah," he said, turning around. "Like I was just sayin' to Sophia, Russians always have a drink to something like this." He gave Mrs. Ware the glass, and to Sophie's horror, she simpered at him.

"This is too much sherry," she said coyly. "I don't drink very often, Alexander."

"Go ahead," he replied. "I don't think it'll make you drunk."

"To the blushing bride, then," said Mrs. Ware, giving Sophie an all-the-same-I-don't-forgive-you-and-we'll-have-a-little-talk-about-this-later look.

"And the pallid groom," said Sophie, tossing back her sherry, Russian-fashion.

"Are you going to stay for supper, Alexander?"

"No, I'll go home. The old people are expectin' me." He put down his glass on the drainboard. "I'll be back tonight to work on that north field."

"Aren't you going to kiss her?" asked Mrs. Ware teasingly.

The awful prospect that Mother might come to approve of this marriage opened up before Sophie and she contemplated it bleakly, staring at her empty glass.

"Come on outside, Sophia," said Alexander.

"See him off, Sophie. I'll do something about this," said Mrs. Ware briskly, taking up the paring knife and positioning herself in front of the window.

Sophie followed Alexander reluctantly outside.

"I'll take the truck, I guess," he said. He usually took the truck. Evidently her mother could make even a man of his massive self-possession faintly uneasy.

"Okay," said Sophie. She, too, was acutely conscious of Mrs. Ware's stance behind the window.

To her surprise, Alexander now seized her about the body in full view of the window and bent her backwards into a long, romantic kiss. After he had stretched this out for some moments, and Sophie was batting her eyes at him to indicate lack of air, he withdrew his mouth.

"This is part of the deal, too," he said softly.

Sophie stared after him stupidly as he drove away, patting the frantic Argus, who was whirling and barking and leaping beside her knee.

Part of the deal, eh? snarled Sophie's mind, as she sat in the jouncing truck that evening. They were going to see

Alexander's parents a few sections away. She had had a long, unpleasant conversation with her mother over dinner about the seriousness of marriage, and the mistaken modern belief that one could rush into it on the basis of a flimsy sexual attraction.

Alexander had worked on the north field until well after nine. Sophie and Mrs. Ware watered the home fields laboriously.

"Rudi sure screwed up your . . . well, he didn't put in that winter wheat right," remarked Alexander, getting out of the tractor and wiping his forehead with the back of his hand.

The plan of introducing her to his parents had come up then. Mrs. Ware declined to accompany them.

"We'll have plenty of time when we get around to making arrangements about the wedding," she said ominously.

Now, in the truck, Sophie was wondering whether her face was dirty. She had looked in the mirror several times before supper: rather merry brown eyes, nondescript mouse-blond hair, the usual sort of nose, with the mouth below it; no smudges. But the march of events today had been overwhelming. Had she washed her face after supper? When had she last washed it?

"This won't be too bad," said Alexander comfortingly, turning his head to look at her in the sunset light. "They're real happy about it. It won't be too bad for *you,*" he corrected himself.

"Like Mother," said Sophie bitterly. "What really bothered her was the possibility that we might be in love with each other. When I explained that we weren't, she was quite relieved."

Alexander laughed. She looked back at him curiously.

"Well, I thought it was an odd reaction," she said, shrugging. "Of course, I've never done anything like this before. How should I know?"

"It makes sense," he said. "She's got a stake in the place, too. You can't just throw it away on some no-good guy."

"Don't mind her—what she said," said Sophie hurriedly. "She's . . . well, she doesn't really mean all that stuff about Ukrainians. My father would never have—"

"Wait till you meet them," said Alexander. "They think I'm marryin' you for your money."

"And you're not?" asked Sophie.

"Listen," he said patiently. "We went through all that. You don't marry someone for money any more than you'd get married for sex."

"Then what do you get married for?" Sophie asked helplessly.

"Mind if I have a smoke?" Alexander switched off the ignition and let the truck roll to a halt.

"Go ahead." Sophie stared through the windshield into the sunset reflected against the eastern sky. Frogs peeped in the ditch.

"Pretty," said Alexander absently, looking at the sky too.

"So . . . shall we just sit here like an old married couple, or shall I move over a bit?" she said self-consciously. She edged toward him.

"Did you ever meet Poppa?" asked Alexander, as she achieved a position about a foot and a half away from him.

"Well, not exactly. I've seen him a lot of times. And your mother, too." She was not going to bridge the final gap without invitation.

"Yeah. The English never did mix with the Russians."

"Why do you say Russians, Alexander? I thought Ukrainians didn't regard themselves as Russian."

"Momma's Ukrainian. Poppa is Russian. But they're all Russians," he told her with unexpected heat. "Momma's parents came here on a cattle boat before she was born. Poppa got out of a camp in Germany when he was twenty-six. What's the difference?"

"Well, but that makes your mother one of the old

settlers. Don't you see?" Sophie was trying to sort this out, to locate a source of indignation.

"Yeah. Maybe that's why Poppa made up the name."

"The name? Bresnyachuk, you mean? Didn't your father come from the Ukraine at all, then?"

Alexander shrugged. "I never did know," he said.

"You've been away a long time, haven't you, Alexander?" said Sophie. She went on timidly, "It's different now. Those old prejudices—even Mother—no one pays any attention to that any longer."

"I got away," Alexander said flatly. "That's the way I see it now. I can come back and I don't care. But prejudice is nothing, Sophia. You don't know what I'm talkin' about."

"What, then?" she asked.

"The way they are, I guess," he said fiercely. "You'll have to see. Anyway, I don't like my family so well they'll always be hangin' around. You won't have to put up with much of this, Sophia."

Somewhat touched by these unguarded utterances, Sophie looked away over the fields, blurry in the dusk, and stretching almost infinitely toward the U.S. border. Sitting amid this vast prairie, the question of whose ancestors came from where should have no significance.

"Tell me about yourself, Alexander. What did you do after you left home?"

"When I left here . . ." said Alexander, slumping in his seat. He paused, but Sophie said nothing, hoping he would go on.

"I thought I'd never come back. I went to Edmonton."

"Go on." She was emboldened to take his hand off the wheel and examine it as he had hers that afternoon.

"The first job I got was dishwasher in the Alberta Hotel. They wanted to move me up to bouncer because of what I look like, but I said no. Then I got work mixin' cement. I did some other stuff, like furnace repairman, drove a taxi, night guarding. When I got to be twenty-two, I thought, What're you doin'?"

"And so?" said Sophie, fascinated, gently rubbing the calluses on his palm.

"I finished high school," he said. "I did it in three months. I was workin' in Leduc on the oilfields by that time. After that, I spent about four years takin' every kind of diploma course you can imagine. I was smarter than I thought, you see?"

"Yes," said Sophie. She did see.

"So I went up north. Thought I could make it on the rigs up there." He put out his cigarette with his other hand. "Well, I did, but what was the point?" He went on, "Money's nothing. I spent it just as fast as I could make it. I thought about gettin' an Indian woman and settlin' down, but the Indians up there, they aren't like ours. They don't know about the horse yet. What else do you want to know?" he asked abruptly.

"Nothing," said Sophie, surprised.

Alexander took back his hand and lit another cigarette.

"About this school principal," he said unexpectedly, sitting forward to look at her in the gathering dusk.

"Oh yes. Robert Markovich. He grew up around here too. He was a grade ahead of me—perhaps you remember him?" said Sophie.

"Your mother thinks he was goin' to marry you."

"Does she now? We had an affair," said Sophie boldly. "It didn't turn out very well. We didn't agree about . . . some things. My father was dying, so I moved in with Mother."

"What didn't you agree about?" asked Alexander.

"About death," Sophie said vaguely. One could hardly explain what was wrong with Robert to a stranger. Or could one? Certainly not to the stranger one had agreed to marry that afternoon.

"Was that why you didn't marry him?" Alexander asked obstinately, still looking at her closely.

"No. He didn't ask!" replied Sophie, laughing.

"Why not?"

"I don't know. What was the point?" she said helplessly. "We weren't in love or anything. We were just sort of using each other."

"Yeah," said Alexander.

"Have you ever been in love with anyone, Alexander?"

He did not reply.

Sophie panicked.

"You're not in love with anyone at the moment?" she asked anxiously.

"No." He seemed startled.

"Oh," said Sophie.

"Now look here," he said. "We're doin' this right, Sophia. This is an old way. Millions of people did it like this. It's a good way to do it."

"Yes, Alexander," said Sophie, liking these platitudes.

"Let's go get this over with, then," said Alexander grimly. He let out the clutch.

As they drove across the uplands toward the Bresnyachuk homestead, Sophie wondered why she had not married Robert. They were suited to one another in many ways. They enjoyed each other's company. It had just never come up. It had not occurred to her to ask him, she corrected herself. It would never have occurred to Robert.

She looked under her lashes at the huge male figure looming beside her. This was a violent infatuation, such as she could never have dreamed of with the intelligent Robert. It was the substance of her mother's nightmares. So at least there was something to it.

Going to bed with Robert was like having an extremely satisfactory chat with a good friend. What it would be like with Alexander she could not now imagine, but she hoped to find out soon.

"Are you cold?"

"No. Oh no!"

4

Momma and Poppa

Sophie got out of the truck in the Bresnyachuk yard and looked around. There seemed to be a great deal of rusting machinery standing around. Alexander had parked next to something that through the dusk looked very much like a steam locomotive. Suddenly she noticed a flock of geese proceeding in her direction at a quick march.

Sophie was justifiably afraid of geese. She appreciated goats and ignored chickens, but geese were a serious kind of threat, especially en masse like this. They appeared around a pile of old truck tires and advanced on her remorselessly, cutting her off from Alexander, who was getting out on the other side.

At the same time, the back door was thrown open and Alexander's father projected himself down the steps, crying, "My son and his bride! They are here, Momma!"

Sophie was surrounded by geese and unable to move. Alexander, moored at the front of the truck, took in her dismay.

"The geese, Momma!" he shouted.

Momma came out on the back steps and rushed down upon the geese, hissing, "Hsst! Hsst! Hsst!"

"Jesus!" said Alexander, reaching Sophie first. "Come on." He quickly put his arm around her and led her past the old man.

"Is just geese," said Momma. She watched Sophie critically as Alexander led her in the door.

"Them birds should have a pasture," said Alexander. To Sophie's amazement, he continued to hold onto her waist.

"If my son would make one," said Mrs. Bresnyachuk with ironic emphasis. She was a tall, gray-haired woman with almost Asiatic features and a wide, heavy build. Perhaps Alexander derived his appearance from her, for his father, who entered now, having shouted "Hsst! Hsst!" fruitlessly several times from the porch, was a small, compact man. He bustled sexily across the room.

"We need fruit, pickles, jam! Where is tea, Veronika? But first we have ham, sausage, fat pork, and we drink to this wedding!"

Mrs. Bresnyachuk ignored all these conflicting orders and stood solidly in front of Sophie.

"This is Sophia, Momma," said Alexander.

"How do you do," said Sophie politely.

"Very well, thanks," said Mrs. Bresnyachuk, with a startling change of both manner and accent. She shook hands with Sophie.

"This is not how is greeted the bride of my son!" shouted Poppa, moving in on Sophie.

Momma glared at him, and he compromised by squeezing Sophie's hand and holding on to her elbow like a grain dealer.

"Here is Luke, also," said Mrs. Bresnyachuk, prying away her husband. Alexander continued to clasp Sophie's waist tightly.

"Pleathed to meet you, Thophie," said Luke, raising a hand casually. He was seated at the kitchen table, and Sophie noticed with astonishment that it was set, almost as though for dinner, with three different bottles, one at each place. In front of Luke was a rye bottle. Mrs. Bresnyachuk had a bottle marked STOMACH BITTERS and a teacup. And the remaining place, occupied by her husband, who now sat down there, was held by a nearly full forty ounce vodka bottle.

"Thith ith quite an occathion," said Luke.

Sophie was already wondering where she would sit. As long as Alexander held on to her it would be all right, perhaps. But Momma was summoning her, and she followed uneasily into the pantry, a room only slightly smaller than the kitchen, and lined with boxes, sacks, jars, and bottles on every shelf, like a dream of World War III.

"Here is pickles," Momma said shortly.

Sophie arranged the pickles on a plate, watching Momma slice up a homemade sausage.

"Good," said Momma, observing her. "Now here is sausage."

She looked over carefully as Sophie laid out the sausage like a pack of cards, meanwhile getting out a loaf of rye bread.

"You are gonna care for my Sasha?" asked Momma fiercely, suddenly relinquishing her knife and taking Sophie's face between her hands. "Is only son I love," she added. "I love in all the years he is away."

Sophie looked into her eyes and saw insincerity mixed almost equally with real emotion. Perhaps Momma was like Alexander, but she was female, and therefore much tougher.

"He is loving his Momma, too," said Mrs. Bresnyachuk.

Rendered temporarily speechless by those mesmeric eyes, Sophie said nothing to this.

"Now he is a man. Then he was only boy," Mrs. Bresnyachuk said enigmatically.

"Yes," said Sophie, finding her tongue. "What do you want me to do with the food?"

"I show you," said Momma, letting go of Sophie's cheeks and going after the rye bread with the carving knife.

"You must preserve a lot," said Sophie, trying to be casual, looking around the crowded pantry.

"You are wise girl, Sophia," said Momma. "Past is past. Over!" She made an alarming gesture with the carving knife above the bread.

"Is this Saskatoon berry jam?" asked Sophie, trying to make out a label—not in Russian, she perceived after a moment.

"I show you lots," said Momma ominously, leading the way back with the plates.

Alexander was sitting beside Luke, a glass of some liquid in front of him. Sophie diagnosed it as orange juice.

"Good! Good!" shouted Poppa. "Sophia will have vodka," he went on magnanimously. "Is a celebration."

"I make tea for you, Sophia," said Momma.

"Vodka! Is good!" Poppa poured a healthy dram into a tumbler for her. "Tea after."

Simultaneously, out of some brotherly impulse, Luke leaned forward and introduced a medicinal dose of rye into Alexander's orange juice.

Sophie sat down cautiously beside Alexander and took up her vodka glass. She found Poppa a known quantity, less threatening but more fascinating than Momma.

Alexander put his arm across the back of her chair and she jumped nervously.

She sipped the neat vodka and looked around the kitchen over the rim of her glass. A garish calendar decorated the wall adjoining the pantry. What Sophie supposed was an icon, a picture painted in the colors of an old violin, hung over the back door. A string of rosary beads hung above another, inner door. Otherwise, the kitchen was furnished in Old Country modern: chrome table and chairs, a divan, an electric stove and refrigerator, cupboards, and a modern counter around an old-fashioned deep sink. This formed a background of unnerving hygienic spotlessness against the situation at the table, where Luke and Poppa were chomping and drinking noisily, reaching into the plates of food greedily with their fingers.

"So," said Momma, sitting down, the teapot adjusted to her satisfaction. "You treat her good, Sasha. Then she is good for you." She nodded oppressively.

"Momma's got high school," remarked Alexander, apparently taking in Sophie's discomfiture. "She's puttin' you on."

"I am taking all subjects in school," said Momma proudly. "Then I marry wrong man, is all."

"Wrong? Right!" shouted Poppa through a mouthful of sausage and rye bread. "You shoulda seen me, Sophia! I was—!" He stood up and pouted out his little breast.

"Yeah. Hero," said Momma wearily.

"I was hero of Vlasov!" said Poppa. "Fighting on the wrong side, okay! But fighting like devils!"

"You were in Vlasov's army?" asked Sophie, amazed. Under the careful direction of the Ukrainian patriot, Robert, she had read a book about Vlasov's army more than a year ago.

"So?" Poppa shrugged. "I am fighting for Gitler, I am fighting for Ukraine! Fight against Gitler? Is fight against Ukraine! Tell this woman for me, Sophia!"

"Gitler was scourge of Ukraine," Mrs. Bresnyachuk said heatedly.

"What the hell are they talkin' about?" asked Alexander in an undertone.

"Your mother . . . Hitler . . ." Sophie began helplessly.

"We are talkin' about marriage," said Poppa, unexpectedly peaceful. "Okay, I am bad man, Sophia. I forgive her that she does not understand. I fight for Gitler. I fight for Stalin. Is the same! To this woman is all the same. Now! Marriage!"

"Okay," said Momma, putting a dash of stomach bitters into her teacup. "Now you tell Sasha, Poppa."

"To Sasha—I leave all land!" shouted Poppa. "To Luke—money! Rudi—money! But to Sasha—all land!"

"Is good, Sophia?" asked Momma, giving Sophie an extremely secretive look.

"I don't want it, Poppa," said Alexander.

"I am telling Sophia," said Poppa. "Is good?"

"Well . . . yes. But—" murmured Sophie anxiously.

"Poppa!" shouted Alexander, standing up. "I don't want any of it!"

Poppa also stood up. They eyed one another for a moment. Momma providently placed two clean glasses before Poppa.

"Now we drink to land!" cried Poppa. He filled both glasses, although he had one already nearly full, and Alexander had touched none of the eccentric mixture before him.

Alexander, still on his feet, said slowly, "To Sophia, Poppa."

"Oh yeah! To Sophia—the bride!"

Sophie laughed. "To him that hath, it shall be given, Alexander," she told him.

"Later we will talk," said Poppa, apparently catching the drift of this. "Tonight—celebrate!"

Everyone drank her health, each from his own selection of liquor.

Alexander remained standing an instant too long. Poppa grabbed Sophie's arm and began to monopolize, moving his chair up closely.

"I am knowing your father a long, long time," he said. "Always an honest man, your dad."

Sophie nodded, sipping, and trying to escape total encirclement.

"He is like a father to me," said the old man. "Like my Poppa. He is saying, 'Rudolph, you must take oats out of west field and sell to so-and-so.' Like brothers we was." He crossed his fingers and looked at Sophie wisely.

"Yes," said Sophie dubiously.

He kneaded her arm.

"Now, at last, we are one big family," said Poppa. "Your father, in his grave, this makes him happy, I know."

"I hope so," said Sophie insincerely, looking around for help.

"My boys is working for him every harvest," Poppa went on relentlessly. "Was then maybe you see this one. You go to Dad, say, 'Poppa, I am seeing Alexander Bresnyachuk. Is good-lookin' boy. Talk to old people, I ask you this, Poppa.' Then Dad he looks out at Sasha. Is hard worker—"

"Yeah. Well, that's not what happened," said Alexander dryly. "I never worked for your dad, Sophia."

"Alexander, my son, with girls is always like this. Even with this one here." Mr. Bresnyachuk ogled Momma for a moment. "For them is only a question of love."

"Leave alone, Poppa!" urged Momma.

Alexander tossed back his vodka, looking for a moment alarmingly like his father.

"I'm takin' Sophia home now," he announced. He stood up and extracted Sophie from Poppa's toils by the simple expedient of lifting her straight out of her chair by the arms.

Momma watched suspiciously from the end of the table.

"Maybe Sasha is loving the girl," she said to Poppa. "But is the girl loving Sasha?"

"Of course!" shouted Poppa, spreading his arms wide,

a foot away from Sophie. She was drawn backwards sharply against Alexander, who was still holding her elbows.

"We're goin' now, Momma," said Alexander, interposing himself skillfully between Sophie and Poppa. "I'll be back in a few minutes."

Sophie faded toward the back door, aware that she must not allow Poppa to kiss her. The Oedipus complex, like baseball and apple pie, had probably been invented in Russia. It seemed that they might come to blows over her mere proximity. She paused a moment, then called loudly and clearly, "Good night. Good night, Mrs. Bresnyachuk. Good night, Poppa. Good night, Luke." Then she slipped out into the cool night air. Instantly she was surrounded by geese, croaking and hissing and snapping.

"Hsst!" said Alexander quietly, following her out. "It's okay, Sophia. They won't hurt you."

"If you're going to drive me home, then Mother or I will have to drive you back," she protested, achieving safety in the cab of the truck. Her mother had been doing most of the commuting with Alexander in the early spring.

"I'll keep it overnight," said Alexander. "Anyway, I'm comin' with you now," he added grimly.

Sophie slid over, and Alexander got in and started the truck. The geese scattered at once.

"Jesus!" Alexander remarked as they turned out of the driveway.

"That wasn't bad at all," said Sophie coolly, reserving to herself certain fears about Alexander's mother.

"Not for you, maybe," he replied. "But, Sophia, that was a bunch of lies Poppa was tellin' you."

"Really?" said Sophie.

"Yeah. About his will. And then about him and your dad. He didn't know your dad. I think Rudi worked on your place part of one harvest. That's all."

"It doesn't matter," said Sophie soothingly. "It was just his way of saying he was happy you were—"

"Doin' so well for myself!" Alexander finished for her.

"And as for that stuff about his will—he's been usin' that on all of us for—"

"Well, don't get mad about it, then," Sophie suggested. "Anyway, you're more like your parents than you think, Alexander. I mean 'old style,' " she mocked. "They're real old style, don't you see that?"

"Yeah, but I don't lie like Poppa," he muttered.

"I like him. He's sort of—well, legendary or something. You don't meet a member of Vlasov's army every day of the week," said Sophie dreamily. She began to inch sideways toward Alexander across the seat.

"What was that all about?" he demanded.

"Oh—Vlasov's army? Well, it was Russian prisoners of war who—"

"Yeah? The last time I heard about it, he was in Auschwitz."

"Oh." Sophie reflected. "Well, it's interesting, anyway." She leaned against his shoulder boldly.

"I'm like Momma," said Alexander, "if I'm like either of them. And sometimes I wonder whether I didn't get changed at the hospital," he went on bitterly. "Except I wasn't born in a hospital."

"Well, your mother is marvelous," said Sophie, feeling her way to firm ground.

He turned up her driveway without comment. Sophie yawned, leaning on his arm. It had been hard work in the garden. She was no longer worrying about whether her face was dirty.

Alexander stopped the truck with a jerk, not his usual glide, in the dooryard, and sat tensely beside her for a moment.

"It's okay," said Sophie, using his words of common comfort. He was behaving very well, she thought, comparing this to her own performance of the afternoon.

"Good night," he said.

"Hey!" said Sophie. "Is that all? We reserve kissing for public performances only?"

"You want to kiss me, Sophia?" he said. "After that?"

"Yes!"

She turned around on the seat, kneeling beside him to make everything easier, and looked down at his face, illuminated by the brilliant light of the dooryard. Alexander leaned back, looking up in surprise, but making no move.

"Like this," said Sophie, putting her lips on his in a long, dissolving kiss.

This was even better than she expected; in fact, she was just giving herself up to it completely when he said, "Good night," and let go of her abruptly.

Sophie sat back on her heels, bewildered and insulted.

"Maybe we better go slow on this, Sophia," he told her. He took cigarettes and matches from his breast pocket, and Sophie withdrew toward her door, quivering with outrage.

"I'm not pushin' you into anything," he said. "You still have to think about this."

"Your intentions are altogether honorable, I'm sure," Sophie snapped, preparing to get out of the truck.

"Yeah. They are," said Alexander. "By the way, mind if I take out your horse tomorrow? He's not gettin' enough exercise."

"If you think you can ride him," Sophie replied sharply.

"I know I can," said Alexander. "Him and me are friends."

"All very well. But he's hard to ride."

"I grew up on a horse," Alexander replied simply. "Me and Benedict Malone . . . well, I'll tell you about him sometime," he added, as Sophie got out and shut the door.

5

Courtship

During the week that followed, Alexander appeared to be *courting* her. This was very startling to Sophie, who had grown up in the ethic of the sixties and seventies, in which even the word, like *eligible* and *ladylike*, had gone the way of the dodo. Up till now the men in her life had, after a brisk reconnaissance, either taken her home to bed or deposited her on the sidewalk outside her apartment.

Alexander usually appeared in the yard immediately after Sophie got home from school, and they had tea together with her mother. In the evening, before he went home in the truck, a privilege he had now firmly assumed, he stayed on for about an hour, mostly chatting about the farmwork. Her mother had begun to take a decidedly optimistic tone after several days of this, and by the weekend she was deliriously happy, almost bridal.

Naturally, Mrs. Ware was supposing that they did

their lovemaking in private, but in fact they did it exclusively in public. When Alexander gave her a light goodnight kiss on Wednesday, Sophie almost bit him.

When she came home after school on Thursday afternoon, she waited in the dooryard, patting the dog and listening for the expected sound of the tractor coming off the fields. It rolled into sight after a moment and Alexander parked carefully beside the barn. Then he advanced toward her, a large bunch of field flowers in his hand.

"Thanks," said Sophie, touched. She sniffed, but they only smelled of dust. It had not rained for weeks. She put her hand determinedly on his collarbone and he paused and looked down at her.

"I'm awful dirty."

"That's all right." She noticed that what he said was true, and compromised by merely putting her other hand with the flowers in it on his arm. She stared at him hard. The situation was bewildering her completely. No new intimacy had been achieved since she had accepted his proposal; on the contrary, the social obstacles between them had become insuperable.

She was aware of her mother spying on them as usual from the kitchen window and thinking, no doubt, what a sweet picture they made together. She sprang backward, tripping over Argus, who had his nose pressed restively against the back of her knee.

Alexander caught her arm cleverly before she capsized completely.

The dog whuffed and showed his teeth on one side.

"Let's go have tea," Alexander suggested. "I can hardly talk for dust."

"Sit down, Alexander," said Mother solicitously. She had the tea ready, as usual.

"I'll just wash up first, Mrs. Ware," said Alexander, going to the kitchen sink, where he attacked his face and hands vigorously with yellow soap. He sat down a moment later, ruddy-faced from the kitchen towel.

"I was doin' the slough field today," he observed.

"Yes, that's usually the last you can get after," agreed Mrs. Ware. "Although this year it's so dry . . ."

Sophie began to arrange her flowers listlessly in a tall jar, her mind only half on this conversation.

"I was wonderin' about that slough," he said. "You could probably get a real good pond out of it if you took the trouble to clean it up."

"Sophie, there are doughnuts in the raising pan. Give some to Alexander."

"It would be good for cattle," he went on.

"Yes, I know," said Mrs. Ware. Sophie noticed that they were both looking at her as she bent over the raising pan in a bottom cupboard.

"Cattle are a great deal of work," said Mrs. Ware. Sophie wondered why her mother wasn't acting to dispose of this proposal with her usual force.

"Horses," said Sophie, puzzled. "That was Dad's idea."

They were both still looking at her.

"You hardly have time to look after the horse you have, Sophie," said Mrs. Ware sharply. "And he's too big for you to handle. I don't like having a stallion on the place, and I told Harry that."

"Well, I'm keeping him anyway," replied Sophie. "Even if I have to get married to manage it." She put down the plate of doughnuts with a click.

"Him and me have been goin' out together in the mornings," said Alexander to Sophie, munching peacefully on a doughnut. "He's a real good guy."

"You said you liked horses." Sophie had suddenly entered into the spirit of this conversation. It had not occurred to her before that she had decision-making powers. It was actually up to her. Sophie felt a curiously lonely thrill.

"We always had 'em," replied Alexander placidly, taking another doughnut between two gulps of tea. "Momma had a couple of good ones, but the rest of 'em were real rough, hard-broke old mares."

"I remember your place in the old days," said Mrs. Ware, speaking quickly and warmly to Alexander. "That was one thing about you children—you always looked like you were having so much fun with the horses!"

"Yeah. Us and the Indian kids," agreed Alexander. "Benedict Malone—"

"Benedict Malone? Oh yes," said Mother thoughtfully. "One of the Malones from the Reserve."

"Benedict, he could talk the language of horses."

"Horses don't have a language," said Sophie. "I mean, they're animals."

"So're we."

"Yes, but . . ." It was Sophie's instinct to agree with him. But a good rider is warned against anthropomorphism, she recalled, simultaneously trying to remember how to spell it.

"Benedict could talk to 'em just like people." Alexander took a cigarette out of his pocket and Mrs. Ware got up silently and fetched the ashtray.

"Poppa had a mare one time," he went on reflectively, striking a match with his thumbnail. "He traded for some wet hay or something. He gave her to Marfa because Marfa was doin' eggs that year and she thought she ought to get wages. Now that mare . . ."

He paused, his nostrils expanded.

"Marfa had your idea," he went on. "But she sure couldn't ride that mare. First she was just usin' a saddle, and then she took a switch, but after that she was tryin' out Poppa's Polish cavalry spurs—"

"Polish cavalry!" cried Sophie, diverted.

"Yeah. You couldn't tell her nothin', not any more than that mare. They were tryin' to kill each other. Then Benedict come along and he saw Marfa lyin' in the muck, cryin', and that mare was over in another corner, probably cryin' too. So he just—"

"What did he do?" asked Sophie.

"Like I said, he could talk to horses," said Alexander.

"Oh yes," she replied cynically.

"Well, that was why Marfa liked Benedict so much," said Alexander. He was looking at Sophie, his eyes a distant, cloudy gray. She had the feeling he didn't really see her.

"Did you ever break a horse yourself, Alexander?" she asked.

"Sure," he replied. "Lots of times. I broke most of the ones we had. You couldn't really say they were broke when we got 'em."

"How did you do it?"

"Haven't you ever done that?" asked Alexander.

"Well, I've seen people do it," said Sophie cautiously. "They showed us at riding school. But I never—"

"You've just got to know the horse. Benedict, he always said you had to know a name. Then you and that horse've got something between you."

"That's not the way they did it at riding school," said Sophie firmly. "You had to go on getting back up till the horse recognized that you were the master. That's what they said."

"Well, probably they did it differently," he said calmly. "I don't know about all that professional stuff. I guess you did that—dressage and gaits and all that." He said this with a certain respectful contempt.

"It sounds as if you'd like to have horses yourself, Alexander," said Mrs. Ware. "But they're even more work than cattle. I told Harry—" Her voice broke suddenly.

"If Sophia wants horses, we'll have horses," said Alexander. He stood up. "She's got to think about it. We'll still need a pond." He stretched. "I've got another hour or so to do on that slough field."

Sophie followed him outside.

"Are you going to be *busy* tomorrow night, Alexander?" she asked sarcastically.

"Not if I finish with the slough field," he replied, evidently surprised.

"Maybe we could go out to dinner or something," Sophie said icily.

"Okay," said Alexander.

"Not to the Buffalo Jump Café, though."

He grinned. "Where to, then?" he asked.

"There's a new place in the Grove. I heard about it in the staff room. We could go there." She had not been expecting he would have any ideas. "I'll pay," she added.

"Nope," said Alexander cheerfully. "Your mother gave me my wages last week."

"Your wages?" This aspect of their relationship had slipped Sophie's mind. She was tempted to laugh, but realized at the last minute that this would be tactless.

"I'll tell Momma not to wait up for me, then."

Sophie thought this was a very good idea.

He gave her the usual light kiss, but she was much cheered by his last words.

They were going to the Pug Dog, a Chinese steak-and-lobster joint on Highway 2.

Alexander had finished with the slough field. He was in a hurry to go home and change. They did not have their usual tea in the afternoon.

Sophie retired to her room. After much thought, she decided to do up her hair and put on a sundress. It was necessary to dress up, but not so much so as to exceed the expectable dreariness of the restaurant. She wanted to look desirable, without any extra flourishes.

After a long struggle with her hair she let it be, curly, useless, and almost brown, and stared despairingly into the mirror. She looked like what she was, she decided; a boring little WASP, the sort of person somebody would want to marry. To describe any of her features as anything in particular would be an exaggeration, especially if the description was favorable. After a further melancholy inspection, she decided to go downstairs. She was ready much too early.

When Alexander finally appeared in a pair of dark corduroy trousers and a white shirt, he was looking both desirable and harassed.

"What is it?" she asked in the truck. This had become, undeniably, his vehicle. "You were later than I expected."

"Oh—Marfa was home," said Alexander.

"Does she live around here?" asked Sophie. "I haven't seen her in years."

"She's got a place over across the Reserve," said Alexander. "She doesn't usually come around, but I guess she heard we were gettin' married." From the tone of his voice, it sounded as though Marfa did not approve of this. "She wants to talk to you."

"Oh? What about?"

"She'll tell you herself," said Alexander curtly. "Marfa's got her own ideas." He drew up in the parking lot of the restaurant. "This the place?"

Sophie looked furtively around the dark interior as they entered. This was her first public display of Alexander, and she felt unreasonably nervous about it. There were sure to be some people from the school present, taking notes.

"Nice place," said Alexander to Sophie, following the waitress to a table.

"Oh yes?" she said, but there seemed to have been no concealed sarcasm in his remark.

Their table was behind an Italianate pillar, probably the remnants of a pizza joint named Zeno's, which had preceded the Pug Dog. A mongrel decor was in evidence, as Sophie noted, looking around. A Chinese lantern hung from a bracket over their heads, establishing the authentic Chinese identity of the present owners.

Sophie ordered a martini.

"Maybe I'll just have wine," said Alexander, looking up at the waitress, a Ukrainian wheat-ear blonde. "I like wine," he added.

He listened appreciatively as they were exhorted to make free with the salad bar. Sophie looked away across the room in simulated boredom.

"Is that what you usually drink?" she asked, watching him sip and sniff when the waitress had returned with the drinks. With a stifled giggle, she thought of the well-set table in the Bresnyachuk household.

"I usually drink beer," said Alexander. The waitress went off in disgust, to Sophie's satisfaction.

"Do you go to the Buffalo Jump Bar, then?"

"Sometimes." He smiled.

"But not usually?"

"Usually Momma makes me a cup of tea and I go to bed," he answered. "I've been workin' pretty hard. Rudi sure run down your land."

"I thought so," said Sophie. "Last year he didn't bother to summer fallow." She disposed her arms on the table. "Let's not talk about that."

He apparently found this difficult. They sat in silence for a moment.

"I used to live here in the Grove," said Sophie. "When I started to teach. I had an apartment. I just moved in with Mother when Dad got sick."

"I've been thinkin' about your dad," said Alexander. "He put his sweat into that land."

"Yes, he did," agreed Sophie, swallowing a chunk of olive with difficulty. "He was . . . he had all kinds of plans."

"Your mother is real great, too."

"He died of lung cancer. For a long time they wouldn't tell him what it was."

Alexander looked at her attentively.

"He went on making plans," said Sophie. "Like the horses—that was one of them. He thought it was pneumonia scars. No one would tell him."

Alexander poured some wine into her glass.

"He couldn't breathe."

"That's bad," said Alexander. "Bein' sick like that."

"I didn't know what to do," she said. "I could have told him. Would he have believed me?"

"Sophia," said Alexander gently.

"I knew what it was from the beginning," Sophie went on, gripping the edge of the table. "I read up on it. But he went on talking as though . . ." She could not continue.

After a moment she regained control of herself. It had not been her intention ever to talk about this again, certainly not in a Chinese steak-and-lobster joint on Highway 2.

"So I didn't tell him," she said flatly. "I don't believe he wanted to know." She sipped her wine, then shook her head and laughed. "It's so cruel," she said.

"When my little sister Alice died, Momma stayed grievin' for months," said Alexander. "I used to get into bed with her and she'd cry."

"When was that?" asked Sophie.

"Oh, about twenty-five years ago," said Alexander. "Matthew and Alice were the last."

"Matthew?"

"They both died," he said.

"So you know what that's like," she said.

"Maybe not," he said gravely. "But Momma does."

They were both having steak. Their snobbish waitress cast a disgusted look at their unused salad plates and flounced away.

Sophie pondered the tenderness she now perceived in Alexander's personality. The fact that he was so inarticulate added to the impression; she had a clear mental picture of the seven-year-old Alexander in bed with Momma, of Marfa crying in the muck.

"Were you very close to Marfa?" she asked. "She's the same age as I am, you know."

"Close?" Alexander lapsed into silence for a moment, his eyes on the middle distance. "We were always together. Her and me and . . . Benedict Malone."

Sophie nodded.

"Benedict played soccer. I guess you remember that," said Alexander. "He was real fast. Benedict was the runner and I was the kicker."

Sophie remembered Alexander very well. He had been the star player in the school in every kind of sport. But she had no recollection of an Indian boy on that team. There were very few Indian kids in the high school. There had been a girl in her class; that was all she could remember. Alexander's loyalty to his friend was charming to her. Not many people held on to their childhood allegiances like this. Perhaps it was because of the emptiness of his life in between, as he described it.

"I remember you, Alexander," she said, smiling at him.

"Benedict was a real Indian," said Alexander. "Like a buffalo hunter. They could run—run all day. But he was fast, too."

"You were the hero of all the little girls," she said, putting down her fork. "I never would have dreamed of this!" She again put her arms on the table, conscious of their elegance, slender and very white.

"Of this," repeated Alexander, smiling. He was looking at her arms, to her great satisfaction. "Who gave you that?" he asked, reaching out to touch the thick gold bracelet on her wrist.

"My father."

This conversation was making her very happy. There was an intimacy between them that had not been there before.

"After harvest," said Alexander abruptly, "maybe I could get you something pretty like that."

"Alexander . . ." Sophie was now ready to broach the main mystery between them. But Alexander was looking up, then pushing back his chair and standing up.

It was Robert.

"This is Robert Markovich, Alexander," said Sophie

resignedly, seeing the sparkle in Robert's eye. Robert was a social scientist. He specialized in uncontrolled experiments.

"A pretty rumor has reached my ear," said Robert. He glanced between them. "Are you engaged to this young man, Sophie?"

"Who told you?" demanded Sophie.

"Yes, we are," said Alexander. He presented a remarkable contrast to the weedy Robert as he continued to stand politely beside his chair.

"Well, in that case, I shall pay for the champagne!" Robert quickly drew out a seat and began signaling to the waitress with one arm. "Even though," he added mischievously, "Sophie is an heiress."

"Go to hell, Robert," said Sophie.

Robert was now conferring with the waitress over the wine list, and Sophie looked nervously at Alexander. The tiny thrill of sexual tension that had held them together after he touched her bracelet had left her completely, and she saw him as Robert would see him, merely as a male animal, entirely and unfairly attractive.

"Well—to domestic happiness!" said Robert, exploding the cork. "Quick, Sophie! Your glass! This is a Canadian toast, I'm afraid. I couldn't see you to a French one."

"Thanks," said Alexander.

"Thanks *anyway*," Sophie corrected.

"So when is the happy day to be? Very soon?"

"We haven't—"

"Probably at the end of the—" Sophie and Alexander spoke simultaneously.

"Oh, I see. You aren't in a hurry, then."

"The baby is due in September," said Sophie coldly. "Stop guessing."

"Just a hypothesis." Robert sighed and lit a short cigar. "We spry and warty bachelors always want to know these things."

"Perhaps you remember Robert at school," said Sophie to no one in particular. "He grew up to be a bachelor. Because of the warts, you know."

"Just wait until you have six children and a mother-in-law, Sophie dear."

"Ho, ho! I do love a mother-in-law joke!"

"But I didn't make it yet. Just wait until you have one," he said. "You'll be making them yourself."

"I bet I won't." Sophie noted how Robert had achieved the complete exclusion of Alexander from this conversation.

"Maybe not, but *he* will," said Robert, jerking his thumb at Alexander. "I know your mother, remember, darling?"

Sophie saw that this exclusion was a test. Robert was sitting around in his chair so as to face her, his back almost wholly turned on Alexander. He was daring her to do something about it.

Sophie frowned at him expressively. He merely grinned, watching her closely.

"Do you think it will rain?" she asked, lifting her eyes innocently to Alexander.

Instantly she saw that she had done the wrong thing. Robert would have seized this glove and run with it. Alexander obviously didn't play conversational games. He looked at Sophie's empty plate, then at Robert, his nostrils expanding slightly.

"Are you ready to go?" he asked Sophie.

"Okay," said Sophie, embarrassed.

"Thanks for the champagne," Alexander said briefly.

"Not at all. See you, then," said Robert, amused. "See you on Monday, Sophie."

"I hope not," muttered Sophie, passing his chair on her way to the hatcheck. Alexander was already paying. She collected her sweater and trailed after him to the truck.

Alexander started up and they drove in silence for a few moments through the warm, exhaust-scented summer air. It occurred to her that he was really angry.

"What's the matter?" she asked sharply.

Alexander turned off the highway onto the Steamboat Lake Road.

"He was just running through his repertoire," she said. "You made his day, I guess."

Alexander drew up by the lakeshore, and stopped the truck. He breathed deeply a couple of times through his nose.

"You like talkin' to that guy, do you?"

"Not exactly." Sophie was not too sure on this point herself. "It's entertaining—sometimes," she admitted.

"Well, I despise fellows like that," said Alexander. "He doesn't like to see people bein' happy together. Especially not you and me."

"Happy?" said Sophie doubtfully. But it was true. They had been being happy together.

"Yeah," said Alexander grimly.

"You wouldn't be *jealous*, by any chance?" she said incredulously.

"Wasn't that the point?"

"Good heavens."

"You can keep him on the string if you want. But don't expect me to be there, too!"

"Well, I'm here, am I not?" said Sophie, utterly charmed by this unexpected development.

There was a silence.

She put her hand on his arm timidly.

"You can't possibly think—" she began.

Alexander turned around and grasped her shoulders, pushing back the sweater, and she felt with a sudden wild delight that he desired her. He was kissing her neck, pulling down the straps of the sundress, the bunchy, longish hair above his ears brushing against her mouth and then her collarbone as he moved slowly downward to the exposed tops of her breasts.

Groping to find her way through his clothing to his back, Sophie thought resignedly, Well, the front seat of a truck . . .

It was not in the least like the light-handed approach of the spry and warty bachelor, Robert. Sophie shuddered under the sucking pressure of Alexander's mouth. Its very artlessness was a source of almost frightening excitement.

A moment later, he stopped. He rested his forehead against her shoulder for a moment, then pushed the straps of her dress back up her arms and kissed her quickly on the lips.

"Alexander! For Christ's sake!" she cried, in a turmoil of frustrated expectation.

But he simply put his arm around her shoulders and pulled her against him. Sophie closed her eyes, feeling close to tears. This was the most ridiculous and humiliating thing yet.

"Sure, I could go on," he said after a time. "But I'm not goin' to. Not when I'm mad."

"Well, stop being mad, then!" Sophie laughed unhappily.

"We're gettin' married for all the things he was heapin' shit on," said Alexander. "To run a farm, have a family, so your mother can stay on if she wants to stay, or go away if she wants to go. Those things are important."

"And this isn't? What if it turns out that we don't suit one another very well—I mean, this way?" she said.

"Do you think it's goin' to turn out like that?" he asked.

"No," she admitted. His hand on her bare shoulder was driving her crazy.

He seemed to sense this, for he shifted it down to her upper arm, still encased in the sleeve of her sweater, and she rested her head against the muscular flesh above his armpit, feeling melancholy.

Alexander lit a cigarette with one hand.

"Robert is just the end of a long line of people you'll never have to meet," she said. "The first one—well, it happened in the front seat of this truck. Or not this one, I guess, but the one we had before. I was eighteen at the time, and just about to go to the university. It was a sort of last-ditch stand with that boyfriend."

"Yeah," he said. She could tell that he didn't like this at all.

"After that," she went on dreamily, rolling her head from side to side on his shoulder, "it was the straight road to perdition. Universities were pretty exotic places in those years—even the University of Alberta."

"I heard," he said ironically. She remembered his description of his own search for self-education. That had seemed pathetic, but like everything else about him, it was different.

"I came out to the country to teach when I was twenty-four. I spent a year bumming around Europe first. With a friend. A boyfriend. I got involved with Robert about three years ago. That ended when I moved in with my parents."

"He didn't like your folks?"

"Not so much that," said Sophie. "He couldn't help, you see. Maybe nobody could have, though."

"What he was sayin' about your mother—" Alexander began.

"No, no," said Sophie. "We just couldn't agree—about Dad. He thought I should have told him." She drew breath. "He said Dad was deceiving himself and I was helping him. Well, that was true. I was. But Robert is the kind of person who just can't leave a thing like that alone. He can say things ten times as well as you can—but sometimes you just don't want them said."

Sophie now felt a subtle change in the muscles of Alexander's arm behind her back. The grip of his hand became a clasp.

"That was a year ago?" he said presently.

"About that." Sophie turned her face into his neck, beginning to feel better. "So you see."

She waited a few minutes. He seemed to be reflecting on this.

"So Robert was the last," she said. "What about you?"

"What do you want to know?"

"The first and the last will do," she replied. "I'm not interested in a head count."

"Well, there was somebody here," said Alexander. "I quit school." He paused.

"Go on," said Sophie. "I'm more interested in the last, of course."

"The last time was with someone I met in the Buffalo Jump Bar a while ago."

"Oh."

"Just after I came back," he said. "I hadn't seen you yet."

"And what did you think when you saw me?" she inquired, trying to suppress all interest in her tone.

"I thought I'd stick around," he replied.

"Oh, I see. Good broad hips, not too bright, six hundred and forty acres—things like that?"

"No," he said slowly.

"Well, what, then? For heaven's sake, Alexander, do we always have to discuss this as though it were a cattle sale? I'll tell you what I thought. I thought I wanted to go to bed with you—or not necessarily to *bed*! I thought I was pretty plainly throwing myself at your head for weeks until you made your—your proposition!" She laughed.

"Were you?" He sounded perplexed.

"You mean you *didn't notice*?" She hit him sharply on the chest with her palm and he caught her hand and held it against his diaphragm. "What *did* you think?" she insisted.

"I thought you were lovely," he said simply.

"I was pitching manure at the time!"

"You'd better start ridin' that horse again," he advised. "He's gettin' used to me now."

"Forget the horse! I was pitching manure, and—" she prompted.

"And after that we had tea in the kitchen," he replied.

He turned to kiss her in his "romantic" fashion, with only a very slight sexual pressure, entirely centered on the lips and tongue. Sophie struggled to get her hands free, but after a short contest of wills she decided to let him do it his own way.

A moment later he yawned and leaned his forehead against the back of the seat beside her temple.

"You're tired, aren't you?"

He nodded. "I could go to sleep like this if I was lyin' down."

"Like this?" Sophie was divided between outrage and the desire to laugh.

"You feel good," he said, yawning again. "And you smell good. You smell like yourself."

"I hate perfume," said Sophie. "You smell good, too. Maybe that's what it all really amounts to," she added dreamily.

With the newborn nose of a sworn nonsmoker, she detected that Alexander smelled of soap and fresh air, a hint of tobacco underlying.

She sniffed appreciatively.

"Let's go home," he said. "I've got to work on that harrow tomorrow." He straightened up and started the truck.

Sophie remembered something that had been in the back of her mind all evening.

"Annie Malone," she said. "That was the name of the Indian girl in my class. Was she Benedict's sister, Alexander?"

"Yeah," said Alexander, driving. "Annie was Benedict's sister."

6

Falling Off a Horse

On Sunday morning, Sophie sat for a long time on a nail keg in the machine room of the barn, watching Alexander tinker with the tractor. It reminded her of old times. He was like her father in his approach. Alexander did not swear as much, but there was the same alternation of frustration and competent action; the same long periods of puzzled silence were followed by exclamations of understanding or disgust. The same radio murmured quietly in the corner.

Just before noon, Sophie got up with a sigh and went for the pitchfork.

"Where are you goin'?" he asked immediately, pausing with the cigarette drooping from a corner of his mouth.

"To change Rosi's straw. I'll take him out, too." She flourished the fork.

"Wait a minute." He took the cigarette out of his mouth and stamped it underfoot. Then he approached her and carefully put his arms on her shoulders so that his greasy hands did not dirty her blouse.

"I like havin' you around like this," he said softly, looking into her eyes. Sophie put up her lips, thinking he might want to kiss her, but he merely brushed them with his own and said even more deliberately, "It's nice havin' you here."

Sophie smiled at this tactful effort. She had decided to stop pushing. It was evident that Alexander would get around to what she wanted in his own way—and if he didn't, she could always leave for Timbuktu before the wedding.

It was apparent after the events of Friday night—she pursued her thoughts, pitching manure—that he was a normal male, but dominated by very abnormal ideas. Or very normal ones, from another point of view. An abnormal male dominated by normal ideas? Sophie laughed to herself.

His being jealous of Robert was simply silly. She might as well be jealous of the woman he had met at the Buffalo Jump Bar.

Sophie had never really been jealous of anyone. She had begun by being the center of her parents' universe, and it had not been different thereafter. She was aware of this in herself; she knew she had not wanted for anything. As a consequence, she was attracted to the poor, the inarticulate, the insecure. Clever Robert, none of the above, knew how to exploit this quality in her, to reveal and mock it.

She led Rocinante out of his stall and into the yard. If only men were like horses, she thought. How simple.

She stood up on the gate and got astride Rocinante bareback. His glossy sides slid firm and smooth between her thighs. She set off at a trot into the ditch trail, intending to take him around the entire circuit of the farm.

Rosi had other ideas. He began by shying at the truck.

Then he started a runaway gallop and she pulled him up with difficulty. He caracoled for a short while.

Sophie slid off his back grimly and led him around to the fence again. Even her horse had contrary notions and was perversely resistant to the simple pleasure of going for a ride.

She gentled him for a while, then mounted again. Alexander, hearing the commotion, had come out of the barn to watch.

Self-conscious now, Sophie started at a walk. Rosi shied at the truck again and she took him around. They stood together by the fence. The horse was panting, it seemed to Sophie. She sat quietly on his back.

"Want some help?" said Alexander, coming over and taking the bridle.

"What's the matter with him?" asked Sophie. "Is he frightened of the truck?"

"Maybe you'd better use a saddle."

She shook her head. "I'll try again."

Rosi got past the truck this time, then began to run. Sophie tried to pull him up and they had a fight. He reared and hit her on the nose with his comb. Then he threw her off forward and she came down hard in the ditch. Rosi cantered ahead, kicking up his heels.

Sophie sat up, dazed, rubbing her forehead. Alexander arrived on the run and knelt beside her.

"You okay?" He began feeling her arms and legs worriedly.

"Mm?" Sophie leaned on his chest. "Nosebleed."

"Nosebleed?" she heard him saying through the fog. "Concussion."

A long while later someone was asking her insistently, "What's your name, Sophia? Sophia, what's your name?"

"Sophia," said Sophie, struggling to remember. She opened her eyes and found a man's face hanging overhead like the moon.

"Sophie," she said weakly. "I think I just fainted."

She was lying on something soft, and she looked around to see what it was. It was the front-room sofa and Alexander was kneeling on the floor beside it.

"Did you catch Rosi?" she asked.

"He's okay. I put him in the barn."

"Oh." Sophie let her head fall back on the sofa cushion.

Sophie's mother appeared in the background.

". . . crazy about that stupid horse . . ." she heard.

". . . got used to me . . ." Alexander was saying.

". . . *dangerous*. I told Harry . . ."

"I must have been bleeding," Sophie said, looking at one rusty hand.

"You had a nosebleed."

Mrs. Ware receded from the room, and Sophie heard the angry clatter of lunch dishes.

She noticed that she was getting a headache. Instantly that she noticed it, it became a terrible headache, the worst she had ever had. She moaned a little.

"You must have got a real good crack on the head," said Alexander, half to himself.

"Hurts like hell." Sophie felt her nose.

"It's not broken."

"Never fell off before. Keep getting back up," she muttered.

"Yeah. Not now. Want anything, Sophia?"

He made a slight movement and she opened her eyes in alarm. "Just stay here, please."

"I'm not goin' anywhere."

"I think I'm cold."

"Just a minute," he said, and lay down full length beside her on the sofa with his arm under her neck. He was very warm.

Sophie let her eyes close again, and instantly a psychedelic light show started behind her eyelids. She opened them quickly and kept them fixed on the pearl-topped snap of Alexander's Western shirt immediately in front of her.

"Did you ever fall off?" It was necessary to stay conscious.

"Sure," he replied readily. "We were always playin' around, back in them days."

"Playing around," murmured Sophie.

"Yeah. Bareback, saddle, clothes, naked—"

"Naked?" she said, arrested by this thought.

"Didn't you ever try that?"

"They didn't teach us. Not at riding school." Sophie laughed. "Ouch!" she said at once.

"Well, we didn't go to riding school," he said. "We rode all the time, clothes or no clothes."

"It must be nice."

"Especially for a girl," he agreed. "You should do it sometime."

"Playing around," said Sophie dreamily. "You and Marfa—" She experimented with closing her eyes again. It seemed to be dark in there.

"And Benedict."

"And Annie?"

"Yeah. And Annie."

Sophie woke up a few hours later. She was in her own bed. Mother was sitting placidly in the chair in front of the dressing table.

"How did I get here?" Sophie asked, struggling to a sitting position.

"Alexander carried you up, dear. Dr. Morrison thinks you have a little concussion. So you're just to stay in—"

"Who undressed me?" demanded Sophie suspiciously.

"I did, of course. Who did you think, dear?" Her mother stood up. "I'll go tell Alexander you're awake. He's been terribly worried."

"He has?"

"Naturally he blames himself for letting you try to ride that horse."

Sophie sat upright and began quickly shifting her legs over the side of the bed. A bolt of pain shot through her head, and she compromised by reclining with one foot on the floor.

"Did he say that?" she demanded.

"No, but of course it's the way he feels." Mrs. Ware's lips momentarily tightened into a thin line. Then she smiled sweetly at Sophie. "He'll tell you himself, dear."

"Rosi is my horse," said Sophie, finding it necessary to lie down flat again.

"I think you could probably eat some soup, couldn't you, darling? You didn't have any lunch."

"Soup and—"

"Crusts. Of course. You always get crusts when you're sick, you know."

"Yes," said Sophie, sighing luxuriously against the pillows.

Alexander visited her that evening.

Sophie had left the virginity of her bedroom intact during the year that she had lived there. Alexander looked rather incongruous against the pastel ruffles of her adolescence. She was amused.

He lounged on the foot of her bed with a cup of tea in his hand and told her what she had begun to recognize as a "Benedict Malone story."

"One time Benedict and me run away together," he began.

"You ran away from home?" Sophie raised her eyebrows, then instantly regretted it. She was getting two magnificent black eyes now. She had seen them in her hand mirror.

"Not exactly. At least, we were goin' to come back. We were goin' to go to the mountains and bring out a herd of wild horses."

"Really? I suppose you didn't have the least idea if there were any, or where you were going."

"Well, there were wild horses," he said. "We would have found them sometime."

"But you didn't. What happened?"

"Poppa sent the RCMP out after us. Marfa said it was because I took Momma's Appaloosa, Bella. I don't guess he'd have been so worried about me."

"Oh, come now!"

"Benedict's ma was drinkin', so she didn't give a damn. But Poppa tried to get us both charged with horse theft."

"But you didn't steal any horses!" exclaimed Sophie in astonishment.

"Benedict did," said Alexander, with a slightly shamefaced grin.

"My God!"

He rested his elbow on the padded pink footboard of the bed.

"Indians don't think horses really belong to people," he said. "Not to white men, anyway."

"But they stole all their horses from white men. I mean, that's how they got them in the first place!"

"Yeah. They did," agreed Alexander. "That's why he—"

"Oh, I see. So Benedict was doing it like his ancestors, was he?" Sophie smiled painfully. "What happened?"

"The principal of the school got us off. Benedict was real good at school."

"When was this? How old were you?"

"Oh, about twelve, I guess."

"Your father would really have let you go to jail for horse theft?" Sophie was outraged.

Alexander shrugged. "Poppa," he said. "That's him."

He put his teacup down on the glass top of the flounced bedside table, leaning over Sophie in the warm yellow light of the lamp.

"We got some real good ones, too," he said, smiling

at her. "We only got caught when we were bringin' 'em back."

"But—what were you going to do with them?"

"Benedict and Annie had a place out on the Reserve. He was goin' to keep 'em there. We were just kids, you know, Sophia." He made a move as if to stand up, and Sophie caught his arm.

"Tell me about Annie, Alexander," she said, unwilling to let him go so soon. "I remember her very well now. She was good at school, too."

Alexander continued to bend over her. "I've been thinkin' about that, Sophia," he said seriously. "I've got to tell you about Annie sometime. At first I thought you remembered, but now I guess you never knew."

"Knew what?"

"I'll tell you tomorrow," he said. "You're not goin' to school in the morning, not the way you are."

"I must look awful."

"Pretty bad," he agreed.

Sophie made a face at him and let go of his arm. He stood up.

"Maybe if I part my hair on the other side . . ." she called after him.

"It won't help," he said, laughing, as he went out of the room.

Alexander was right about how she felt in the morning. She still had a splitting headache. She took a couple of aspirins, but it seemed senseless to go to school. Her mother had already called in to say she was sick.

After breakfast she staggered out to the machine room of the barn. Sitting on a nail keg was about all she was up to, and she was looking forward to one of Alexander's extraordinary stories. The way these stories revealed the unbridled emotions of his family interested her more than the hero, Benedict.

Alexander was finished with the tractor. He looked up as she entered, then came over and silently led her back to Rosi's stall.

Rosi whickered and Sophie went over eagerly to make up. But his eyes were trained on an object beyond her shoulder: Alexander. Sophie did her best to ignore this as she patted his nose.

"What if you can't forgive your horse?" she inquired rhetorically.

Alexander leaned on the stall door, lighting a cigarette.

"I do tend to hold grudges," she said. "You could go too far some day, darling," she went on, addressing the horse.

"It's probably just because he's—" Alexander began.

"Because he's a male chauvinist pig?" Sophie said coldly. She was not going to have Alexander explain Rocinante to her. The horse continued to regard him adoringly while Sophie scratched his ears.

"You were going to tell me something about Annic," said Sophie, turning away crossly and seating herself on a straw bale. She put her hand momentarily on her forehead, a little dizzy.

"Yeah," said Alexander. "I didn't think you'd forget." He looked down at his cigarette.

"I don't know how I could have forgotten her," said Sophie carelessly. "She was a really unusual person. There can't have been more than two Indians from the Reserve in the whole school. She was one and Benedict was the other."

"Yeah."

"I didn't know her all that well. She was so shy. But she was really pretty. What happened to her, I wonder? She dropped out of school, I think. That must have been the year you were in grade twelve." Sophie glanced up, smiling. "Oh my God!" she said a moment later.

"I got her pregnant," said Alexander. "That's why I left." He dropped his cigarette into the dust of the barn floor, then bent to retrieve the end.

"You left?" said Sophie vacantly.

"Yeah. I left town when I was eighteen."

"And Annie was pregnant?" Sophie was getting herself together slowly. Annie had been pregnant and so she had been expelled from school. They handled things like that very quietly in those days.

"She had a boy. Named him Benedict," said Alexander, tucking the filter end into his breast pocket. He usually smoked the other kind, without filters. Sophie could see why.

"You just left?" Shock was making her inarticulate.

"Yeah," said Alexander.

"You left her all alone to have a baby? And then what? Why didn't you tell me before?"

"I'm tellin' you now."

"But I wouldn't have—" Sophie was panting slightly. "I knew her! You wrecked her life! And you didn't even stick around to—"

"Benedict wanted to kill me," said Alexander.

"Are you kidding? Benedict was only eighteen!"

"He tried to kill me," said Alexander. "He come after me with his bare hands down by the bridge on the Reserve." He stared somberly at the floor.

"But—"

"So Poppa told me to get out. He didn't want any trouble with Indians."

"Didn't you try to take her with you? Why didn't you take her?"

"You don't understand, Sophia. She was fifteen."

"I remember," shouted Sophie, standing up. "She was beautiful! She was perfect! Then she disappeared! Why didn't you leave her alone?"

Alexander was silent.

"Couldn't you have done anything?" she raged at him.

"There wasn't much I could do," said Alexander. "Poppa gave me a hundred dollars and an old wreck of a car. Told me not to come back except in a coffin. Or unless I got rich."

Sophie stared at him, speechless, her mind reeling.

"I tried to send her some money once," said Alexander. "I got it back. Benedict sent it back."

"She was all alone." The mother was an alcoholic; Sophie remembered this clearly from the story he had told last night.

"Benedict was there," said Alexander. "You don't understand about Indians, Sophia. They look after their own."

"And the baby? What happened to him?"

"He's fourteen now. He lives with Annie."

Sophie's rage, until now purely abstract, took an unexpected turn. Of course he had seen her again. Annie was the woman he had met in the Buffalo Jump Bar, the woman he had slept with. She became quite calm suddenly.

"Are you giving her money now?"

"She wouldn't take it."

"Don't you think you owe her something?"

"It doesn't work that way with Indians," he said. "If it'd been a Ukrainian girl—or someone like you—it would have been different." He laughed shortly. "For one thing, I'd have gone to jail."

"Or you'd be married!" said Sophie. "You never thought of that, I suppose. Maybe Annie would like it if you said, 'Come on, Annie. Let's get married. Let's have a *place* together!' "

Alexander folded his arms, a patient, defensive expression on his face.

"Well, what about it?" she demanded. "It's not too late, surely? She has your child!"

"Are you trying to make me marry Annie?" he asked. "I'm not goin' to marry Annie, Sophia," he went on.

"Why not?"

"She drinks like her ma, for one thing."

"Oh—that's your reason, is it?" shouted Sophie, thinking again of Alexander meeting Annie in the bar.

"Hey! Where are you goin', Sophia!"

"I'm going to school!"

Alexander followed her out of the barn and watched from the doorway while she got into the car. Sophie clutched her forehead for a moment like a Romantic poet, then fumbled with the key in the ignition. Alexander began to walk rapidly and anxiously across the farmyard to the car. Sophie let out the clutch, stalled in third, then readjusted the gearshift and started off with a shower of gravel spurting from under her wheels.

7

Annie Malone

"My God," said Robert. "You've got a black eye!" He came a little farther into the classroom, then, as usual, returned to secure the door. "Two black eyes," he said, standing in front of her.

Sophie had spent the lunch hour with a box of pancake makeup borrowed from Madeleine LeJeur, who had acne scars. But nothing could hide the swelling, which was still coming up.

"I fell off my horse," she said shortly.

"Oh yes," said Robert, seating himself sideways on her desk. "You fell off your horse. Was that before or after he beat you up?"

"Oh, for Christ's sake, Robert! Do you have to?" Sophie surprised herself by bursting into tears. She had been icily calm for hours now.

Robert continued to sit in front of her, interest flickering across his face. Unlike most men, he rather liked seeing women cry.

"I was wondering where you were at recess this afternoon," he said presently. "I assumed you were avoiding me. And now I see you were avoiding me."

Sophie got some Kleenex out of her desk drawer and turned her back on him.

"Well, I suppose one can't help drawing certain conclusions from all this," he said gaily, coming around the desk to stand beside her. "I would say that this was done by a horse. A male horse," he went on thoughtfully, peering at her face. "An Arab stallion, I should say. Poorly broken." He shook his head. "A poorly broken Arab stallion, brown, with a white blaze on its—"

"Very funny," said Sophie in a choked voice. She blew her nose.

"Ah, but there's more to it," said Robert, extending a forefinger and catching a tear from her chin. "*This* was never done by a horse!"

Sophie got up and went over to the windows. Robert followed and put a kindly arm around her shoulders.

"Why don't you tell me all about it?" he suggested.

This was the trouble with Robert. You could tell him things. But sooner or later you saw that he liked it entirely too much.

"I'll just ask, shall I, darling? You know my methods. Have you broken off your engagement, then?"

Sophie was mute. But she knew it was hopeless. Robert was never satisfied with anything less than the complete story.

"There are two reasons why women break off their engagements," he went on smoothly. "One of them is jealousy, and I'm not sure what the other one is. That probably explains why I'm single to this day. Now in your case . . ."

Sophie shook her head, making a negative noise.

"Now you," Robert continued, paying no attention to this, "are the sort of person who either doesn't know or will not admit she is jealous even when various antique methods of torture are applied. So your opinion is worthless."

Sophie knew that she was not jealous. What she felt was outrage. She remembered Annie, so shy and pretty and good. Alexander had no conscience about this, apparently.

"The work of the analyst is to bring certain facts to consciousness," said Robert smugly. "The cooperation of the patient is only vital in the later stages. Now that we know what is *wrong* . . ."

"I'm not jealous!"

"No, no. Of course not," he said soothingly. "Your sympathy lies entirely with the other woman, doesn't it? What he did was quite wrong. Very wrong indeed. You see how well I know you, Sophie?"

"You don't know a thing!"

"Okay. That's agreed, then. Now, obviously you think he ought to be doing something about it, right? So you told him to go and marry her, didn't you?" He closed one eye slyly. "Entirely overlooking his feeble protests that he doesn't want to marry her."

"You're on the wrong track, Robert!" said Sophie, amazed by this clairvoyance.

"Well, I do think he has something there, Sophie. Of course, I don't know Annie myself, but—"

"Cheat!"

"But I know you through and through, darling. Through and through!" He was delighted with himself.

"How did you—"

"We all went to high school together, don't you remember? I know you were still in the egg at the time, so I've been wondering what you would do when you found out."

"Pig!"

"In fact, we've all been on tenterhooks for weeks—"

"We?"

"Oh, roughly the classes of '67, '68, and '69, you know."

Sophie stared at him. This aspect of the matter had not yet occurred to her. But of course, everybody knew.

"Why do I tell you these things?" Robert inquired, leaning against the windowsill. "The analyst always has mixed motives, of course. At some point the patient should subject these to a critical evaluation."

"Shut up, Robert." Everybody knew. So it followed that Alexander had really thought that she knew.

Robert was looking at her kindly. "I can probably help you out a bit there, too," he suggested. "Let us suppose that your analyst has an emotional attachment to you. He may want to reinforce certain hasty resolves. . . ."

Sophie had stopped listening. A new and even more excruciating thought had occurred to her. Perhaps Alexander believed that the reason she was angry was that everybody knew. Perhaps he thought she cared about their opinion.

"So what have we established?" Robert asked rather pathetically, trying to break in on her abstraction.

"Nothing!"

"Absolutely wrong!" he cried gaily. "We've made massive strides in one short afternoon session. Let me just do some of the, ah, intellectual work for you, Sophie. One! You're jealous as hell! Two! You're pretty self-righteous, you know. Three! You don't know anything about Annie. Four— You're not a very cooperative patient," he complained.

Sophie had gone back to her desk and was putting on her sweater.

Alexander probably believed that she was angry because she adhered to the same vicious, backbiting, middle-class standards as the classes of '67, '68, and '69, the standards that had had Annie expelled from school.

"Where does Annie live, do you know?" she asked.

"Ah," he replied, "now if I were to give you some

advice—which I certainly shall not do, as I never give advice—"

If everybody knew, so much the worse for them! They would see her, Sophie, taking Annie's part. Annie had been destroyed first of all by Alexander, and then by this "everybody," so eager to be cruel.

"I never give advice," Robert repeated.

"No," said Sophie absently, her tears long gone.

"She lives in the Buffalo Jump Bar," said Robert thoughtfully. "Would you like me to go with you?"

"No!"

"Wait!" he cried, following her out of the classroom. "Don't go yet! She won't be there till nine o'clock or so! We must talk some more!"

But Sophie was already out the door.

Sophie went home and had supper. She went to her room and thought for a while, then grimly helped water the garden. Mrs. Ware conversed sporadically with Alexander, but Sophie worked furiously, her head down. Anger and determination churned confusedly inside her.

At nine o'clock she checked her makeup and then went out to her car.

"Where are you goin', Sophia?" asked Alexander quietly, materializing out of the shadow of the barn. He was wearing his "harassed" expression.

"To the Buffalo Jump Bar," said Sophie shortly. "To see Annie."

"I could take you later," he offered.

"No," said Sophie, getting behind the wheel of her car.

He sighed. "You don't understand, Sophia. That's a real rough place. And Annie—"

"I've been there. And I used to know Annie. Anyway, I'm going."

She had no real plan of action. She was going to find Annie, that was all.

So many layers of motivation. And who was to say which was the real one? According to Robert, it was really only jealousy. This was perhaps the male interpretation. Sophie was going to put paid to this. It would be one in the eye to all those who had been so eagerly watching to see what she would do.

As for Annie . . .

"I'll just propose to her straight off, and then when she says no, I'll go home," Sophie told herself, laughing through her clenched teeth. "I don't really want to marry her anyway."

Sophie knew the Buffalo Jump Bar very well, having frequented it with Robert. Robert liked to amuse himself by setting conundrums for the local drunks.

It was a small-town beer parlor. The interior was arranged somewhat like a café, with a central row of booths divided by a partition, and tables along the sides. A dance floor separated this area from the bar proper. It was illegal to dance in Alberta's bars, but a kindly management recognized dancing as a need of country people with grain checks.

Sophie approached the beer taps and leaned up in front of them, her jeans and cowboy boots serving as a sort of protective coloration. Robert liked to wear his academic costume to drink in: a tweed jacket with leather patches and a discreetly striped tie. It occurred to Sophie to wonder just how often her presence had kept him from getting beaten up on such occasions.

She ordered a beer from Bobby Boy. Bobby Boy had been in grade three with her, but she had lost him somewhere behind after that. His parents owned the bar.

"What's new, Sophie?"

"Oh, nothing."

Sophie spotted Luke Bresnyachuk at a corner table. She waved vaguely and turned back to Bobby Boy.

"Is Annie Malone here?" she asked.

"Yeah." Bobby Boy was flicking a rag around the

counter, keeping an eye on three things at once. Already an evangelical type whose company Robert favored was acting up:

" 'In my father's house there are many mansions! If it were not so I would have told you!' " he was screaming to the bar at large. "I'll give you five hundred bucks if you can tell me what it means!"

Bobby Boy sighed and hunched his shoulders. Meanwhile, Sophie looked carefully at the Indians lined up against a far wall, stolid, morose, and silent over their glasses of draft beer. A beautiful black-haired teenager in a turquoise T-shirt flitted away from them among the tables, looking for an oilman or a rich farmer on a spree. She leaned over somebody's shoulder and her hair spilled down onto the filthy table like oil or clean water. But this was not Annie.

"Where is she?" asked Sophie.

"Over there." Bobby Boy pointed, loading a tray. "What d'you want with Annie, Sophie? She's a real mean broad."

"I know her," said Sophie simply. She paused a moment, looking at Annie, before she made any approach.

Annie had changed. She still had her thick dark hair, but it was frizzed around her head into a meaningless short permanent, now beginning to unravel. Her face had hardened into inscrutability; her lips were thin, almost cruel. She looked mean.

She was sitting at a table with two men, oilmen by the looks of them, in Stetsons and string ties. Annie appeared to be ignoring them, however. She had a glass of draft in her hand. The men were drinking whiskey, not talking to one another. The whole setup had an unwholesome look to Sophie.

She went over slowly, feeling self-conscious. She was twenty-eight and Annie was twenty-nine. But Annie could have been forty. This, too, was Alexander's fault. Sophie pushed indignation to the forefront of her mind. "Hello, Annie," she said.

"Yeah?" said Annie. "Who're you?"

"I'm Sophie. Sophie Ware," said Sophie. "May I sit down?"

"Sure. Make yourself at home," said one of the torpid oilmen, pushing out a chair with his foot. "What'd you say your name was?"

"Mind if I sit down, Annie?" repeated Sophie.

"Nope." Annie looked her over with hostile interest. "Sophie Ware?"

"Sophie?" said the oilman, waking up fully. "That's a weird name. What've you been doing with yourself, Sophie?" He leaned toward her.

"Annie," said Sophie, pressing on, "I've come to see you. It's been a long time, I know, but I've got to—"

"Yeah," said the oilman. "Too long. Why didn't I see you here before, Sophie? Buy you a drink?"

"I already have one. I want to talk to Annie."

"Well, like I say, what've you been doing with yourself these days, Sophie?" As with most men in bars—she had observed this before—a firm grip on the name was the first step toward serious acquaintance.

Annie continued to regard her with displeasure.

"Oh, I've been busy," Sophie told the oilman. She glanced anxiously at Annie. Bobby Boy brought beer and two more whiskeys in response to some concealed command, and she was only able to beat the oilman to the draw with a twenty-dollar bill on the basis of greater sobriety.

"I bet you're a teacher," said the oilman. "Live around here?"

"I own a farm."

"Oh yeah. One of them acreages, probably. Got your garden in?" The man put his twenty on Bobby Boy's tray as a tip.

"I have, as a matter of fact." Sophie again glanced at Annie, but she was addressing herself indifferently to her beer.

"What're you growing? Bananas?" The oilman laughed, and the other one, barely alive, made laughing gestures.

"Cabbage," said Sophie.

"Yeah?"

"Rutabagas." Sophie had a sudden inspiration. "Tomatoes," she added.

"Oh boy! Hear that, Ed? Sounds like quite a—"

"Green peppers."

"I bet." But a slightly dizzy look crossed his face.

"Zucchini."

"What's that?"

"With garlic?" said Sophie in mock astonishment. "Or, you know, souffléed?"

Annie was now taking an interest.

"Garlic," said Sophie quickly. "Garlic and onions. Creamed onions."

"Creamed onions?"

"Yes, with buttered carrots. Mashed potatoes. Turnips and mushrooms."

"Turnips and—?"

"Baked squash, pea soup, brussels sprouts with cheese sauce. Dill pickles . . ." Sophie continued her litany. A faint smile had appeared on Annie's hard lips. "French beans—you know, those red ones with strings—and then—"

"Okay! Okay!"

"Sauerkraut," she went on inexorably. "And buttered carrots."

"You already said that," Annie told her.

"Oh dear."

"Let's go to the can," said Annie.

"Good idea," agreed Sophie. Annie was cooperating.

She followed Annie across the floor to a door on one side of the bar counter marked with a crude, hand-lettered sign: WOMAN. As soon as they were inside, Annie turned around quickly, her back to the mirrors above the sinks, and gave Sophie a narrow look. After a moment she withdrew a crumpled package of cigarettes from her back pocket and put one between her lips.

"Some broad attack me in here once," she said in a

dry, low-pitched voice. "Broke a mirror and went after me with the glass. I like to be sure it not goin' to happen again."

"We were in grade ten together, Annie," said Sophie vaguely. She had caught sight of her own reflection in the glass behind Annie, and was horrified to see herself under the brilliant fluorescent lighting. Makeup did not help at all. If anything, it made it worse. With an exclamation of dismay, she went over for a closer look.

"Someone been beatin' up on you?" asked Annie harshly, as Sophie took her makeup case out of her shoulder bag.

"I fell off a horse."

"You sure did," said Annie skeptically.

The fact that the swelling around her nose had gone down did not improve matters much. The skin under her eyes looked like Danish bleu cheese. Sophie gave a muffled snort of laughter and put the compact away.

"Well, I can't wait all night," said Annie. "I guess you got something to say to me."

Sophie turned around and leaned against the sinks herself. How to put this? Now that she had gotten to the point, she had no idea what to say. Her tragic consciousness had departed entirely.

"Alexander Bresnyachuk—" she began, hesitating.

"Sasha? You can't tell me he did that!" Annie's lips curled with scorn. "Sasha never beat up on a woman in his life!"

8

You Might Call It a Talent

"No, no! It's just that you—I—he wants to marry me," said Sophie in desperation.

"Oh yeah?" said Annie. "Here, hold this. I'm goin' to do what I came here for." She gave Sophie her cigarette and went into one of the cubicles.

"You don't mind?" Sophie took a long drag on the cigarette.

"Do you?" asked Annie dryly.

"No." Sophie was smoking rather hard. "But he just . . . er . . . this morning he told me about you."

"Oh?" Annie emerged, still zipping up her jeans. "So what do you want to know?"

"Hey! This isn't an interrogation. I just wanted to see you again."

"Like hell you did," said Annie.

"No! I really did! I wanted to make sure you were—"

"Stop shaking, Sophie." Annie rinsed her fingers. "I

won't bite you." She looked into the mirror and drew a wet forefinger over her eyebrows, then glanced critically at Sophie.

"Do you want to marry him yourself?" said Sophie directly.

"Here, have another cigarette. I still got three," said Annie generously. "You're askin' me?" she went on.

Sophie accepted a cigarette and smiled uncertainly at Annie. "You might say so."

"Well, then—no," said Annie bluntly. "You got my answer." She lit a cigarette for herself. Then she regarded Sophie with a genuine smile. "You're crazy," she remarked. "I remember you."

"Yes. We were in the same grade. But then you just . . . disappeared. They expelled you, I guess."

"They never expel me. I couldn't go no more," said Annie. She made this distinction a little stubbornly, as though it mattered.

"Oh God, Annie!" said Sophie, on a rush of sympathy. "I didn't know, you see. If only I had known!"

"What could you have done?" inquired Annie coolly. "I had the boy, anyway."

"The baby?"

"He fourteen now. Doin' real well."

"Is he?"

"Sure he is," said Annie defensively. "He like my brother Benedict."

"It was you I was thinking of," said Sophie timidly.

Annie shrugged. "Don't worry about Annie," she said. "Annie'll be okay."

"Sophie'll be just fine too," murmured Sophie darkly.

Annie laughed.

"I got used to dealin' with social workers," she said.

"Social workers?"

"Yeah. They come mooning around sometimes," said Annie. "Then they go home and get divorced or something. I think maybe you are one till you start that stuff about vegetables."

"Oh yes. That stuff about vegetables," said Sophie, remembering.

"So you're goin' to marry Sasha?"

"Yes, I guess so," said Sophie, wondering how Alexander felt about this now.

"You look like you could use a social worker yourself."

"Maybe I could. Do you want another beer, Annie? We could find a different table."

"Sure. I'm broke, though."

"That's all right," said Sophie hastily. "I'll pay. Your consulting fee."

"Yeah. My fee." Annie looked at her sharply and then laughed. "If you say so."

They took a corner table in the front, recently vacated by one of those dark, dirty men who sit apparently in torment through a couple of beers, and leave halfway through the third. The bar was stirring into the loquacious phase that was Robert's particular specialty.

Annie listened intently as Sophie described the courtship of Alexander. Her hard face had relaxed somewhat. Sophie was hamming it up. But she felt quite comfortable with Annie now.

"Jeez," said Annie, when Sophie had finished describing the proposal.

"Well, and then—" Sophie went on relentlessly.

"Boy, you need a friend," said Annie.

Sophie ordered another set of beers.

"You have a point," she said. "But after you reach about twenty-five, they begin to drop off like flies. I mean, I had friends—in college and so on—"

"Is that why you're gettin' married to Sasha?" asked Annie curiously.

"No. But—"

"So why are you?"

Sophie paused. Certainly it was an interesting question.

"There has to be some progress," she said.

"What do you mean by that?"

"I mean, he's right," said Sophie, marshaling her thoughts. "You do this, and then you do that—all very well, but what are you going to do when you grow up?"

"Want to have kids?" asked Annie.

"Well, I suppose so. But it's not just that." Swept away by her own articulation, Sophie began to enlarge on Alexander's proposal, suddenly changing sides.

One of the men from Annie's table, the other one, now approached them and knelt at Sophie's elbow.

"Haven't I seen you somewheres before?" he asked.

"Don't bother," said Sophie faintly. "We've already settled it."

The man looked up at her in perplexity, one hand on the back of her chair, the other still groping for her knee. "Nothing you can do will stop us," said Sophie. "We're getting married tomorrow."

"Who?" he demanded.

"Annie and I. I'm a man, didn't you notice?"

"Yeah. I'm not," contributed Annie, chuckling.

The oilman took his hand off Sophie's knee hastily, then put it back more firmly.

"You coulda fooled me!" he said.

"You've heard of these sex-change operations?" said Sophie with a sigh. "Well, one day, about last February—"

"Oh yeah? Which are you now?" He withdrew his hand again.

"The trouble is, I still can't resist women's clothes," said Sophie, looking down at her man-tailored shirt and jeans. "Luckily, Annie doesn't mind."

"I had a dress once, me," said Annie thoughtfully.

The oilman was fidgeting.

"Let's tell him the truth, Annie," said Sophie soberly.

"Sure," agreed Annie.

"Nope," said the oilman, standing up. "Three's a crowd, I guess." He moved off in the direction of another table.

"Sorry, Annie," said Sophie ruefully. "I just can't help myself."

"Well, you sure good at it!"

"I suppose you might call it a talent."

"Would you like to dance?" said Annie ironically.

Sophie now caught sight of Alexander at the door, looking out over the tables. He began making his way toward her, an expression of relief on his face. Annie looked behind her, following the direction of Sophie's eyes, and saw him too. He was coming slowly through the close-packed bar, narrow-hipped, broad-shouldered, taller than anyone else in the room.

"Want me to go now?" asked Annie, swinging around.

"No, no!" said Sophie nervously, catching hold of her sleeve.

"Okay. But I don't want no hassles, is all!"

"Hi, Annie," said Alexander, standing over them.

"Hello, Sasha," said Annie. "We just been talking." She indicated Sophie, her tone defiant.

Alexander sat down. Bobby Boy instantly appeared at his side with a bottle of beer on the tray. He had been watching her all evening, Sophic realized uneasily.

"How's Bennie?" Alexander asked Annie. "Doin' good?"

Sophie suddenly felt like throwing her arms around his neck. He had a gift for the simple and the good; she had never met anyone like him before.

"He doin' okay," said Annie.

Alexander drank some beer out of the bottle.

"Her and me are gettin' married," said Annie to Alexander, breaking the silence. "That what she tell that guy over there," she added, jerking her thumb at the oilman, who was now making some headway with a dyed blonde over by the shuffleboard.

Alexander frowned, and Sophie watched him anxiously, but he only seemed to be trying to make sense of this remark.

"I kind of got the idea by that time," Annie said to Sophie. "But let me tell you, when a tough-lookin' broad with two black eyes comes up to my table and begins pullin' off a vegetable stunt like that, I—"

"A vegetable stunt?" Alexander was looking curiously at them both. "What in hell are you talkin' about, Annie?"

"I had to get your attention somehow," said Sophie, beginning to laugh.

"Yeah. Well, you did," said Annie.

Sophie smiled tentatively at Alexander. To her intense relief, he smiled back. It was going to be all right.

"Sophie fell off her horse," Alexander told Annie.

"So she say." Annie took out her last cigarette. "How you been, Sasha?"

"Okay." Alexander struck a match absently. "I guess Sophia told you we're gettin' married?"

"We talk about that, yeah." Annie's lips curled upward in a faint smile.

"Well, that's good," said Alexander, sighing. "How're you?" he added.

"Still drinkin'," replied Annie, with a careless gesture that brought Bobby Boy flying with more beer. He waited patiently, ignoring Sophie's money on the orange towel that was the tablecloth, while Alexander found three dollars in his wallet.

"Too much, to tell you the truth," she went on, after Bobby Boy had departed.

Alexander said nothing. Sophie felt there was a criticism implicit in this.

"My old man drive for Northern," said Annie. "He's all right—especially when he not drinkin' himself. But he's away a lot."

"Drivin'," agreed Alexander. "That's the way it is."

Sophie had a slight feeling of unreality. Surely they knew each other better than this.

"Yeah," Annie went on. "Benedict drive for Northern for a while. That's how the old man show up. He from another Reserve, but Benedict bring him home one time, and he kind of hang on after that."

"When was Benedict drivin' for Northern?"

"That was after he got hurt at the Stampede," said Annie.

"I heard about that."

"He got hurt real bad."

"Remember how I told you he could ride?" Alexander said to Sophie.

"What happened?" asked Sophie.

"I was there, me," said Annie. "He doin' great all afternoon. He can ride just about anything. They got some real mean ones at the Stampede."

"Yeah, they really hurt them," said Alexander.

"I guess Benedict, he don't do it like that," said Annie. "He get hurt instead." She looked across at Alexander. "But he never fall, Sasha. He jump. I was there."

Alexander nodded, frowning. Annie seemed to expect some comment, but he said nothing.

Listening to this conversation, Sophie once again caught a hint of the glamour of Benedict Malone. He could never have fallen, of course.

"He stay up in Foothills Hospital for a year while they pick his ribs out of his lungs," said Annie.

"What happened then?" asked Sophie in alarm. Annie spoke of her brother as though he were dead.

"He start to drive for Northern," said Annie, looking up. "I'm goin' to the can again."

She stood up, not waiting for Sophie to follow this time. Sophie watched her walk away. She had a surprisingly feminine way of walking, despite the overall flatness and narrowness of her figure.

"So now you saw Annie?" said Alexander. Sophie turned around, trying to interpret the expression on his face. It astonished her, this expression. It was a protective expression, almost proprietary.

"Want to go home?"

"Okay," said Sophie, still amazed. "But what about Annie?"

"She'll stay on." He shrugged. "She's drinkin'. Drinkin' and cheatin' on her old man."

"I like her," said Sophie. "I want to wait until she comes back."

Annie returned after a minute or two. Alexander stood up immediately.

"Come see me sometime, Sophie," said Annie.

"I'd like to."

"It's on the Reserve. Anyone could tell you where." She looked down at the beer bottles on the table. "I got to get off this after tonight anyway."

"So long, Annie," said Alexander.

Sophie led the way out of the bar. One or two male hands reached out to seize, and then were quickly withdrawn as she made her way through the press. It was the effect of Alexander behind her, she guessed—a sort of continuation of the meaning of that look he had been giving her. "Buttered carrots" would probably not strike him as a fine self-protective device. He really knew nothing about her. Annie already knew more than he did.

"Where's the truck?"

"I walked," he replied. "It's only about three miles."

"Good heavens!" Sophie smiled into the soft summer darkness. "Were you expecting to get drunk or something?"

"I don't know what I was expecting!"

"Anyway, I'm apologizing, Alexander. I said a lot of mean things." She stopped under a streetlight.

"Don't feel bad," he said.

"I really didn't know, you see." Sophie looked up at

him earnestly. "It took me by surprise. And then—you must have thought I was a real bitch!"

"Nope," he said cheerfully.

"What *did* you think, then?" Sophie asked. But the unanalytical quality of male thought, she already knew, made him unable to answer this question. So she merely continued the conversation in her mind as they got into her car.

"What are you laughin' at?" asked Alexander.

"Me? Oh, I was just thinking how much I like you," said Sophie cautiously.

Alexander stretched out his legs uncomfortably in the little car as Sophie started up.

"Yeah. That's what I was thinkin' too," he said.

"You were?" said Sophie happily.

"I was thinkin' that when I went in there," he said. "When I saw you over there talkin' to Annie."

Sophie now began to feel rather pleased with herself. It had been the right thing to go and see Annie; she already knew that. But apparently he knew it, too. She saw suddenly that the innocent silence she had maintained on the subject of Annie must have caused him real dread.

"You know," he went on, "something else I was thinkin'. I was thinkin' how many times I went lookin' for a woman in a bar like that. The only ones I ever wanted were the ones who weren't lookin' at me."

"I was looking at you," remarked Sophie.

"Yeah. You were. But even if you hadn't been, I'd have gone over there and tried to get you."

"You mean if you didn't know me?"

"And you'd have told me to go to hell, most likely."

"Well, I'm not so sure of that," said Sophie. She thought about "buttered carrots" again and gave a guilty laugh.

"It's not your way," said Alexander.

"I'm not as naïve as I look, perhaps."

"You're a real beautiful girl," he said. "Know that, Sophia?"

"And the marrying kind, you think?" Sophie was touched, however.

"Yeah," he said contentedly.

Sophie drew up into the farmyard and stopped beside the truck. She got out of the car.

"Well . . ." she said, beginning to yawn, standing between the two vehicles.

Alexander smiled at her, putting his hands on her shoulders, and she leaned against him confidently, finishing her yawn. It was all right. In fact, it was a good deal better than all right, she realized a moment later, as he showed no signs of wanting to stop this kiss.

She sighed with pleasure, pressing herself a little forward and feeling Alexander's quick intake of breath. Hard, warm hands were on her waist above her belt, drawing her body toward him.

A thought struck her suddenly. There was something else she had to explain.

"Perhaps I was a little jealous," she murmured.

"Of Annie?" He sounded startled.

"Well . . . yes."

He withdrew a little, still holding her, but by the arms.

"That all happened when we were kids, Sophia."

"No, it was when I was thinking of you being with her after you came back."

"After I came back?"

"When you met her in the Buffalo Jump Bar." Sophie tilted back her head, speaking precisely. It was necessary to be honest about this.

"What do you mean?" asked Alexander.

"Annie was the person you slept with—you know—the last time, wasn't she?"

The look of perplexity on Alexander's face faded into comprehension. He let go of her arms and began lighting a cigarette.

"No," he said. "That was somebody else. That wasn't Annie, Sophia."

9

Going to See Annie

It was lunchtime. Sophie, her raccoon eyes discreetly masked by dark glasses, was doing yard duty. Caterpillar fights were going on in all corners. She had just stopped a particularly messy one over by the swings.

"And now," said a suave voice by her elbow, "I perceive you have time for another one of our fifty-minute sessions."

"Oh, hello, Robert," said Sophie, smiling at him absently.

"My spies tell me that you went to the Buffalo Jump Bar last night."

Sophie laughed.

"I see," said Robert wisely, looking her up and down.

Sophie now admitted to herself that he had been partly right about her yesterday. She was not going to tell him this, however. It would not be good for him to know, and besides, she was no longer the slightest bit jealous of Annie.

"Well, I'm glad to see you're still intact," Robert went on. "Rumor has it that Annie Malone once cut some woman into two hundred and fifty thousand tiny pieces in the, uh, powder room of the Buffalo Jump Bar."

"But that wasn't Annie's fault," said Sophie quickly.

"Oh?"

"No. The other woman attacked her."

"She did get off with a fine," said Robert thoughtfully.

"*She* got a fine!" Sophie was shocked. "But—"

"Annie is an Indian, Sophie. I hope this does not entirely escape your well-meaning liberal attention. The other person was probably white."

Sophie looked down at the caterpillars crawling over the asphalt at her feet. Her father had been responsible for the liberalism of her views. Mother's family, Social Credit to the death, didn't go in for this wishy-washy, bleeding-heart business. From an entirely different point of view, neither did Robert.

"So you talked," said Robert.

"Yes," said Sophie guardedly. She saw that Robert was embarking on a new investigation.

"Let me guess!" he said eagerly. "First of all, you told her that poor old Sasha was negotiable, didn't you? You would do that, you know, Sophie!"

"Well . . . anyway."

"Must have been quite a conversation!" Robert began lighting one of his short cigars. "You can see why I had a fleeting worry on your behalf, I hope."

"We had a good time together," said Sophie with dignity. "First of all, we drove away some oilmen, and then—well! Then we drove away some more oilmen," she said, laughing helplessly.

"In short, not a very profitable evening!" said Robert.

"Profitable? Do you mean to imply—?"

"On the contrary! Meaning to imply, like giving advice, is something I never do! Let me introduce you to Thomas," said Robert, pointing to a small, bespectacled child over by the seesaws, an onlooker. "You had him in your class three years ago, I believe?"

"Thomas Jones," agreed Sophie, still somewhat upset. "Bright, but weird."

"Perceptive as always," murmured Robert. "A four star kindergarten teacher. Weird, if I may say so, but perceptive."

Sophie watched Thomas with sympathy. He was trying to get along with the others, but it was merely imitative behavior in his case. They all knew it.

"That downy brown hair. Those sweet, myopic brown eyes. You know," said Robert, "he even reminds me of you somewhat."

"A misfit," said Sophie sadly, taking in Thomas trying to act tough with a baby of a girl who had climbed aboard the seesaw ahead of him. She was reminded of the many times she had tried to find a playmate in this very schoolyard.

"Thomas Jones," said Robert reflectively. "Funny name for an Indian kid."

"Thomas is not an Indian."

"There you go, you see. Stereotyping. Sweet, myopic, downy—obviously not an Indian!" Robert turned his face around triumphantly in the brilliant sunshine.

Sophie looked at Thomas again. It was true that she had never met the parents. It had taken her well up to Christmas to discover that Thomas was a conformist, not a halfwit. After that she had put him with the advanced phonics group.

"Annie Malone's child," said Robert austerely.

"Jones?" Sophie was stricken.

"Well, why not?" he replied.

"My God, Robert!"

"Don't take on so," he said irritably. "These things

happen." He rocked back and forth on his heels for a few moments, one of his school-principal gestures.

Sophie pulled herself together. As usual, Robert knew it all. He was watching her with interest.

Sophie realized he was giving her the option. She could crawl back into the old Sophie Ware now, and know nothing about this. It was not too late. Probably, like the rest of the class of '69, that was what he expected her to do.

"What about . . . Benedict?" she asked, gritting her teeth. "Benedict must be in—"

"Grade eight. Good! So you do have deductive powers!" crowed Robert. "Over there," he said.

Sophie shifted her glance from the disconsolate Thomas, following Robert's discreetly pointing chin. A tall, skinny Indian kid was playing a game of murder ball with some young toughs of about the same size over by the fence.

"I teach grade eight, as it happens," Robert informed her. "Benedict Malone: not a good student, inattentive, too involved with his body, no doubt." He glanced at her slyly. "A feeble intelligence struggling with early sexual awareness," he added.

"Bugger off, Robert."

"You should teach grade eight sometime," he moaned. "What is the capital of Ecuador—or do you remember?"

Sophie continued to watch Benedict. He didn't look at all like Alexander, but he was very good with the ball.

"Argentina, on the other hand," Robert complained. "Do you know anything about Argentina, Sophie?"

"Gauchos," she murmured. Annie thought he was like the other, the original Benedict. The one who had tried to kill Alexander with his bare hands.

"Gauchos! Right you are! And for that answer I was able to give him fifty-two on the geography exam at Christmas. That was after he became a horse thief. I always think it helps to relate these things."

Sophie was riveted. "A horse thief?" she said. "Are you kidding?"

"You say this to me—principal of the school?" inquired Robert. "I got him off."

"Wait!" said Sophie, inspired. The bell was going to ring in a moment, and she was poised on the cusp. "I know how you did it, Robert! I'll tell you what you said to the police! You said he was your best student. You explained that Indians have no concept of property! You said he had a romantic infatuation with horses! You said—"

The bell rang and, classically conditioned, they began to crunch through the caterpillars on their way to the door.

"Early intelligence," muttered Robert darkly. "But who told you, I wonder?"

"Summertime—and the living is easy!" sang Sophie.

She was in her car on her way to visit Annie.

There were a number of different possible ways of characterizing her motives for this. Jealousy—Robert's candidate—topped the list. Then there was a certain unwholesome fascination with the details of Annie's existence—a hypocritical desire to help, perhaps? Or merely the impulse to violate the common dictates of reason and middle-class prudence?

She saw that Robert thought she was getting in over her head. The class of '69 silently urged her to go to bed with Alexander and do her best to forget about Annie. A summer eternity of not going to bed with Alexander and not forgetting about Annie stretched bleakly before Sophie, and she dismissed it with a snort.

"Summertime—and the . . ."

Besides, Annie had invited her.

She pulled into Joshua Joe's garage on the edge of the Reserve. Everyone in Buffalo Jump knew Joshua Joe and his two sons, Eddie Joe and John. Joshua was either a bad white man or a bad Indian, depending on your point of view. He always flew Louis Riel's flag on Dominion Day.

His sons worked on the harvest and spent the rest of their lives lazing around the gas pumps.

"Hello, Eddie," said Sophie, getting out of her car.

Eddie gave her a gap-toothed grin and began to clean her windshield.

"Check your oil, Sophie?"

"Just gas, please."

"Had a guy in here yestiddy who wanted twenty-five cents worth." Eddie jerked his thumb in the direction of the Reserve. "Guess he was savin' his money for something else."

A zephyr of whiskey-laden breath reached Sophie's nose as Eddie leaned across to dump his rag in the bucket.

"So how're you doin' these days? I hear Sasha Bresnyachuk's workin' your farm."

"Yes, he is."

"Lookin' for Annie?" Eddie inquired innocently.

Eddie's membership in the class of '68 was purely honorary.

"Them kids of hers was just here a minute ago," he said, looking around. "Oh well. It's real close." He began giving Sophie detailed directions.

Annie lived in a fairly modern brown bungalow on the main road through the Reserve. There was no real village. The houses stretched in a long line along the highway, or scattered outward on the dirt roads into the uplands. There had been a good deal of controversy in Sophie's childhood about the closing of the Reserve school in favor of consolidation, but the Indian Band never put up a real fight in those days, before the oil money began to roll their way. Recent years had radicalized them, especially on the subject of irrigation. They owned a stretch of the Steamboat River.

"Summertime . . ."

Sophie parked across the road. She was now very nervous. She did not think Annie had been insincere in inviting her. But Sophie was wondering, aside from the question of her motives, whether she could live up to a set of constraints alluded to last night by Annie in the bar, and further clarified to her by Robert on the playground today. Sophie felt that she looked rather like a social worker—or a public-health nurse—as she crossed the road in her school dress and sweater.

The house, conventional from a distance, was perched on concrete blocks atop a pile of gravel. A tricycle with one wheel off impeded progress up the broken porch steps.

Sophie knocked.

There was no answer from within. A faint sound indicated that someone was there, however. She knocked again. The sound, something like a moan, was repeated. Sophie paused for thought, then tried the door handle, swallowing her terror.

An old woman peered at her like a badger out of the gloom in the front hall. She raised the stick in her claw at Sophie, an ambiguous gesture of hostility or greeting. They stared at one another, and the woman let out a louder moan.

"Who is it, Ma?" came Annie's dry voice, a little plaintive, from the depths of the house.

The old woman now turned sideways to Sophie and began to shuffle toward a doorway on the right. Annie appeared at the end of the hall.

"Sophie!" she said in surprise. She was looking a little the worse for wear, rubbing her eyes and yawning.

"Maybe . . ." Sophie was hesitant. "I could come some other time if you're not . . ."

"Come into the kitchen, Sophie," said Annie. "I wasn't expectin' you today." She turned around and led the way, looking over her shoulder to make sure Sophie was following.

The kitchen was a barren room containing a metal table, a few cracked chairs, a sprung sofa in one corner. It looked clean.

"Well," said Annie, sitting down on the couch. "Tell the truth, I'm not expectin' you at all."

Sophie sat down gingerly on the edge of a kitchen chair.

"Do you have a hangover, Annie?" she asked.

"Yeah." Annie gave her an inscrutable look. "Want some tea?"

"Don't go to any trouble." Exactly what a social worker would say, Sophie thought, her heart sinking.

Annie made no comment. She went over to the stove and picked up a glass coffeepot that Sophie perceived was full of simmering tea. She paused, pot in hand.

"What'd I say to you last night?" she asked.

"Well . . ." Sophie considered. Had she really forgotten? "For one thing, you refused to marry me."

Annie laughed. She hesitated for a moment with the teapot, then set it back down on the stove.

"What the hell," she said, and went back to the sofa, where she withdrew a quart bottle nearly full of rye from under the cushion.

"Hair of the dog," said Sophie mildly.

"Yeah. I already had some." Annie produced a mug for Sophie and poured some rye into it. "It not like this around here every day," she said defensively, finding her own cup and sitting down with it.

Sophie went to the stove to put some tea in with the rye. She had evidently gotten over the first hurdle. But when she turned around, she saw that Annie was examining her critically, lighting a cigarette.

"You come to see Bennie?" she asked acutely. "He not here."

"Well, that's okay. I came to see you."

"You did?" The aggressiveness had gone out of Annie's tone.

"I like you," said Sophie, plunging boldly forward. "I always did. We used to know each other a little—in school—before—"

"Yeah. A little," agreed Annie. But again, her expression relaxed after a moment.

"And your brother, too," Sophie went on, panting slightly in her nervousness. "Alexander always—I mean, he's been telling me about him."

"He has?" Annie stared at her for a moment. "Yeah," she said slowly. "I guess he would."

"All about—well—the things they used to do together. Breaking horses and—" Sophie began to find this level of hypocrisy hard to sustain.

"Bennie and Sasha," said Annie, her eyes on the middle distance.

"They were friends."

"They were blood brothers. You know what I mean?"

Sophie took a sip of her whiskey, feeling uncomfortable. Now that she had managed to start a conversation with Annie, her real motive for visiting her was becoming unpleasantly clear. She did not want to talk about Benedict. In fact, she had a slight allergy to Benedict.

"You ever seen that scar on Sasha's wrist?" Annie asked abruptly.

Sophie shook her head.

"It mean they die for each other." Annie smiled, a dry smile, but she was looking at Sophie again. "Sasha damn near bleed to death that day," she said.

Sophie also smiled, politely. Even Annie was afflicted with this foolishness. Benedict, the hero, who never fell off a horse.

"I never had a brother," she remarked. "I was an only child. That's why I was so lonely—at school." She looked timidly at Annie, afraid this confidence might be rebuffed.

Annie gave her a penetrating stare. "Lonely?" she said. "You?"

"Well . . . yes."

"Me, I was scared."

"I remember you were shy." Sophie remembered Annie standing by the school fence in the afternoons. She looked like a deer, her face a little anxious, her books pressed close in her arms.

"Benedict, he pick me up every day, he walk me to school. That's why I went to school, Sophie. He make me go."

Annie bent forward to put out her cigarette.

"Maybe you don't know," she said. "You never had an Indian big brother. He God. He tell you to do something and you do it quick. But he look after you, too."

There was something to this. Sophie nodded attentively.

"Benedict, he look after me. He always look after me, ever since we were kids, Ma—" Annie made a vague gesture toward the hallway. "I belong to Benedict."

The mother was an alcoholic, Sophie recalled. Alexander had told her.

"I guess you seen me in the bar the other night. But you know what I was scared of back then, Sophie?" Annie laughed harshly.

"What?" Sophie was a little frightened herself.

"Whitemen."

"But," said Sophie after a moment, clearing her throat, "what about you and Alexander?"

She looked at the hardened face of the woman lying on the sofa, her brown skin lined with alcoholism and the despair of ill treatment, her eyes, once so soft and bright, now as dull as pebbles. She was terrified. But she had to know about it.

"Yeah, Sasha," said Annie. "You know what Benedict was like? He was like this." She lifted up the whiskey bottle and held it to the light. "With Benedict you know he's goin' to kill for you, die for you! Sasha—you know how we think water got no taste? Well, Sasha, he was just like a cup of water to me."

"I don't understand," said Sophie. She had no idea how to interpret what she was being told. Benedict! They all talked about Benedict! What had he to do with anything? It was now impossible not to ask. "You . . . you were in love with Alexander, weren't you?"

Annie lowered the rye bottle to her lap and began unscrewing the top. She carefully poured some whiskey into both cups. Then she lit another cigarette and sat down again.

"You want to know about that, Sophie?" she said.

10
What Happened to Annie

Sophie nodded dumbly, appalled at herself. This was the very thing she disapproved of in Robert. The fact that she resisted it so strongly in him just showed that she was that way herself. She wanted to know all about it.

"I never in love with Sasha," said Annie. "Not what you would call love." She smiled.

"You weren't?" Sophie reflected. "I wouldn't?" She asked cautiously a moment later.

"I guess you think it was his fault," Annie went on.

"Well . . . yes." Sophie leaned forward nervously. "After all, you were only fifteen. And he ought to have—"

"I'm not talkin' about that," said Annie impatiently. "You just let me tell you, Sophie. Maybe it better that way."

Sophie was silent. She was ready to hear this story on any terms now, even if Benedict was going to be the hero.

"You never had a brother," said Annie. She stopped, looking down at her hands. "Benedict, he walk me. Every day we walk."

She looked up. Sophie nodded obediently.

"Then he don't walk me," said Annie. "I guess something happen to him that year. Bennie stop wantin' to be an Indian. Maybe he want to be a whiteman."

"What was it?" asked Sophie, trying to be a slave to the story.

"All he care about was what was goin' on at the school. He hang around all the time. First I don't know what it was. But he hangin' around a girl."

"What was her name?" asked Sophie curiously.

"She was a whiteman." Annie ignored Sophie's interruption. "Benedict forget about everything else. He forget all about me. He let Sasha pick me up after school. He always want to stay on, him."

Sophie strained her memory, trying to remember a tall boy by the fence with Annie. She couldn't remember—only that sad little face.

"I was real mad. You got to remember that, Sophie."

"Because Alexander was picking you up? Oh, Benedict told him to, did he?"

"No, Sasha pick me up because he know he ought to. I was mad at Bennie, Sophie, not Sasha."

Sophie didn't see this at all. They were still talking about Benedict.

"Alexander was picking you up," she repeated.

"Yeah. But Bennie, he know about me. He know I'm scared. He stick around so he could screw that whiteman."

"Oh."

Annie stretched and stood up to put more rye in her cup.

"You don't mind me tellin' you all this, Sophie?" she asked.

"Of course not," said Sophie, amazed. "Go on."

"Sasha, he had a car that year," Annie continued, resuming her seat. "One time we have a flat tire and we got to walk. I never walk nowhere yet without Bennie. Sasha, he say, 'We got to, Annie.' I say no. He say, 'What's the matter?' He don't understand. He call me 'Annushka,' he take my books. Finally I got to go. I never so scared in my whole life."

"What happened?" asked Sophie anxiously.

"Along come a fast car. Sasha, he say, 'Crazy nut!' Me, I'm just like a rabbit in that ditch. He makes me get goin' again. Benedict, he would have hit me. But Sasha, he wasn't like that. He was just worryin' about me—gives me a piece of gum."

Sophie drew a breath of relief.

Annie looked at her sharply. "You don't know anything about him yet, do you?" she asked.

"I guess I don't." Relief still gripped her. So it hadn't been like that, in some ditch. She had been imagining all kinds of things.

"You know what they shout when they're passin'?" said Annie, watching her. "Whitemen? They shout, 'Squaw cunt!' Sasha, he shout, 'So's your sister!' "

"My God!"

"I guess maybe that was when I notice," said Annie.

"Noticed what?"

"That Sasha was a whiteman."

Annie's fear was beginning to make sense to her. She had never thought of this before. Annie at her desk at recess. Annie alone by the fence.

"We were at his place, fixin' that tire," Annie continued.

Sophie realized that she had not been listening.

"His ma lit into him about where was Marfa. I'm not scared of Sasha's ma—"

"I am, though," muttered Sophie.

"But she ought to know that Sasha, he can't tell Marfa

to do nothing. He tell Marfa what to do and she say, 'Get lost, muscle man!' Benedict, he the only one who can tell Marfa anything."

Sophie laughed.

"I would have run away when Sasha's pa catches us. But we were gettin' along good, fixin' that tire. You know, I really think I'm helpin' him. Sasha make me stand on the rim; I think he needs me. So I stick around while the old man yell at him in Russian."

Annie lapsed into silence for a moment.

"Sasha never talk Russian," she said. "You notice that, Sophie? Maybe he can't no more, but he never did. I'm like that with Ma, too," she went on. "It the same thing. I know what she say, all right, but I never talk it."

"What was Alexander's father mad about?"

"Oh yeah," said Annie. "He shout, 'Squaw cunt!' "

"Oh, Annie!"

"That what he say. I start to run. I just run!"

Sophie shuddered.

"When Sasha catch up to me, he sayin', 'I never hit him, Annushka! I never hit him!'

"Then he cry," said Annie.

They were still sitting in the kitchen. Annie had poured some more tea and whiskey and opened the back door. A poor pasture stretched out behind the house, breaking into the bush country leading down into the river valley. Sophie's hands had stopped shaking.

"That's where you used to keep the horses, is it?" asked Sophie, thinking of Alexander's story of the horse theft.

"You been down by our river?" asked Annie.

"No."

"That fall—that was another time. You ever go swimmin' in October?" she asked.

"October! In Alberta?"

"It was real warm that fall. I remember. Sasha and Marfa, they come over ridin' pillion on that horse of Marfa's, Egg Money."

"Oh yes. That was the horse Benedict broke for Marfa," said Sophie. "Alexander told me."

"He broke her. But she still couldn't ride her. Sasha was the only one who could make her do anything but walk. So Benedict told me to let Marfa ride my pony, Star."

"You didn't mind?"

"Benedict told me to," said Annie.

It was a real allergy, Sophie noticed, not just a minor rash. She didn't like Benedict. He seemed to get away with murder. He hit Annie. He broke horses, but only Alexander could ride them. And still they were both infatuated with him.

"Marfa liked Benedict, didn't she?" Sophie remarked.

"Until that whiteman came along."

"You mean—his girlfriend," Sophie murmured.

"I want to go swimming. But Marfa and Bennie, they got so far ahead of us—I got Sasha to make a dam in the creek."

"Why didn't Alexander have a girlfriend?" Sophie demanded, pursuing her own thoughts. "He could have. I remember what he was like. He could have had anybody." She amended this hastily. "I mean, someone of his own age."

"Maybe Benedict got there first," said Annie.

"Oh!"

Annie laughed.

Sophie was suddenly touched. She saw them riding pillion together, the two who were left out, babyish Annie, wanting him to make a dam, and Alexander, tender-hearted, looking after his friend's little sister.

"It was real warm," said Annie. "I guess you never done that. Those creeks are so shallow you can sit in them, even in October."

"It sounds nice."

"Yeah. I unbraid my hair. Sasha take his clothes off right away, but I didn't want to."

"But I thought you even *rode* naked!" exclaimed Sophie.

"When we were kids. Then Benedict wouldn't let me," said Annie. "Sasha was watchin' my hair float."

She paused.

Sophie took a nervous sip of her whiskey.

"We were sittin' in the water. And then—"

And then. And then. Was Annie really going to tell her?

"You ever see how Sasha's eyes get dark when he's excited, Sophie?"

Sophie didn't want to hear about this. She produced a strangled noise of dissent.

"We were kissin'," said Annie, these innocent words coming oddly from her lips. "You don't understand, do you, Sophie?"

"No." Sophie forced herself to say this. They were kissing. What was wrong with that?

"Benedict," said Annie. "He never would have let me. He would have killed me."

"What? But he—"

"Don't you see? I made him. I made him because of that. I made him because of what Benedict was doin'. Don't you see?" whispered Annie, her voice dry and soft.

It was getting late. Sophie looked at her watch. It was nearly suppertime.

"It was because of that whiteman," said Annie.

Sophie concentrated on Annie's children. She had nearly forgotten them. Or didn't they bother to come home for supper?

"So that was when he kiss me," said Annie prosaically.

"He just kissed you?"

"I made him swear not to tell Benedict."

What did Benedict have to do with it—again? Would he have killed her?

"I should go home," said Sophie.

"Don't go yet," said Annie. "Want some soup or something?"

"No, no."

Annie lay back, lighting another cigarette. Where had she gotten the money for whiskey and cigarettes? She had been broke last night, Sophie remembered. But maybe she had had a visit from the social worker in the meantime.

"I want you to understand this, Sophie. Maybe Sasha never will, but you got to."

"Why?" asked Sophie. "Why do you want me to understand? Maybe I can't."

"Yeah, you can," said Annie. "And the reason is, I spoil everything for Sasha. I see him last night, lookin' at you. He want something, Sophie."

"Well, I thought I explained all about that," said Sophie sharply. "What he wants, I mean."

Annie laughed. "Why are you talking to Annie, then?" she asked.

"Just go on, Annie," Sophie pleaded. "Maybe I can understand. You were trying to get even with your brother, is that it? But Alexander—didn't he love you?" she asked doubtfully.

"Oh yeah, he did. I was the only thing he had left. His ma and pa were real down on him. Marfa always just treat him like a moose. And Benedict went off with that whiteman. He was all alone except for me."

"But all the same, Annie," Sophie said, "you couldn't really have *made* him." She was finding this interpretation very unexpected. It was far from the story of seduction and betrayal she had steeled herself to hear.

"I know what I was doin'. Even then I know." Annie's voice was sad. "That night his ma made him come over here lookin' for Marfa—I know what I was goin' to do."

She paused, smoking introspectively.

"What—what did you do?" asked Sophie, looking away.

"I was mad. Bennie was out, and there was Sasha

stompin' around, tearin' his hair out about what Momma'd do to Marfa. I just blew up at him. I told him I didn't want him lookin' after me no more."

"I can see how you might have felt that way," said Sophie cautiously.

"Well, Sasha couldn't. It got him all roused. He never even knew he was lookin' after me till I tell him to stop. Sasha don't think in words, you know, Sophie? He thought it was him I was mad at—because of what he did when he made that dam."

"But you said that was just kissing!"

"Yeah, it was. But he know what he want when we were doin' it. And now I'm standin' there right in front of him in a flannel nightgown, screamin' and throwin' my chemistry book. You think he don't know he want it again? He try to make me stop cryin'. I'm shoutin', 'I hate you! I hate you!' And he's shoutin', 'Shut up, Annushka! Annushka, shut up!' But I wouldn't. I was just yellin' every dirty thing about Bennie and him and what Bennie was doin' with that girl and Sasha couldn't stand that."

"I suppose he was jealous himself," murmured Sophie, watching with a detached eye as the whiskey wavered in her cup.

"He was all mixed up about how he felt. Me, I was the one who was mad. Sasha, he was tryin' to comfort me." Annie indicated the sofa she was lying on.

"And you let him?"

"I made him," repeated Annie.

It was well after suppertime. Sophie had finished her whiskey. Why was she still here? She had heard it now.

"But you needn't have gotten pregnant," she said, after a moment. "He could have prevented that, at least."

"You know, I see why he want to marry you, Sophie," said Annie, sitting up and frowning a little. "You think the same way."

"Did he feel guilty about it?"

"He felt bad all the time, even when he was doin' it. But he want me. He didn't have nobody else. I ask him, 'Don't you wish I was a whiteman?' "

"I don't suppose he wished you were a man at all," said Sophie, laughing feebly.

"He was just a boy, Sophie. They want that more than eatin' and drinkin'. I don't see it at the time, but later on I know it was like that for Benedict, too. But he don't feel bad about it the way Sasha did."

"How awful for him," said Sophie. "How awful for you!" she exclaimed, raising her eyes seriously to Annie's face.

"No," said Annie. "He got that scar on his wrist. You look at that scar sometime, Sophie. That was what was makin' him feel sorry. He just couldn't see how he was doin' this to Benedict."

"To Benedict! But you were the one who—it was you he got—"

"That's why I was glad when I got pregnant," said Annie. "I knew I couldn't have Sasha forever. But I had the baby. He was mine."

"You can't be serious!"

"You never have a baby yet, Sophie."

"But your brother—"

"Oh yeah. He slap me around when I tell him. Then he go after Sasha. But you know what, Sophie? He love my baby," said Annie. "He love Bennie better than anyone."

She turned and looked at Sophie with her dark, impenetrable eyes, and Sophie saw that they were soft with tears.

The screen door into the kitchen opened with a sudden bang, and Thomas entered.

"Ma, I'm—" he began, and stopped short as he caught sight of Sophie.

"Yeah, well, it's goin' to be soup," said Annie sharply, getting to her feet. "And go get the others first."

Thomas receded swiftly after another quick, anxious glance at Sophie.

"Want to have some with us, Sophie?"

"I'd better go home." Sophie watched Annie operating the can opener for a moment. So much for Robert Markovich and the class of '69.

"Well, come again if you want," said Annie. "I like talkin' to you, Sophie."

11

Poppa's Birthday

It was June 21, a Friday. The hot, dry weather continued, and the children were sweltering in the classroom.

After Sophie got home that afternoon, she showered and changed her dress, then went out into the yard. Alexander was taking her home overnight for his father's birthday celebration. Sophie was hoping to see Marfa. The whole family would be there.

Alexander emerged from the barn, taking off his gloves. He was sweating heavily and she looked in fascination at his forehead, beaded with perspiration, and then at the wet black hair of his chest showing through the front of his unbuttoned shirt.

Sophie got behind the wheel of her car, and Alexander got in on the other side.

"Like my dress?" she asked, glancing at him sideways.

"Yeah," he said. "Just don't stop, okay? I'd wreck it,

probably." He lit a cigarette and Sophie noticed that it stuck wetly in his fingers.

Satisfied with this exchange, Sophie began to sing:

"She wheels her wheelbarrow,
Through streets broad and narrow,
Crying . . ."

"You been goin' to see Annie?" he asked.

"You don't mind, do you?" she asked.

"Nope." He reflected. "I'd say it was pretty nice of you."

"It's not nice," Sophie corrected him. "I want to."

"Just as long as you don't get jealous again." He glanced at her uneasily.

"I don't think I am," Sophie said stoutly. "It's just that I seem to be marrying into her family, that's all."

"Yeah," said Alexander, as she turned up the Bresnyachuk driveway. "This one is bad enough. Let's just get this over with first." He gestured at the lineup of cars in the yard.

The Bresnyachuks were having a barbecue. Like everything else Alexander's father did, it was a barbecue on a colossal scale. The outside tables were piled with every variety of food and liquor; a mixed grill of steak, fish, and deer sausage sizzled on the coals. The old man was already in full swing, kissing the women on both cheeks or pulling their ears, slapping backsides, and hitting the men on their arms and shoulders.

Alexander disappeared immediately to change, so Sophie ran this gantlet alone. The last person to greet her was Marfa.

"Hello, Sophie." Marfa was dark and slight, with beautiful eyes the same cloudy gray as Alexander's. Sophie took refuge with her behind the drinks table.

"You're going to marry my brother, I hear," said Marfa, opening beers for herself and Sophie. "I must say, that's not something I ever would have predicted."

"Alexander has been running our farm," said Sophie noncommittally.

"Does he have any other good points?" asked Marfa.

Sophie laughed.

"What are you doing these days, Marfa?" she asked. "I haven't seen you in about ten years."

"I was married for nine of them," said Marfa. "But now I'm through with that, thank God. I'm farming over in Bitter Root."

"Your husband let you keep the farm?" asked Sophie, surprised.

"No. He died. Rolled a Cat while he was grading a hillside. He was drunk, of course. I bought the farm with the insurance."

"You're really doing it alone?"

"Me and two kids. Cattle," said Marfa, lighting a cigarette. "It's easy," she added bitterly.

"You could have picked something easier, I guess."

"Bohunks are all the same, Sophie. They're crazy for land. You ought to realize that." Marfa smiled.

"Yes, he told me," said Sophie calmly.

"Well, in that case . . ." Marfa gave her a curious look. "Sasha's not such a great catch. If you want to keep the place, why don't you farm it yourself?"

"But I don't know anything about farming. I was letting out the place to Rudolph last year. I don't want to go on doing that."

"No. I can see why. Well, I guess you've thought about it." Marfa grimaced and put down her beer bottle. "Boy, I hate these parties! See those two over by the swings?" She pointed out two children approximately eight and nine, a boy and a girl. "They're mine."

Alexander appeared beside Sophie, wearing clean clothes, his rough, bunchy hair combed straight back.

"You found each other, did you?" he asked, opening a beer.

"A tiny island of sanity," replied Marfa. "I only came because I wanted to see Sophie, actually."

"You used to be friends, didn't you?"

"Not really. I didn't go to riding school or take dancing lessons or play in the band," said Marfa.

"You were a cheerleader," Sophie pointed out.

"It was already out of style."

"Come on," said Alexander. "We're not going to go through all that, are we?" He glanced around, frowning, and absently picked up his sister's cigarette. "This is a madhouse. Look at the old man."

Mr. Bresnyachuk was on the swings. There was an incredible amount of noise. Poppa was shouting and laughing, swinging wildly back and forth, with a screaming tot pressed to his hairy decolletage. A file of anxious mothers was already lined up to collect the baby and three other displaced toddlers who were crying with displeasure.

"Oh Christ!" said Marfa. "Where are my two?" She went off, leaving her beer bottle behind as a place-holder. Alexander went on smoking her cigarette.

"She's gone a little sour," he remarked. "That guy she was married to was a pig, as you would say. A real German hog. He killed himself on shaving lotion and hair spray."

"Marfa's got guts," said Sophie, looking up at him. "She's doing her own farming."

"Oh yeah? She didn't mention the guy she lives with, I guess. She wouldn't bring him anyway. Poppa'd have a stroke."

"Why? Because they aren't married or something? Even your father—"

"Nope. He's an Indian," said Alexander. "Seems to me I told you about the Russians and the Indians the other day."

Sophie looked away. She now knew more, much more than he had told her. She wondered how he would feel if he realized this. But you couldn't just slam the door on the past. She wanted to understand it. She had to.

Alexander's brother Rudolph staggered up to the drinks table, puffing and blowing. He had been arm-wrestling. Sophie compared him covertly to Alexander. The things that made Alexander irresistible were reproduced in repulsive genetic imitation on Rudi: Where Alexander was heavy and muscular, Rudi was fat; an infantile bald spot peeked from his curly black hair.

"Still the champ!" he cried sportively, slapping Alexander on the back. "You'll drink to that, Sasha?" He poured vodka into two plastic glasses.

"Want some vodka, Sophia?" asked Alexander.

"No, I'll stick to beer."

Rudi put his foot up on a folding chair in classic style, and downed the inch of vodka in his glass. The sweat poured down his face. He looked like a caricature of Alexander coming out of the barn an hour ago.

Alexander looked cynically into his glass, and sipped.

"Jesus Christ! What a lady!" exclaimed Rudi, helping himself to a dill pickle. "Put it back like a man, Sasha."

Alexander's younger brother, Luke, was helping himself out of the vodka bottle, too. He was much younger, about twenty-six, and bore the Bresnyachuk mouth and hair, but his lisp feminized that exuberant masculinity in an unfortunate way.

"Thweet Jethuth, it'th hot," he remarked to Sophie. "You look cool enough to eat, Thophie."

"Have a pickle," advised Rudi, chomping on a slice of ham and wiping his fingers on his pants. "That's the way to cool off in this weather."

The old man, seeing his three sons together, now leaped down off the swings with the cry of a predatory bird, and approached swiftly, patting a few backsides en route. He put his arms around Luke and Rudi, who were each involved in the identical act of putting down a vodka glass, and said something loudly in Russian.

All four of the men looked at Sophie.

"What's this?" she asked in alarm.

"Something complimentary," murmured Alexander.

The old man seized the vodka bottle and poured out half a tumblerful, which he now placed in Sophie's hand. He raised her elbow to about the level of her eyes.

"Now—holding the throat open! Now closing the throat!" he ordered.

Sophie choked, then swallowed hard. Poppa had taken up a stance close beside her and she was aware that he would have put his arm around her waist if Alexander had not suddenly been holding it himself.

"You know I am leavin' Russia when I am twenty years old," the old man said confidentially.

"Really?"

"Yeah. I am refugee from communism. In Russia maybe I make babies, one, two. Then Party can tell me I gotta stop! Here damn Trudeau tell me I gotta stop with six and I vote for Conservatives. See? Is very democratic in this country."

"I see."

The old man moved a bit closer, and Sophie felt Alexander's fingers tightening on her ribs.

"So. How many kids you gonna get, Sophia? Maybe you start tonight. Stay here and I show you?" He laughed uproariously and compromised on physical contact by pinching her cheek.

Sophie was laughing too. Poppa was like some kind of uncontrollable natural force, a volcano or a tidal wave. She was not the slightest bit frightened of him.

Alexander's mother towed Poppa away, listing some things in Russian. The list was either of sins or things to eat, Sophie could not tell which. The old man was supposed to be doing the barbecuing.

"I told your mother you'd probably be staying over," said Alexander moodily, looking after them.

A new, more interesting thought struck Sophie. Where was she going to sleep, then?

By midnight the children were tucked away, and the

men had settled down to arguing about farming and business, mostly in English, but entirely in Russian on the old man's part. Sophie was helping with the dishes in the kitchen and listening a little anxiously to the voices outside. Rudolph and Alexander had already almost had a fistfight over the mustard in the Ware fields. Poppa was playing the peacemaker, a role he seemed to enjoy as much as he enjoyed everything else, and now they were all drinking a round of vodka.

Alexander's mother rinsed the dishtowel and Sophie perched on the drainboard, eating a pickle. Marietta, Rudolph's large, loose wife, rolled out into the backyard and sat down at the picnic table with Luke, who was largely ignoring the discussion in favor of killing the moths settling on the table in the dying glow of the barbecue.

Marfa taped up a package of food and put it in the refrigerator to take home the next day.

"You know all about Annie, I guess," she said abruptly. She shot a sharp glance at Sophie.

Momma ceased sopping the dishcloths in the sink and looked repressively at both of them.

Sophie nodded self-consciously, finishing her pickle.

"I thought so," said Marfa. "When I saw Sasha last, he was pretty sure you didn't, but I told him he was crazy. You were *there,* after all, even if you weren't very—"

Momma turned around, wiping her hands on her apron.

"I guess he thought he was going to have to make some big deal out of telling you," Marfa went on.

"We are not talkin' about this anymore," said Momma.

"Why not, Momma? We're all over twenty-one."

"It's okay," said Sophie.

"It is not okay, this talking. I will not listen to any more of it."

"Well, then, don't listen!" said Marfa impatiently.

"Sophia is in love with my son and you are not gonna

spoil it!" said Mrs. Bresnyachuk with equal heat. "You are jealous of her good luck, that's all."

"Just aside from that, are you in love with Sasha, Sophie?" asked Marfa curiously. "I can't believe it."

Sophie blushed.

"My goodness!" said Marfa. "I didn't know that happened anymore."

"I need someone to work my farm," Sophie said defensively. "I told you—"

"Yeah, I heard all about it. Mustard. Well, well."

"Is a very good farm," said Momma, now continuing placidly with the dishcloths.

"Not that I'll mind having you for a sister-in-law. It'll mean someone to talk to at these godawful parties. He's probably okay in bed, is he?"

Sophie was tongue-tied.

"I suppose you can't help turning red like that? I wish I was a blonde. Even Momma thinks you've got to check out things like that, don't you, Momma?"

Momma smiled enigmatically and went outside to the clothesline.

The men had begun to sing, stamping their feet. Even Luke was singing. Sophie could see him through the open back door. She wondered whether Alexander was singing, and decided not to look.

"How's your mother taking it, by the way? Has she met Momma yet?" Marfa was evidently determined to torture her until she revealed some information.

"I came to a birthday party at your place one time," Marfa went on. "I guess you remember that. You had little heart-shaped pink cakes for each kid." Marfa's lip curled slightly. "Anyway, if you and Sasha get tired of doing it in a field, you can come over to my place."

"Thanks," said Sophie.

"Oh, for Christ's sake!" said Marfa, going to look out the window. An argument had started again, and hoarse male shouts could be heard from the yard. "See what you're getting into, Sophie? God knows why you want to have anything to do with this! I can barely stand it, and I was born here."

"Who's fighting?" asked Sophie nervously.

"It looks like all of them. Here comes Sasha. I guess he had the sense to stay out of it this time."

Alexander entered the kitchen behind his mother. She looked back and up at her tall son, and Sophie suddenly saw where the eyes had come from. Momma must have been beautiful as a young girl, like Marfa, only, as Sophie romantically pictured her, gentler, softer, more innocent and secretive.

"I've had it, Momma," said Alexander. He was drunk, Sophie perceived. "Why didn't you divorce him before you had any of them kids!"

He put his arms around his mother and she stood on tiptoe to give him a kiss on each cheek. Sophie witnessed this uneasily. It was the Oedipus complex again, she supposed.

"My Sasha," said Momma proudly.

"Where's Sophia?" asked Alexander, shaking his head like a buffalo. He caught sight of her, and Marfa smiled sarcastically as Sophie jumped down off the drainboard and went over to him.

"We've been talking in here while you were out there—doing whatever you were doing," explained Sophie, leading him to a chair.

A crescendo of shouting outside was followed by comparative silence, filled only with the voice of Poppa. Momma stood in the doorway, looking out over the dark yard.

"And while we're about it, let's have another drink," said Marfa, getting out a bottle of vodka from behind a flour bag. "I was just telling Sophie you're welcome to a free bed at my place whenever you want it." She poured a measure into three clean glasses. "Here's to it!"

"I'll drink to that!" said Alexander.

"I will too," said Sophie, giving him a significant glance. She was still wondering about tonight. His intoxication seemed a hopeful sign.

"Well, better have another. Hurry up, Sophie. Poppa showed you how it's done." Marfa poured out again. "Jesus, he's going to sleep!"

Alexander opened his eyes, then closed them again.

"He was working pretty hard today," Sophie explained.

"I better go lie down," mumbled Alexander. He rose unsteadily and went to the kitchen divan, then slumped into a snooze in a half-sitting position.

"Some Ukrainian," said Marfa scornfully.

They had started singing again outside.

Sophie went over and with great difficulty began trying to settle Alexander into a supine position. He had very heavy legs.

"I'm wakin' up in a minute," he muttered.

She pushed a cushion under his head and spread an afghan over his knees.

"How touching," said Marfa cynically.

"Come on, Marfa. He's just tired."

"Tired, eh?" Marfa lit a cigarette. "Boy, they don't make 'em like they used to!" She gestured in the direction of the old man's voice, raised in song. "Of course, Sasha—he could go to sleep in the middle of a plane crash. He was always like that," she went on pensively.

Momma, who had been watching Sophie approvingly from the inner doorway, now went out of the room and a moment later could be heard going upstairs to bed.

"So what'd Sasha say to you about all that, Sophie?" asked Marfa coolly.

Sophie came to with a start. She had been looking sadly at the sleeping Alexander.

"About—? Oh, about Annie?"

"Yeah. He's got some funny ideas about that. I want to know what they are," said Marfa bluntly.

"Well actually," said Sophie, considering, "he hasn't told me very much about her at all. He talks about Benedict, though," she added cautiously.

"About Benedict," Marfa said slowly. She put her feet up on a chair and blew smoke from her nose. "Sasha doesn't know anything about Benedict," she said.

12

Benedict

"Talk to Sasha and all he'll tell you is what a hero Benedict was," said Marfa. "Benedict this and Benedict that and Benedict can do no wrong!" she went on vehemently.

"Yes, I know."

"That's all bullshit," said Marfa, and lapsed momentarily into silence.

"I was wondering about that."

"Yeah. First of all, what happened to Annie—well, that was all Benedict's fault. In spite of what Sasha thinks."

"But it was Alexander who got her pregnant," said Sophie obstinately. Whatever mystical desires Annie now ascribed to herself at the age of fifteen, this was the inescapable biological fact.

"Yes, but Benedict couldn't see that as just—well, something that happened. He went after Sasha down by that bridge on the Reserve—"

"Alexander told me."

"Oh, so he did say something, then?" said Marfa with a scornful lift of her eyebrows. "I told him that this was the 1980s, but Sasha lives in a world of his own. I think he still feels guilty about it!"

"Well, but Annie suffered," said Sophie timidly.

"Not as much as Sasha would have suffered if Benedict had kicked his balls off," said Marfa harshly. She looked at Sophie. "Oh, so he didn't tell you that? He wouldn't, of course. Benedict was a mean fighter. You don't think he'd have gone up against my hulking brother without anything, do you? For one thing, he was only half Sasha's size. Steel-toed boots," she explained.

"My God!"

"Well, don't worry. Sasha still has them, I guess, or you wouldn't be—" Marfa laughed. "No, whatever Annie suffered, that was because of Benedict," she continued. "He wouldn't even let her go back to school. And he quit school himself."

"Did you see her after that?"

"Are you kidding? She was in quarantine. Bresnyachuk was the name of a germ! He always did have crazy ideas about what the white man did to the Indians." Marfa snorted. "But, boy! After Annie got pregnant he sure went overboard."

"Weren't you sort of—?" inquired Sophie cautiously. "I mean, Alexander said Benedict broke that horse, Egg Money, for you."

"Yes," said Marfa. She leaned back in her chair and a curiously gentle smile appeared on her lips. "He did, you know."

"Alexander says he was fantastic with horses," said Sophie, trying to be loyal.

"Oh yeah. All that hocus-pocus about stardust and secret names. I don't say he wasn't a great rider. He was. But I'll tell you something, Sophie."

"Yes?" said Sophie attentively.

"Sasha can ride a horse," said Marfa.

"He's been riding mine."

"Well, watch it! It'll be his before you know it. There isn't a horse in the world that can resist him. And it's all straight. A horse just has to look at him to see he's the kind of guy a horse can trust."

"That's nice, isn't it?"

"Well, there's something to it, anyway. He could have been like that with women, too," Marfa looked around the kitchen, her nostrils flaring like Alexander's. "Want to smoke some dope, Sophie? My purse is somewhere."

"Okay. But what about—?"

"Oh, Poppa, you mean? He's tried it. He likes vodka better. Don't worry about that." She found her purse behind the same flour bag that had concealed the vodka.

"Homegrown," she said briefly, licking the cigarette paper. "We had a good crop last year. It's the only thing the Indians know how to grow!"

"This man you're living with—"

"Yeah. You'll meet him," said Marfa, lighting up. "No, Benedict screwed Sasha up about women. Remember Mae Ellen Ballotine, Sophie?"

"Yes," lied Sophie. She eyed the joint.

"Big, huge boobs—and hips to go with them! Oh well," said Marfa. She blew out a cloud of herbal smoke. "You can see why Sasha was lusting after that—even if it doesn't really make sense at all! Shit, he was only eighteen!"

"But I thought he didn't have a girlfriend." Sophie reluctantly accepted the joint from Marfa. "Benedict got there first," she repeated, remembering Annie's words.

"The hell with Benedict!" said Marfa sharply. "Use your mind, Sophie! Sasha was a big beautiful white boy. Benedict was a skinny little Indian kid who could run fast. If you were a snotty eighteen-year-old girl with huge tits, which one would you choose?"

"So why *did* she go for Benedict?" insisted Sophie.

"She didn't. Sasha could have had Mae Ellen Ballotine

on toast! But he wouldn't compete with Benedict. Oh no! He wouldn't do anything to show up Benedict!"

"Oh."

"Don't get excited, Sophie," said Marfa kindly. "This was all years ago, remember? I know about it because Benedict told me." She laid the roach in the ashtray delicately, with the tips of her fingers. "There was just no way Sasha was going to get laid first. So rest your soul!"

"I see," said Sophie. There was a good deal more to this story than Annie knew or cared to remember.

"Wait! Now I'm going to tell you how Sasha did get laid!" said Marfa, groping in her purse, her eyes alight with a manic enthusiasm. "You want to know, don't you? Just a sec." She began expertly making another joint.

Sophie opened her mouth and then closed it again. She thought she already knew. But did she? Marfa had been giving her quite a new angle on Benedict.

"There was a school dance," said Marfa, inhaling luxuriously. "Benedict went with Mae Ellen. He must have told her Sasha was going to be there. Benedict was smart, Sophie. He was as smart as a woman!"

"He was good at school," Sophie agreed.

"Yeah. He was on the debating team and the school paper and the soccer team. That's not what I mean. He was really smart," said Marfa. She passed the joint and Sophie inhaled this time.

"I was there," went on Marfa. "I went to the dance with a little snakelike guy called Robert Markovich. I guess you wouldn't remember him. I fooled around with him a bit, but that was because Benedict . . ." She trailed off.

Sophie looked up. But Marfa was already continuing, "Mae Ellen had to go home early, or so she said. Sasha wasn't there, you see. So Benedict took her in her dad's car and then he came back to get me. He used to walk me home sometimes," she said, looking slantwise at Sophie.

"Alexander used to walk Annie home every day," said Sophie in an undertone. Marfa wasn't listening.

"That snot-faced girl!" she exclaimed. "How did she get so important to him! He couldn't talk about anything else, all the way home! And after that, too. We went to a place—where we used to go," she went on secretively, "and he told me all about it. About going to college and law school and about how he was going to give Mae Ellen his debating pin, and about her dad's car, and how he was such a big important surgeon—and incidentally about what a bitch she was!" said Marfa viciously.

"You weren't impressed, I take it," said Sophie, slightly alarmed.

"It was pitiful! Pathetic! At least I knew that, even then. He wanted all the middle-class trimmings, see. He wanted to be Prime Minister and Louis Riel, the greatest lawyer, like—I don't know! And the biggest horse thief! He wanted to take Mae Ellen to the prom in white gloves and a gardenia, but he expected to be Poundmaker and Sitting Bull back on the Reserve! Jesus Christ!" Marfa rested her forehead on the back of her hand momentarily. "Well, I knew he couldn't settle for me. He was telling me so."

"Were you—?" Sophie hadn't thought of this before.

"Were we?" Marfa mocked. "Were we what, Sophie? Let's have another drink," she added.

"I'll get it," said Sophie hastily. She poured out a dram in each glass and carefully went to the sink to mix them with water.

Alexander rolled over on the divan with a grunt, and began to breathe deeply and evenly. You couldn't really call it snoring, Sophie comforted herself, returning to the table.

"It wasn't sex," said Marfa, her eyes very bright as she watched Sophie sit down again. Sophie perceived that Marfa was in what they used to call a state of expanded consciousness. Marfa seized her glass and lifted it in accordance with Poppa's instructions. "To sex!" she said, downing about half the contents.

"To sex," agreed Sophie. "What was it, then?" she

asked curiously. This was not the story she had been expecting to hear.

"I guess you know what I mean. It was just the kind of stuff we'd always done," said Marfa.

"Actually, I'm not sure I do know," said Sophie nervously. "I mean, I never had a brother or any—well, any friends. Not at that time," she added.

"Well, it isn't sex," said Marfa. "Benedict knew all about sex. He'd have to, growing up on the Reserve like that—and with his mother the way she was. In fact, he had this thing about purity. Annie was a complete innocent—a virgin—because Benedict was so strict. Oh, yes, I'm getting to that," she said, with a malicious grin at Sophie. "No, what I mean—it's like this."

She picked up Sophie's hand off the table, almost as an idle gesture, and separated the fingers, twining her own around them.

The hair on the back of Sophie's neck prickled. Marfa curved her narrow palm around Sophie's wrist.

Sophie blushed.

Marfa smiled.

"I'm not bent that way either," she said. "But that's what I mean. Not just that."

"Sort of like foreplay."

"As they say in books. Benedict thought he could get away with that with me forever. It never occurred to him to stop, not even after he started making Annie wear a bathing suit and sit with her legs crossed."

Sophie shook her head. "I just can't get Benedict together," she said.

"You've been listening to Sasha," said Marfa. "That's why."

"So what happened that night?" asked Sophie.

"Oh yes. Back to that. We got cold. It was November or something. So we went back to Benedict's place. And there were Sasha and Annie. Wait!" She raised her hand imperiously and had some more of her drink.

There were Sasha and Annie. The words reverberated in Sophie's ears. Wasn't it already enough? What more did she have to hear?

"You never had a brother?" said Marfa. "Well, then, you can't have any idea. It's almost as indecent as seeing your parents! Annie was crying, of course. They usually do," she went on, for the benefit of some unseen listener as scientific as herself.

"But he was comforting her!" shouted Sophie, standing up.

Marfa looked up at her, on the edge of a laugh. But apparently, even through her veil of stoned cynicism, she saw Sophie's expression of fear and horror.

"I'll tell you what, Sophie. *She* was comforting *him*! They were lying on that sofa in the kitchen and she was petting him and talking to him in that funny little voice of hers while Sasha lay on top of her like some big, humble kind of animal. They hadn't even taken their clothes off. I bet it just happened like that!" Marfa snapped her fingers.

"Oh God!" said Sophie, sitting down and beginning to cry a little, partly from relief.

"Well, what did you think?" asked Marfa, diverted. "Poor, sweet, innocent little Annie. Do you think anyone could have wanted to hurt her? Not my brother Sasha, at any rate."

"Didn't Benedict see them too?" asked Sophie.

"No. He knew Sasha was there to take me home when he saw the truck outside, so he just went to bed," said Marfa. "It never would have occurred to him that Sasha would do something like that."

"Why not?" asked Sophie, beginning to recover. "After all, he was competing with Alexander—for that girl." "That whiteman," she wanted to say.

"You think Benedict would have seen it that way? As far as Benedict was concerned, Sasha didn't even exist when he wasn't thinking about him. None of us did," said

Marfa. She sat still for a moment, resting her palms flat on the table. "Maybe something happened to change that later," she said.

"When he found out about—?"

"No. After that."

"What happened after that?" asked Sophie.

"What happened after that?" said Marfa, looking up satirically. "Why, Annie got pregnant, Sasha took off, Benedict quit school, and I lived happily ever after!"

"Well, I'm glad somebody came out whole."

"Oh yeah. I guess Sasha's pretty whole, too, or I wouldn't be telling you this at two o'clock in the morning with him snoring over there." Marfa jerked her head casually in the direction of Alexander, sleeping heavily with the afghan rucked up around his shoulders. "Talk about the kitchen couch! Too bad men aren't what they're cracked up to be, Sophie!"

Somewhat later, Sophie woke up with a start.

Marfa and she had gotten rather drunk together, and she had only a dim recollection of going to bed in Alexander's room.

She was wearing a nightgown Marfa had given her out of an elderly collection she kept in a suitcase in the boot cupboard.

"I got these when I was engaged," she told Sophie, laughing uproariously. They were both very stoned at that point. The nightgown was a flimsy piece of black nylon, frothed out crinoline-fashion about the knees, and ending in an unnecessary ruffle of lace.

"I'll wear one to your wedding!" shrieked Marfa over a pink affair with a collar and no bodice at all.

Sophie woke up alarmed, at first for no reason at all, then because she realized that there was a fight going on outside. Hoarse male cries were punctuating a fairly continuous background of female screaming.

She leaped out of bed, too frightened to look out the

window. Instantly she became furious. If it was Alexander again, she intended to give him a piece of her hangover.

Sophie arrived in the kitchen ready to break up a pair of orangutans with her bare hands, if necessary.

Alexander was sitting up on the divan, looking rather pale.

"Sophia?"

"Alexander? Thank heavens! I thought it was you out there."

"What's goin' on?"

"Someone is beating up on someone else." Sophie pointed in the direction of the yard. "At first I thought it was you and Rudi. But that sounds like a woman." Her voice trembled.

Alexander rolled off the divan and went to look out the window.

"Who is it?" Sophie was clutching him from behind as he leaned over the sink.

"Rudi and Marietta," he said disgustedly. "Hey! Just relax."

"Why are they—? Is he hurting her?" Sophie dug her nails into his arms as he turned around to look at her. "Let's go out there!"

"There's nothing we can do, Sophia."

"What do you mean? Surely we could—" Marietta had burst forth into louder screams. "Aren't you going to stop him?"

"How do you expect me to do that?" Alexander was now holding on to Sophie, who tried, shuddering, to wrench herself away.

Alexander's father strode past them, majestic in a pair of purple and white striped pajamas. He gave Alexander a significant nod, indicating, as Sophie interpreted it, *Get her out of here.*

"Come on," said Alexander briefly, and led her back upstairs. "Poppa'll take care of it."

"What if he hadn't? Wouldn't you have done anything?" Sophie demanded fiercely, as he pushed her ahead of him into the bedroom and shut the door. Muffled shouting could be heard outside.

"Would you like a glass of water?" Alexander asked. Sophie sat down slowly on the edge of the bed and nodded, looking at him wide-eyed. He seemed utterly heartless.

"Stay here, Sophia."

Alexander went out of the room, shutting the door carefully behind him. He returned some moments later with the water. His hair was wet and his face was ruddy and shining; evidently he had put his whole head under the tap.

"Drink up," he suggested.

Sophie drank and then turned again to look at him with hostility. All that was to be heard outside now was the reasonable voice of Poppa.

Alexander sat down beside her.

"Jesus Christ!" he remarked. "Russians!" He put his arm about her shoulders and Sophie wriggled away.

"Everyone in your family thinks he's a sort of changeling," she said coldly. "But when you get right down to it, you're very much alike! You got into two fights with Rudi tonight yourself, Alexander! And the only thing that stopped the second one was that you were too drunk to get on with it!"

He grinned sheepishly. "Well, at least I didn't mix with a third one."

"Rudi was beating up his wife!"

Alexander sighed. "You're as brave as a lion, aren't you, Sophia?"

"No, but if I'd been you, I'd have gone out there!"

"And then what? Do you want to see me get hurt? He's jealous."

"Was that what it was—jealousy?" said Sophie incredulously. "Rudolph is *jealous* of Marietta?"

"Yeah," Alexander said.

"And who?"

"Oh . . . Luke. I don't know."

"Luke!"

"Yeah. Or whoever was around. He accused me of messing with her once or twice, but I wouldn't play the game."

"That's disgusting!"

"Sure it is." He folded his arms and looked at her intently. "Some people are like that," he said.

Sophie looked into his eyes and suddenly quailed.

"I'm not like that!" she said aggressively.

He sighed. "You goin' to stay mad?" he asked.

"No," said Sophie humbly. "I'm sorry."

The screen door slammed, and they heard the murmur of voices in the room below.

"It was just a reaction," said Sophie, looking at him sideways. "I woke up suddenly, and then I was a little scared."

"Scared? You?" He smiled. "I didn't notice."

Sophie leaned back against his arm. It had just come to her that he was talking about himself, not her. He was a very jealous person. And he didn't know about her conversation with Marfa.

"Where'd you get this thing you're wearin'?" he asked.

Sophie giggled. She kicked out the froth below her knees with a bare foot. "It's part of my trousseau."

"Really?"

"Of course, really. Marfa gave it to me."

"You were talkin' to Marfa when I went to sleep, I guess."

"Yes. We had a lot to drink and some dope and—we admired you, sleeping!"

"So maybe I'd better let you get some sleep yourself," he said, moving a little away.

"No!" Sophie clutched him again, hearing raised voices in the kitchen. "Stay here with me!"

"Okay." He looked uneasily at her, and Sophie promptly lay down flat on her back with her arms at her sides. He looked away immediately.

"So this is your room," she said dreamily. It was a barren room: the bed, a chair, a white-painted bureau with a pile of clean laundry on it, a collection of ancient leather workboots visible through a partially opened closet door.

"I sleep here," he said.

"Was this always your bedroom?"

"Yeah. I had to share it with Rudi, though."

There was an explosion of screaming downstairs, and Sophie shot upright in alarm. The screams died away into soothing murmurs. Alexander's father was a genius at this kind of thing.

"It's all right," said Alexander.

"This household is so violent," said Sophie, pressing her nose into his shoulder. She noticed with secret amusement that he was trying to keep his hands off her.

"After I got away," he began, clearing his throat. Sophie shifted herself onto his lap and put both arms around his neck. "When I was workin' up north," he went on, putting one hand on the small of her back and then quickly removing it, "I heard myself once or twice," he said. "And I noticed I sounded just like them. Like Poppa." He rested his unshaven chin lightly against her forehead. "It gave me a shock, I'll tell you."

"So what did you do?" asked Sophie, idly unbuttoning his shirt.

"I didn't like it," he said. "I quit."

"What do you mean? Fighting and things like that?" she inquired ironically, resting her palm on his flat, hairy stomach.

"Yeah. Except that here—when I get a little too much vodka in me—I can't always— Cut it out, Sophia!" He took her by the elbows and held her away from him.

Sophie smiled demurely.

The look of annoyance slowly faded from his face,

and was replaced by quite another expression. They regarded each other closely for a long moment.

"You really want to, Sophia?" he asked.

"Why not?" replied Sophie. "I'm not the one who's marrying for money."

"But for this?" he asked softly.

"How should I know?" Sophie rolled her eyes.

He laughed.

"Don't you want to get to know me?" he asked. But she had already seen the change in his face.

"It isn't nice to tease!"

"I'm not teasin' you, Sophia."

"Oh no?"

"Listen to them down there. That's in my blood too!"

"Do I have to wait till you get the mustard out of the fields, then?"

"No. Just—" His eyes were dilated and his hands were not so firm on her arms. She saw that she was not winning this battle with words.

"Just?"

"Just—" He put his mouth down on hers, and Sophie's arms slid easily, loosely, around his neck. A moment later he moved her off his lap onto the bed and lay down to kiss. Sophie raised her knees and he slid his hands up under the layer of froth. She heard him sigh with satisfaction as the nightgown came off over her head and she clasped him, hard and almost fully clothed, to her naked body.

"So white," he murmured in surprise.

"So black," whispered Sophie mockingly, tugging at his shirt.

He rolled aside and undid his belt buckle cooperatively, gazing at her with eyes that were now, indeed, almost black.

Sophie looked at the heavy pelt of curling black hair covering his chest and descending in a V under his belt. She lifted her arms to him with a little moan.

Alexander shed his shirt quickly, then stood over her, struggling with his trousers.

Sophie sat up and pressed herself against him, putting her arms around his waist and sliding them down with his jeans. He was shy. She suddenly knew that whatever his experience had been, she had powers he knew nothing about, that would bewilder and astonish him.

"Jesus God!" Alexander groaned, and caught her face between his hands, the long fingers finding purchase in her tangled hair.

Sophie tilted back her head, flushed and triumphant, and laughed at him wickedly.

Heavy, stumping footsteps ascended the stairs and a door opened down the hall. There was a gust of rapid Russian in the corridor. Another door opened and Sophie heard the cross, waking-up voice of Marfa. A moment later Momma said, "Where is Sasha?"

Sophie and Alexander remained frozen in place for a moment.

"Sasha!" shouted Poppa.

"Shut up, Poppa," said Marfa in a high, clear voice. "He's probably in bed with—"

"Sasha!" Momma called, and approached the door with a brisk shuffle of bedroom slippers.

Sophie whisked herself under the bedclothes, taking her ridiculous nightdress with her. Hastily pulling up his jeans, Alexander went to the door. Sophie was cleverly getting into her costume under the covers.

"Momma? What do you want?" He opened the door with a gesture of exaggerated patience. Giggling softly to herself, Sophie read frustration and fury in the posture of his broad, bare back.

"Were you sleeping through all that noise?" asked Momma in disbelief.

"No. Sophia woke up, so I—"

"One can get no sleep here in the nights," said Momma irritably. "It is the madness of this family!"

"Sophia, you are not being scared by all this clatter?" shouted Poppa jovially from the hall.

"That's the way it goes, Sophie!" cried Marfa satirically, evidently unable to resist joining the crowd in the doorway. "Would you like some hot milk?"

"I am getting everybody hot milk," said Momma. "Stay in bed, Sophia." Apparently something occurred to her for she added: "Alexander, my son, it is not right for you to be in her room."

"Keeping her awake like that," added Marfa.

Alexander shut the door very firmly and went over to pick his shirt up off the floor. Discussion outside indicated that everyone was going to have hot milk except Poppa, who was going to have a beer. Alexander pulled on his shirt and buttoned it, turning even farther away from Sophie to tuck it in. Then he turned around, running a hand through his thick hair, and glanced at her.

"That was exciting," said Sophie. "I feel about ten years younger."

He grinned suddenly.

"I might have known that nothing that nice was goin' to happen to me in this house!" he said.

Sophie hopped out of bed, first establishing that she was fully dressed again, and gave him a brief and charming kiss. The whole episode struck her as extremely amusing.

"I have to go," he said reluctantly.

"Some other time, maybe," said Sophie lightly, touching his unshaven cheek with her fingertips.

"Not less than four hundred miles from the nearest Russian," he said, detaching himself gently and going to the door. "I think I'll have a beer with Poppa."

13

Ring

Marfa drove Sophie home the next morning. Alexander had already gone, taking her car. Apparently all of the Bresnyachuks had stayed up drinking beer. Only Momma and Sophie had had hot milk. Sophie continued to hold Momma in awe.

Sophie recognized Marfa as the only one in the whole family who spoke her language. The trouble with Marfa was that she was too articulate, if anything.

"Yeah, I know what it's like," she was saying. "It's a real piece of luck that I got myself an old man Poppa won't even let in the house. Saves quite a lot of trouble that way." She stuck an unlit cigarette between her lips, then checked her reflection in the rearview mirror and began fumbling in her purse for a tube of lipstick.

"You're not going to marry him, I take it." Sophie glanced over her shoulder at Marfa's children, but they were inattentive to all this.

"Why should I? I own the house, the land, all the stock except his horse. I'll keep him on till he notices that it's a free hotel and figures he can check in with a girl. Then—" Marfa drew a zero in the air with her lipstick.

"He doesn't help with the farming?"

"Are you kidding? He's an artist." Marfa chuckled. "Real grade-A, hot stuff, fake, pseudo-Indian art. It almost pays the bill for the beer he drinks." She slowed for a crossroads, carefully applying her lipstick. "Come over any time you want, Sophie. It's just across the Reserve on the road to Bitter Root. My name's on the mailbox. Harthog," she added. "A classic, isn't it? Always makes me think of warthog, for some reason."

"Oh, I see. Your husband's name?"

"Yeah. I keep it around for a souvenir." Marfa turned up the driveway. "I'll just drop you off," she remarked. "Save your mother for the wedding. When is the wedding, by the way?"

"I don't—we haven't decided." The children in the back seat were having a dispute over who was to sit in front as Sophie got out. "Thanks, Marfa."

"Not at all. Shut up, you two! Well, come over, like I say, and I'll give you the best bed in the house. Or just come over. We've got a really good swimming hole."

"Okay, I'd like to."

"Jeez, is that Sasha out there on the tractor? I never thought I'd see a Hunky working this land. Better him than Rudi, I guess. Stop that, Herbie! It's Emmie's turn! See you later, Sophie."

Sophie staggered into the house and took a long shower. Then she went back to bed, suffering poorly the inquisitive interest of her mother in the details of the party.

When she woke up, it was to the sound of lunch dishes. She could hear Alexander's voice in the kitchen; like an auditory hallucination, it echoed the sound of Poppa's voice. Sophie got up and pulled on jeans and a Western shirt, listening to this dismally.

"Sophie, darling, will you lay out a towel?" called Mother. "Alexander is going to have a shower before lunch."

Still listening to Poppa in the kitchen, Sophie found a towel and put it on the edge of the bathtub. Was marriage such an intrinsically positive thing that your parent came not to care whom you were marrying? Of course, Alexander himself had pointed out the resemblance to her. Was there supposed to be some comfort in that?

She lingered in the hallway, feeling ill and obscurely annoyed.

"That lower garden needs water," said Alexander at the bottom of the stairs, still talking to Mother. "Especially them potatoes."

Perhaps he should marry Mother, Sophie thought. She was the one who would appreciate it most.

Alexander's face appeared between the pickets of the bannister on the landing, shining like the sun. It was another scorching day.

"I'd get after that this afternoon, but I've got to go to the Co-op," he was saying. He caught sight of Sophie and smiled at her.

"Don't you ever sleep?" she hissed at him.

"Marfa bring you home?" he inquired.

"Yes. We had another lovely chat," said Sophie abusively.

"Oh, Marfa'd be okay if she hadn't married a drunk," said Alexander seriously, standing over her. He radiated heat and moisture. His shirt was sopping wet with sweat, sticking in patches to his hairy chest. It was the same shirt he had been wearing at the party.

"I see. I'll have to remember that when I decide who I'm going to marry myself," said Sophie.

"Do you mind if I borrow your toothbrush?" asked Alexander, proceeding to the bathroom.

"No, no," said Sophie, pointing it out quickly and then retreating as he began to undress. She could suddenly appreciate his reluctance to make love to her last night. It was all very well for her in the Bresnyachuk house, but Sophie could not imagine doing it here at home, with Mother frying potatoes in the kitchen below.

It struck her, as she continued to linger in the hallway, that she was going to live in this house with Alexander. Which bedroom were they going to have? The thought made her positively ill. *He* might not mind, but she . . .

To her horror, Alexander now began to sing something in the shower. Fearing that it was in Russian, Sophie fled to the lower story.

She was feeling slightly better when Alexander arrived back in the kitchen, drier, and with his hair slicked down as usual. Mother gave him a glance radiant with love.

"Want to come with me to the Co-op, Sophia?" asked Alexander.

"No. I'll water the potatoes."

"Leave it till tonight. It's too hot."

"I'm going to take Rosi out tonight." She noticed that Alexander and her mother exchanged a significant look. "He just has to get used to me again," she said defiantly.

"I wish you had a nice gentle mare," said Mother, setting a plate of food in front of Alexander.

"Some of them mares can be pretty tricksy too," said Alexander.

"Anyway, I want to take you shopping this afternoon, Sophie," said Mother.

"What do you want to go shopping for?" asked Sophie, privately resolving to leave the potato garden altogether and take her horse out.

"Your trousseau, of course."

Alexander shot Sophie a quick smiling glance and she recalled Marfa's foolish nightgown, now in a paper bag in her bottom bureau drawer.

"Oh good. We'll get something to match my black eyes."

"They've almost disappeared," said Alexander comfortingly.

She put a saddle on Rosi that night, but it did not help. He had noticed that she was afraid of him. They had a very nasty walk around the pasture, since she did not dare try to take him down the road. Alexander watched, covertly at first. Then he strolled over to the fence.

"He's in a weird mood," said Sophie, pausing at the gate. "You must have been spoiling him."

"We get along pretty good," said Alexander.

"Well, he used to get along with me, too," said Sophie. She put Rosi into an awkward trot, and he pretended he was going to bolt, rolling his eyes. Sophie pulled him up sharply and the horse laughed at her.

Alexander sat on the gate, chewing a timothy stalk.

"All right, then!" muttered Sophie, dismounting. She began to lead Rosi back to the barn.

"Maybe you shouldn't leave him like that," suggested Alexander. "He's all excited."

"Well, he'll just have to put up with it," she snapped, undoing the saddle girth. "If he wants a ride, he has to behave better."

"He wants it," said Alexander, lifting down the saddle and setting it on the fence. "But he doesn't know how to handle you." He looked at her sideways, smiling to himself.

Sophie caught this and burst out laughing.

"Did you buy a lot of things today?" asked Alexander, mounting Rosi cleverly with a bound. He did not have to use the fence.

"Mother did. She's full of girlish anticipation," said Sophie, watching her horse fawning on Alexander with irritation.

"I'll just take him around a few times," said Alexander calmly. "I wanted to get you a ring this afternoon," he began as they galloped off in perfect harmony.

"But I got you something else instead," he told her, passing by the gate again. "I'm not sure you'll like it."

He dismounted. "Want to take him now? I think he'll be okay."

"Just go ahead," said Sophie. "Take him out on the road. I'm going to water the potatoes."

She was trying to be generous, she convinced herself half an hour later. When he had married Mother, she could give him Rosi as a wedding present.

She drove Alexander home that night.

"Did you have a lovely ride?"

"Mm." He slumped in the seat and a large, heavy head came to rest against her shoulder.

"You must have been feeling like shit all day," she said sympathetically.

"Yeah."

"There's nothing like a hangover to put things in perspective," she went on.

"I don't know about that." He sat up. "Poppa's birthday only comes once a year. You won't have to put up with much of that, Sophia."

"What about Christmas and so on?"

"As far as Poppa is concerned, Christ was born in June," said Alexander, lighting a cigarette. "Other holidays are just holidays."

"Well, it was certainly an experience," said Sophie, laughing. "My favorite fight was the last one, of course."

"I liked what happened right after that best," Alexander exhaled a plume of smoke.

"Oh." Sophie glanced at him in the darkness. "What *didn't* happen, you mean."

"We better get married, Sophia."

"Yes, these teenage escapades in single beds and trucks and things! Have you thought of taking me to a drive-in movie yet?"

"What about settin' the date?"

"Just a number?"

"Don't be scared, Sophia."

"I'll think about it," said Sophie uncomfortably. She drew up in the Bresnyachuk dooryard. "Couldn't we just go to a hotel or something first?"

Alexander sighed. Then he yawned, putting out his cigarette.

"I'll think about it," he said. He kissed her on the forehead and got out of the truck, shutting the door. Then he opened it again and said, "I'll be over early tomorrow. I've got something to show you."

Sophie woke up at six o'clock the next morning, feeling full of energy. She sprang into the shower, then ran down to the barn, looking for Alexander. Her hair fluffed out prettily in the breeze. Her pink shirt suited her. Alexander was not entirely unsusceptible; that much had been established at least. There were serious grounds for optimism.

He was not there yet, so she went in to chat with Rosi, who was still asleep, standing on three glossy brown feet. Alexander was keeping him up very well. Rosi opened his eyes and grinned at her. She put on his bridle and began leading him out to the pasture, talking to him:

"Going over to the Cossacks?" she inquired. "I've got some news to whisper in your ear, darling. You're an Arab, not a Russian."

Rosi stopped dead and neighed.

"What is it now, you pig? Communist!" she shouted at him, tugging on the bridle.

Rosi neighed again, lifting his nostrils to the breeze.

Alexander rode briskly into the yard on a pretty little strawberry mare. The mare stopped, tossing her head, flirting with Alexander and eying Rosi doubtfully.

"What's this?"

"Just a present," said Alexander, dismounting. "I'm calling her Ring, because that's where all the money went."

Ring extended her neck in Rosi's direction, savoring the air, her teeth exposed.

"Well, well." Sophie put her hands on her hips. "This is supposed to make it okay, is it?"

"What okay?" he asked, patting Ring's neck and letting her sidle toward the other horse.

"You and Mother seem to have the same opinion of my riding!" Sophie was humiliated, furious.

"We've got to have two anyway," he pointed out.

"Yes, but I already had one. I guess he's yours now, eh?"

"Hey, come on, Sophie! They're both yours!"

Sophie glanced at Ring, her eyes bright with anger. She looked like a gentle little mare, just Mother's idea of a horse. She was much too small for Alexander.

"Well, thanks. Have a good time riding them," she said flatly. She dropped Rosi's bridle and began walking in the direction of the north field, swallowing tears of rage and injured vanity.

"Sophia!" said Alexander. She heard Rosi neighing and hoped Alexander would be quite busy with the two of them for some time to come. Rosi tended to dislike strangers.

She sulked away the early part of the morning under a poplar hedge at the end of the north field. Later on, she saw Alexander advancing on the tractor and she got up and walked back to the house. Passing the corral, she noticed Ring and Rosi standing nose to nose. They turned around to watch her passing, and Rosi gave Ring a nasty nudge with his huge shoulder.

"Attaboy!" shouted Sophie. "Bite her! Show her who's the boss!" She went on into the house.

"What is it, dear?" asked her mother. "Did Alexander give you a new horse?"

"So you weren't in on the plan?" asked Sophie coldly.

"I've just been thinking about travel arrangements," said her mother pacifically. "Since you won't be able to honeymoon until after harvest—"

"Oh, I wouldn't worry about that!" said Sophie, snorting.

"Well, but you won't want me in the house, dear. So I thought I'd go to the Coast in July. Then you can—"

"I'm going out for the afternoon," said Sophie. "Don't expect me for supper, either."

"So soon?" said Marfa.

Sophie had considered visiting Annie, but Annie had gone over to the enemy completely. Annie wanted Alexander to be happy with her. His sister had a more detached view.

The farm was very small, set in a creek ravine running down to the Bow River. A long, precipitous driveway led to the hidden, ramshackle farmhouse. It was very pretty, verdant from the mists of the river. Sophie, whose two-and-one-half section farm was conventionally flat, arid, and caterpillar-ridden, looked at this prettiness with a professional eye. They probably made more money from art than from cattle, she surmised.

"Well, luckily we always have dope on hand," said Marfa, leading Sophie out behind the house to some garden chairs. "I'd have laid in something if I'd known you were coming."

"Sorry, Marfa. I could have called or something."

"Don't be silly. Not at all. You had a quarrel with Sasha, I suppose. Wait. I'll get the lemonade."

Sophie waited in a lawn chair, meanwhile bitterly watching Emmie ride her pony across the pasture with artless skill.

"Nice garden," she remarked, pointing to it as Marfa returned with a pitcher and two glasses. "Are you going to sell tomatoes? This will probably be a good year for it."

"Tomatoes?" asked Marfa quizzically. "Oh yeah. That's Tim's garden, Sophie. And it isn't tomatoes."

"I see," said Sophie quickly. "I don't know why I . . . I've seen it growing before, when I was in East Pakistan." She now began to see how this farm could be a paying proposition.

"Better land in Alberta, I bet." Marfa sat down and lit a cigarette, gesturing hospitably at the lemonade. "So what happened?"

Sophie realized suddenly that she could never tell Marfa about the cause of their quarrel. It was a completely ridiculous thing to be mad about.

"I thought this deal was crazy when I first heard about it," said Marfa helpfully. "I mean, Sasha's just a great big, rawboned Bohunk. What's he got that a refined little thing like you needs?" She smiled maliciously. "I've already guessed," she added. "You don't have to tell me."

"Well, but we haven't—" began Sophie tentatively.

"No doubt you think you're in love with him."

"Yes, but you see—"

"Hell, I'm even in love with this bum who's boarding with me, now."

"Alexander hasn't—"

"Men don't use that word the same way," said Marfa. "When he says it, you don't understand what he means." She shrugged.

"But he doesn't say it!" cried Sophie desperately. "We haven't even—"

"What?" asked Marfa, taken aback.

"No."

"So what were you doing all night in Sasha's bedroom?" inquired Marfa. "Talking?"

"How did you know?" said Sophie. Herbie now rode into view, also on a pony, and began to chase Emmie down the pasture. Sophie watched moodily.

"God! What stake have you got in it at all, then?"

Marfa shot Sophie a sort of are-you-lying-to-your-mother look. "You're not kidding me, Sophie?"

"No," said Sophie. She drank some lemonade. "People don't get married for sex," she said distantly. "They get married so they can have a *farm*!"

Marfa burst out laughing.

"Boy! This is my brother?" she shrieked. "I mean, I always wondered if we were related! All the excess fat on Sasha is between his ears."

"Alexander isn't stupid," said Sophie sharply.

"I'll give you that," said Marfa, enjoying herself. "He isn't stupid. In fact, he's a hell of a lot brighter than I would have thought! Most men looking into those soft, lust-filled brown eyes of yours wouldn't be able to hold out for your land!"

"He's trying to be fair. He thinks I may want to back out of it."

"The buyer's dilemma, eh? He wants her land and she wants his body!" Marfa addressed the impartial scientific observer, invisible at her elbow. "The thing is, they have to do the deal at the same time, otherwise one of them might fail to deliver!" She roared with laughter.

"It's not really like that, Marfa," said Sophie helplessly.

Marfa drew a pre-rolled joint out of her hip pocket and prepared to light it, still chuckling.

"Anyway, that's not what we . . . had an argument about," went on Sophie, still unwilling to tell about it.

"It wasn't? Believe me, Sophie"—Marfa inhaled, rolling her eyes—"that *was* what you had an argument about! Those gorgeous, hairy Ukrainian legs, that sweaty Ukrainian forty-six-inch chest, not to mention—"

"Yes, well, we won't mention it, if you don't mind," said Sophie crossly.

"On the other hand," Marfa went on, pursuing a private good time of her own, "I suppose it's reasonable for you to begin to wonder. I mean, could it be all that great? He may look sexy, but—"

"Very funny," said Sophie.

"Relax," Marfa said, patting her arm. "I actually do think he's pretty good at it."

"I wasn't wondering about that!"

"Yes, you were. That's all you've been wondering about!" Marfa stood up, passing Sophie the joint. "Come on inside and I'll show you around. I'm glad you came. Stay for supper. We'll probably go for a swim tonight. Meet the tribe."

"Wait," said Sophie, pausing to inhale. "Marfa, do you think—? Do you think I'm attractive to him at all?"

"You?" Marfa paused and regarded her narrowly. "The way you are now? If I could believe he didn't want to, I'd get you a ticket to East Pakistan tomorrow! He wants to, all right! But anyway," she went on, "you can check all that out tonight if you like. Just stick around, Sophie!"

14

Marfa

Before supper, Marfa's friend, Tim, drove into town to get some beer from the bootlegger. Sophie helped Marfa with the cooking. They were making a very large meal: deer meat, mashed potatoes, great quantities of salad, Jell-O, and pie.

"Tim'll be back with the tribe," explained Marfa.

Tim seemed perfectly all right to Sophie, not the shiftless, wasteful character of Marfa's ongoing conversation. She let up on this, but only slightly, in Tim's presence. He was an oil painter as it turned out, not the sort of basket or belt-buckle maker that Sophie had been led to expect. She had already admired several canvases in the sitting room and was wondering whether she could buy one without hurting Marfa's feelings.

The "tribe" turned out to be a classical-guitar-playing Scandinavian, about six feet eight. Sophie began to worry about him immediately. She had the feeling she was being pushed into something. No overt pressure was being applied, but she felt more comfortable talking to Tim.

"So, what do you do, Sophie?" They were washing dishes. Marfa had disappeared with the children, and Sven was in the dimly lit, plant-crowded sitting room, tuning his guitar.

"I teach kindergarten," said Sophie.

"That's cool," said Tim, squinting against the smoke of the joint in his mouth as he dried a plate. "How did you get to know Marfa?"

"We went to school together." Sophie glanced sideways at him, wondering if he knew any more about her. Marfa probably didn't tell him about her family, under the circumstances.

"A good grade, kindergarten." Tim was almost excessively handsome in a lithe, silent-walking, impassive-faced Plains Indian way. It went very well with his laid-back manner.

"Yes, it is. Come to think of it, it was always my favorite, even when I was five!" said Sophie with a drug-induced giggle. Feeling lighthearted, she began to sing the alphabet song. The guitar in the sitting room picked this up and started to elaborate.

"Boy, you must have a lot of fun!" said Tim when she had finished. He was amused. "Is that all you do? Kindergarten?"

"No." Sophie drew breath. "Old MacDonald had a farm!" she began, and this time Sven sang harmony with her as he picked out the chords.

Tim opened a beer, leaning back casually against the large round kitchen table. Sophie noticed with pleasure that he was now giving her a definitely sexual inspection, not bothering to hide his interest at all.

Marfa came down the stairs that led eccentrically up from the back porch.

"Ee-eye-ee-eye-oh!" concluded Sophie.

"Well!" said Marfa. She regarded them for a moment,

her hands on her hips. "Kids," she said briefly to Tim, who was giving her a look of lazy inquiry. "They want you to come up."

"Okay." Tim went toward the staircase, taking his beer bottle with him. "See you later, Sophie."

"He's nice, Marfa," said Sophie, rinsing the dishcloth. she felt that Marfa must secretly agree with this judgment, especially as he was now putting her kids to bed.

"Let's go down to the river," said Marfa, picking up a carton of beer. "There aren't very many mosquitoes this year."

They went out the back door and across the pasture in the cooling, blessedly humid night air.

"What do you think of Sven?" asked Marfa.

"Well, he's nice, too," said Sophie uneasily. "He's not really my type, though, Marfa. Musicians are always so taken up with themselves. The instrument, you know—they're more interested in it."

"I'd been wondering about that myself. Well, if you don't want him . . ." Marfa shrugged.

Somewhat taken aback by this forthrightness, Sophie was silent. She certainly did not want Sven, and she did not want Tim either, although she had been enjoying his company. She wanted Alexander. A wave of longing for that heavy head, that thick, bunchy hair, those strange, cloudy eyes, that sweaty, forty-six-inch chest, and all the other charms to which Marfa had so indelicately alluded swept over Sophie.

"Maybe I'll go home soon," she said.

"What's this? Getting cold feet? Stay here and have a swim, at least. Nobody's making you do anything you don't want, Sophie," Marfa told her kindly.

"No, no," Sophie agreed nervously.

A mist was rising from the river in little wisps as they came out at the end of the path.

"Don't you wonder how the Indian lived before the horse?" said Marfa. "Sometimes, when I'm down here real late and there's a mist coming up, I think the kids' ponies *are* Indians."

"Coming back to the old places?" said Sophie dreamily. "This river valley . . ."

There was a nice soft sward to sit on above the pool in the stream.

"All I know is, it costs nearly as much to keep one of those ponies as it does to keep an Indian," said Marfa.

"Oh, come off it, Marfa!"

"Yeah. All that crap about how good he is with the kids and how he sold a painting last winter and blah, blah!" said Marfa energetically. "That's not why I keep him around, so don't tell me about it!"

"Sorry."

"Every time I see Sasha, he gives me a long harangue about all that. So what? I didn't mean to bite your head off," she added, lying down on the turf.

"I shouldn't have . . . I mean, it's your business."

"It is my business," Marfa agreed. "You want to know why I do keep him around, Sophie?"

"Well. Only if—"

"Because he reminds me of somebody," said Marfa.

This thought had already occurred to Sophie. Perhaps one of Marfa's problems was that she was too honest with herself.

"He doesn't look like him and he doesn't feel like him. Christ, he doesn't even smell like him. But you know how sometimes a person can remind you of someone else, even if they've got nothing much in common?"

Sophie had occasionally had this very feeling about Alexander in relation to her father. She said nothing.

"I guess Sasha doesn't know about that," said Marfa abruptly. "It happened after he left, anyway. After Benedict quit school. I was eighteen."

"Oh. So you did—"

"Yes. We did," said Marfa, tilting her head to look up at the darkening sky.

"I thought he wasn't letting you see Annie."

"No, and I never did see her again. I met him at a rodeo. He was riding in one of those poky little one-horse things in Steamboat. He was already good enough for the Stampede, but that came later."

"He'd given up on being Prime Minister."

"Yeah," said Marfa dryly. "But you know," she went on, "I hate rodeos. You go see some young punk sit on a horse that's half-dead anyway and kick it till it gets it up enough to throw him. Not Benedict, though. He'd ride a horse like that around the ring three times and then make them take the straps off its balls. It was a crowd-pleaser. But he had to do something in between, so they really let him do it, at least once an afternoon. And he sure as hell did it! Maybe it was cruel, but only a great rider could have done it."

"That's how he got hurt in the end, right?" said Sophie.

Marfa did not reply for a moment. Sophie heard the clinking of beer bottles on the dark grass.

"It looked effortless," she said, giving Sophie a beer and lying down again. "It *was* effortless. But that was mostly because he didn't give a damn. If you want to kill yourself, you can ride pretty well anything. The horse has got more to lose than you do."

"But it takes a certain amount of psychological effort to be suicidal on command," Sophie protested.

"Not for an Indian. They've got a death wish. All of 'em." Marfa lit a cigarette. "He was already going on drugs and drink, just like what you see in all those cheapo rodeo movies on TV. And he was only twenty-one."

"Why? Because of Alexander getting Annie pregnant?"

Marfa shrugged. "It was his destiny," she said. "You should have seen him, Sophie. Jesus! He was beautiful!"

"What did Benedict look like?" asked Sophie, swept

once again into the strange communion of those who loved Benedict Malone.

"He wasn't very big," said Marfa. "About five feet eight, I guess. But his body was like a rattlesnake whip. And he had the face to go with it. You'd better believe he would have killed Sasha! Those eyes—my God! He didn't walk like one of those hokey rodeo players—you know, that kind of stiff walk they put on, as though they had a hard day in the saddle. When Benedict walked, it looked like—well, it looked like scx," said Marfa simply.

"I bet," said Sophie, laughing. "So you just went up to him and said, 'Don't I know you from somewhere?' Or what?"

"Yeah," said Marfa, and Sophie could tell she was smiling. "Yeah. That's what I did."

They sat in silence for a while. The pale moon had risen on the dusky horizon and Marfa's ponies-and-Indians mist was swirling up from the river.

"I wasn't too bad-looking myself in those days," said Marfa. "If I do say so. Pity I didn't have the brains to know what I was getting. I'd give almost anything to go back to then—knowing what I do now—even if I had to look like this!"

"Come on, Marfa! You know you're gorgeous!"

"Have another beer, Sophie. I like the way you talk when you're drinking."

"Great figure. Wonderful eyes. You and Alexander—"

"Yeah. We're the pretty Bresnyachuks. We haven't got anything else in common. Let's have a joint, shall we?"

"Or would that be too much?" pondered Sophie, giggling. The excessiveness of this family fascinated her.

"Started smoking this stuff with Benedict," said Marfa, lighting up the joint between two different fingers of the hand in which she was holding a cigarette. "We'd lie in bed in some filthy motel on the circuit and he'd smoke until he couldn't remember his name or my name or the name of the horse he'd half killed in the afternoon. The only thing it doesn't wipe out is the sex drive—or so they say. I always read the pamphlets in my doctor's office."

"Me too. Only they say it does wipe out the sex drive."

"Well, they're wrong," said Marfa flatly. "It sure as hell doesn't! But nothing could have wiped out the sex drive in those days, of course. I was crazy for him! I couldn't have enough!" Marfa shivered. Then she said, "But maybe it wasn't enough for him at all. Benedict had to have something addictive. At first it was just speed."

"Did he do it before the shows?"

"Do what, Sophie?" Marfa asked mockingly.

"I mean drugs, Marfa. Speed."

"He didn't need to take anything before the shows. Wanting to get killed is the biggest upper you can imagine. What Benedict really needed was to take the kind of drugs that'd make him, you know, a little depressed about dying." Marfa laughed and Sophie joined in nervously.

"Where were Momma and Poppa in all this, incidentally?" Sophie asked.

"Back at the ranch," said Marfa coldly. "Benedict wouldn't play any of those games, like dropping me off in a borrowed ten-year-old Cadillac three miles from home and letting me walk in in my bobby sox: 'I know it's two o'clock in the morning, Momma, but I was kept after school.' We just had one big blow-up, with Poppa oiling his Luger for the duel, and then I got out."

"But weren't you still in school?"

"Yeah. But then it was summertime. What a summer!" Marfa lay back, crossing her arms behind her head, her fingers still lined up with the glowing embers of the joint and the cigarette. "I was either drinking with Benedict or stoned with Benedict or screwing with Benedict all the time!"

"You were in love."

"You might call it that. Whatever it was, it was something I never got from anyone else. Sometimes I wonder whether I'm the only person in the world who knows what it's like. Most people"—Marfa sat upright suddenly—"look at sex like it was a fast-food chain. 'Let's see: shall I have this little sandwich or that one? Mm, that was good—now where was I? A pickle? A french fry? Well—just one, then.' " She roared with laughter.

Sophie looked at Marfa apprehensively. She was approaching the burn-out phase of liquor and marijuana where the manic entertainer suddenly falls to the brimstone lake in a shower of sparks. Sophie took charge of the joint. "Oh yeah," said Marfa, gasping and brushing tears of laughter from her eyes. "That's the way it is now. Snacks!"

"So what happened?" asked Sophie, suddenly impatient to get this over with.

"What happened?" cried Marfa. "You want to know what happened, do you? I got pregnant, that's what happened! A crazy little Hunky like me couldn't have done it differently! He got me pregnant!"

"What? After all that outrage about Alexander and Annie?"

"Are you kidding? You never heard of justice? It was what he meant to do! Benedict had a very good mind, Sophie!"

"He *meant* to do it? You mean—?"

"Sure, that's what I mean!" Marfa was hitting the top of the long parabola she was describing through space. "He meant to do that all the way! It was his revenge! You know—like all that bullshit about how the white man killed the buffalo and screwed the Indians? Annie was the case in point. An eye for an eye, a tooth for a tooth, a sister for a sister! Sasha screwed Annie, so Benedict screwed me!"

"But—"

"The only thing was that he didn't know what a tough bitch I was!" cried Marfa, still screaming through the air. "I wasn't like Annie! I could defend myself! I didn't have

Sasha around to stand over me and see that I ate my spinach! I got rid of it!"

"Oh God! How?"

"I fell off a horse! Someone was going to get killed that way in this story, Sophie!" Marfa shrieked with laughter. "Weren't you expecting that?"

Marfa continued to laugh and sob for some time. Sophie watched the moon, pocked and kindly, looking down on Marfa and irradiating the tears on her face.

"Does Alexander know?" she asked presently.

She knew he didn't. But Sophie wondered whether Annie knew. She had a pretty good idea that Annie wouldn't have been left out of this sequel. Big brother Benedict always told her everything.

"Sasha? He wouldn't *approve,*" said Marfa, a last tiny explosion of laughter emerging from her throat. She rolled over facedown on the soft grass.

Sophie began to have a horrible feeling of dread about this. Not only would Alexander not approve; it would destroy the four corners of the world for him. Sophie was aware that she was not one of these corners.

"What's going on here?" asked Sven, easing himself into a reclining position an even distance from both of them.

"We've been talking," said Marfa in a muffled voice. "I was just telling Sophie about the lost love of my life."

"Are you still into love?" inquired Sven.

"See what I mean, Sophie?" Marfa lifted her head. "Junk food is all I can get these days!"

"Are we going for a swim?" asked Tim, emerging silently from the shadow of the trees. He was naked but for a pair of moccasins. Sophie glanced away, a little embarrassed.

"Right," said Marfa briskly, taking off her blouse. "Coming, Sophie?"

"Is it warm?" asked Sophie, undoing a button reluctantly. It was all right, though. No one was watching her.

* * *

Somewhat later, enervated by the long midnight swim and the new layer of drugs and liquor that had replaced the old, Sophie found herself lying face downward on the greensward, her head on her arms. There had been no sound in the clearing for some time.

She raised her head cautiously, recognizing that she was intellectually deprived. She had not heard Marfa's voice for some time.

"Where's Marfa?" she asked of no one in particular.

"She went in."

A voice, not necessarily from behind her, but from somewhere close by, had said these words. Sophie raised herself on her arm.

"Goodness!" she said, staring at the stars, a little dimmed by the dawn. She flopped on her back to look at them more closely.

There was a quiet movement at her side. A brown, sinewy arm grasped her across her belly and she made out against the growing brightness of the sky the head and shoulders of a man.

It was Benedict.

Sophie gasped, freezing with terror. The body that now fitted itself over hers was like a braided whip. The lips were unexpectedly soft.

"No!" she cried, turning her head away violently and thrusting at his chest with her hands. "Stop! Wait a minute!"

He drew away a little, his head raised arrogantly.

"Who are you?"

"Don't you know?" He laughed, not a pleasant sound. He was still pressing her remorselessly against the earth.

"I—" said Sophie, swallowing panic.

"You weren't expecting this?" he asked ironically. She could see his face, his eyes dark, almond-shaped, and impenetrable, like Annie's.

She wanted to get up and run. But she couldn't move.

He would be fast, faster than she was. He could run like a buffalo hunter.

"What about Marfa?" she cried.

"Don't bother. She went with Sven."

Sophie was conscious that what she was feeling was not just fear. She was gripped by the most vicious form of desire, thrilling and primitive. She struggled not to give in to it, not to move even her hands, flat against his hairless upper body.

Choking a little, she tried to stop herself. "I'm going to marry Alexander."

"Who's Alexander?" he said dismissively. His knee was pressed between her thighs.

"You should know! Marfa's brother—your friend!" said Sophie through her teeth. It was all she could do not to drag him down against her in a betrayal of her words.

"Oh—Sasha."

Hard, slim fingers began to caress her insistently, stroking down the soft skin of her stomach.

She was close to tears.

"Please don't!" she said. "I know about it. I know about all of it. You can't—you mustn't! Not with me."

"All of it?" he said. His hand continued in its lazy, persuasive movement, but more slowly now.

She remembered how he had tried to kill Alexander by kicking him to death with his boots, how he had destroyed Marfa. It was not going to happen again, not with her.

"No!" she said violently, removing the hand. It curled possessively around her fingers, then lay still.

"What do you mean," he asked, "you know about all of it?" The hand was suddenly withdrawn.

Sophie sat up slowly, wanting to say something that would irreparably destroy the attraction she felt for him, something in revenge for what he had done to the other three. She knew that she hated him, but this was the source of the attraction. It always had been, she realized.

"You don't know anything about me," he said, lying back on the grass. A moment later, Sophie heard a match striking. The scent of marijuana rose to her nostrils, and taken up in her thoughts as she was, she knew that this was not Benedict.

Sophie found her shirt and put it on, feeling very cold suddenly. She did not bother to button it, looking for her jeans. Tim, a little distance away, lay smoking.

"I thought you were Benedict." Terror had been replaced by embarrassment.

"Benedict," said Tim meditatively. "He was some kind of monk, wasn't he?"

"Yes, a monk," said Sophie. "A saint, too, I believe."

"I've heard the name." There was amusement in his tone, faintly defensive. But he really didn't know whom she meant, she realized.

"I'm sorry, Tim," she said. "I should have told you before that I—that Alexander—" She began pulling on her jeans virtuously.

"I guess maybe Marfa is the one who should've told me that."

"Marfa!" Sophie reflected. Marfa had gone with Sven.

Tim sat up beside her and passed the joint.

"Did you and Marfa—er—plan this?" Sophie took a drag, looking at him nervously. Now that he was not Benedict, his attitude was even more of a mystery.

"Not me. She did. Get some beer. Bring Sven. Yeah," he replied moodily.

"Oh." Sophie was aghast.

"Not that she's much on planning things. They just happen to her. Sometimes I think she hates men."

"She doesn't hate you, Tim." You just remind her of somebody, Sophie thought uncomfortably.

"Not me especially. I wish she hated me a little more, as a matter of fact. She just doesn't give a damn one way or the other."

Sophie gazed at him unhappily. He had a beautiful

body, smooth, brown, perfect, unselfconscious in its nakedness. What he didn't have, she now knew with certainty, was that cruel force she had desired in him when she thought he was Benedict, the force that Marfa was committed to forever. Sophie was ashamed.

"She wants a man to kill her," he said. "But I don't get off on that."

Sophie shuddered and he roused himself from his abstraction.

"This isn't really your scene, is it, Sophie?"

"No. No, it isn't." Sophie shivered again, and he put a kindly arm around her. "I just came over to talk to Marfa. I had a quarrel with Alexander."

"You have two black eyes," he said. "Maybe you didn't notice." He wasted the rest of the joint in the grass, and Sophie saw that he was slightly—absurdly—concerned.

"I fell off my horse."

"They look great," said Tim, putting his other arm around her.

"That's what it was all about," she said. "He can ride my horse better than I can."

"I can't ride too good myself," said Tim, hugging her. "I know how you feel."

"You really can't ride? Even though you're an—" Sophie bit her tongue suddenly.

"I grew up in Calgary," he replied. "What the Indians ride there is cabs, mostly."

Sophie burst out laughing. She liked him for this joke. He was really very nice. She started to button her shirt as Tim, less amused, continued.

"I drove a cab while I was going to college. That's how I know."

"You did?" Sophie was astonished. He mistook the cause of this.

"Yeah. I drove one while I was going to college and I drove one after I was finished. That's about what you can do with an education these days."

"You have a B.A.?"

"Fine arts," he said briefly. "My father's a lawyer."

Sophie paused, drawing on her boots. There weren't any Indian lawyers—none that she had ever heard of. Not in Alberta.

"He's been doing the job for this Reserve here to stop the Steamboat Irrigation Project. You probably heard of him?"

"Tim Barret!" Sophie named the most hated man in the county.

"That's him," Tim agreed. "He wants me to do something—like, you know—for my people. We don't agree about my life-style," he concluded abruptly.

"I like your paintings, Tim," said Sophie, putting on her other boot. "In fact, I think I want to buy one."

"Oh yeah? Which?"

Sophie deliberated. She had forgotten which. Was it the one hanging behind the spider plant, or . . . ?

He seemed not to mind.

Sophie began to detach herself from his embrace, fully dressed.

"Hey, are you really going to marry Sasha?"

"Yes!" she said breathlessly. "Yes, I am!"

At the mere mention of his name, she wanted to see Alexander immediately.

"And take on that crazy family?" Tim seemed reluctant to let go of her.

"I'm in love with him."

"So I guess you wouldn't—" He kissed her.

"No. No, I—I'm sorry, Tim. But I don't think I—" She recalled the way he had been looking at her when she sang "Old Macdonald's Farm." Some of this was her fault, after all.

"That's cool," he said, kissing her again. "Sasha's okay. He's quite a bit different from Marfa."

"He is! He's very different!" She felt that little rush of joy again.

"Well . . ." Tim yawned as Sophie stood up. "You've got to go teach kindergarten in a couple of hours, haven't you?"

"Oh my God!" Sophie had completely forgotten about kindergarten. It was Monday morning. The sun had dawned.

"It'll be okay. Want to get some sleep?"

"I have to!"

"I've got a place you can camp in," said Tim. "Come on. I'll show you."

He led her up the dark path, holding back the willow branches kindly, and then down the pasture to the darkened house and barn.

"My studio's up there." He pointed out a second-story window on the end of the barn.

"Where are you going to sleep?" Sophie thought again of Marfa and Sven together as Tim went ahead of her up the ladder.

"I'm taking off," said Tim, turning on the light. The room was very orderly, stacked canvases against a wall, a made-up camp bed in one corner.

"Oh." There was nothing to say to that.

"Sure you want to sleep alone?" He was looking at her calmly, still naked, but no longer aroused.

Sophie nodded, not even slightly embarrassed. She found an alarm clock beside the cot and began to wind it.

Tim was stuffing some things into a rucksack. He had pulled on a pair of jeans.

"Are you going to come back?" Sophie asked. She felt that she should be worried about him.

"Maybe," said Tim, taking a last look around and shouldering the rucksack without bothering to don the shirt in his hand.

"I hope you will."

He smiled. "Maybe I'll come to the wedding."

"Yes! Please do!"

"I guess I'll kiss the bride now," he said. "Just in case I don't get back in time."

He put a hand on her shoulder and gave her a brief kiss on the lips.

"See you," he said. Then he ran lightly down the ladder.

Four hours later, Sophie was on the road to Buffalo Jump Consolidated Elementary School.

Hollowly she sang, trying to keep her spirits up:

"The farmer takes a wife!
The farmer takes a wife!
Heigh-ho the dairy-oh!
The farmer takes a wife!"

15

The Lovemaking of Horses

Alexander was sitting on the corral gate, and he turned around as Sophie approached. He had been watching the horses. It occurred to her that he was angry, but his face was expressionless.

"Hi," said Sophie.

"Where have you been?" asked Alexander, looking away.

"At school. Oh, you mean last night? I went to visit your sister."

"You didn't come home."

Sophie got up on the gate too.

"Are they getting along?" she asked, gesturing at the horses.

"Not very well, no." He looked at his hands, scrunching them to show the knuckles. "Sophia, if you don't want to go through with this, why not say so? You didn't have to make a scene about something else."

"You're right," said Sophie guardedly. "Sorry I made a scene."

"What shall I do with the mare? Do you want me to take her tonight?"

"Well, as you say, that's beside the point."

"Sure, but I could probably still get the money back. I bought her off this guy I met at the Co-op the other day."

"Rosi is a stallion," Sophie remarked idly.

"Sophia, I'm not goin' to— Let's keep it on the level," he said coldly. "You can back out now if that's what you want."

"I was just going to say that he'll probably get used to her."

Alexander stopped making his hands into fists. "So you think that was what was wrong with him before?" asked Sophie. "He needed a mate?"

"I wanted to give you a present," Alexander said stiffly.

"She's very pretty." Sophie noticed that this was true. The mare was standing beside Rosi in a docile way, and he was ungraciously letting her stay there.

"So you want her?" he asked after a moment.

"Well . . . yes. Thank you," she managed to say.

"All right. You're welcome. But that's not all, Sophia."

"What else, then?" Sophie asked, her heart sinking. Was he going to back out now that he had seen how petty she was?

"I could see why you'd be havin' second thoughts," said Alexander. "Anybody would. I should never have taken you near Poppa's birthday."

"But it wasn't—" said Sophie, astonished.

"Now you've seen what they're like, I guess maybe you think I'm like that, too. Or maybe you just realized you'd have to have them around sometimes."

"No! Alexander! I didn't think that at all!"

"Well, what was it, then? Why did you stay out all night?"

"I just . . . I had a talk with Marfa. Then we had a midnight swim. I forgot about the time."

"What else happened?"

"Nothing. What do you think?" Sophie was amazed by his perspicacity.

"You know what I think," he said. "Sure, it's natural, it's a reaction, maybe it's even a test. So don't tell me all that."

"But, Alexander—" Sophie began to laugh.

"It isn't funny," he said grimly. "I know what it's like over there. I've been there too. How many guys did Marfa have lined up for you? That's a lousy way to start something as serious as this, Sophia. Like I say, you just have to tell me to forget it, that's all you have to do."

"Good heavens! Is it always like that over there? Well, anyway, you're right. I could have. I had an offer. But I refused."

"Any special reason?" he asked, frowning.

"Well," said Sophie, considering, "I thought it would be a lousy way to start something as serious as this."

Alexander drew in a deep breath and let it out slowly.

"In a way it was a good thing I went there," said Sophie ruefully. "I mean, I wasn't expecting to—er . . . But anyway, I found out that I didn't want to, either. Your sister's life-style doesn't exactly appeal to me."

They sat in silence on the fence for a while, watching the horses in the gathering dusk. Rosi did not seem to be getting any friendlier toward the mare. But Sophie felt that she was beginning to understand Alexander a little better at last.

"Have you ever seen horses makin' love?" asked Alexander.

"We had Rosi at stud."

"I don't mean mating," he said, turning his head to look at her. "I mean makin' love."

"Well . . . no," said Sophie. "I suppose that isn't quite so clinical? At stud, it's—it isn't very nice for them."

"It's real beautiful," he said. "You'll see. When they get used to each other."

"Alexander!" Mrs. Ware called from the doorway.

"We better go in," said Alexander, jumping down.

Sophie followed him more slowly, noticing how he walked: a steady, powerful gait, without the swagger of his father and brothers. There was a hint of stiffness in it, too. He was tired. He had been working all day.

He put his hands in the pockets of his jeans as he went up to Mrs. Ware. She was inviting him in for coffee.

"Then I'll drive you home," she said, casting a coldly reproving glance at Sophie.

"I'll take him home, Mother," said Sophie promptly.

Alexander sat down at the brightly lit kitchen table and stretched his arms out over the top. They were bare where the sleeves of his shirt were rolled above the elbow. The veins stood out on the backs of his wrists, swelling the smooth brown skin and the dark hairs. On the inside of his right arm there was a tiny cicatrice over the artery, the long-healed scar of the cut of Benedict's pocketknife.

Sophie sat down beside him, looking at it thoughtfully. Mrs. Ware swung around to the stove, pressing her lips together in a thin line.

"I better not have coffee, Mrs. Ware," said Alexander. "Momma always gives me tea before I go to bed. I wouldn't get to sleep with too much of that stuff."

"Would you like some ginger ale?" asked Sophie, her sense of the ridiculous secretly tickled.

"Okay."

She got the ginger ale out of the refrigerator and poured a juice glass full of it. Alexander was lighting a cigarette. Mrs. Ware fetched the ashtray. Was it always going to be this way, the tired man with the women waiting on him? Mother took it for granted.

"Are you keeping that horse?" said Mrs. Ware sharply

to Sophie. "Because if so, you'd better start looking after it yourself. Alexander doesn't have the time."

"Yes, Mother."

"It was thoughtful of him to buy you a horse you can ride," said Mrs. Ware. She had a far less devious theory concerning Sophie's recent behavior than Alexander did. On the other hand, she was more fully aware how petty Sophie could be. "Did you say thank you?" she demanded.

Sophie stirred instant coffee into a cup of hot water. When she looked up, she saw that Alexander was giving her a slow, speculative smile.

"Thank you, Alexander," said Sophie deliberately.

Mrs. Ware sighed.

"I'm goin' to work on the big fence along the road tomorrow," Alexander said. "Some of them posts are hangin' on the wire."

"I know." Mrs. Ware nodded. "Harry put in that fence, oh, just after the war, I guess."

"Crops are comin' along," he said. "But the drought's goin' to kill 'em."

"The Dust Bowl is coming again." Mrs. Ware shivered. "I don't want to be here to see it."

"You'll be in Vancouver, Mother."

"Will I?" Mrs. Ware gave Sophie another one of her withering looks.

"Yes," said Sophie firmly.

"What are you going to do with this house?" said Mrs. Ware, suddenly relaxing. "You'd better start thinking about how you're going to change it around. I'm the one who's going away on the honeymoon, it seems."

"We don't need to—" Sophie began.

"I've been thinkin' about that," said Alexander. "Maybe if I get the time later on, I could fix up that basement."

"What for?" demanded Sophie.

"Your mother's got to have a place to stay when she comes back here," he replied.

"A room in the—" Sophie was outraged.

"Of course," said Mother placidly. "There isn't anywhere else, after all."

"I was thinkin' of maybe puttin' in two rooms and a bath," said Alexander.

"There's a perfectly good bedroom upstairs," said Sophie, struggling with strange ideas. "I mean, you could even keep the one you—"

"Don't be silly, dear. You'll need my room. Probably you'll have to add on later. Harry always intended to, but when we stopped with you, it didn't seem to be necessary."

The even stranger idea of her parents contemplating having more children than she herself stopped Sophie's mouth entirely.

"It's a good high foundation," said Alexander, blowing smoke through his nose. "We could cut a couple of big windows."

"Perhaps I won't be here very much at all," said Mrs. Ware wistfully.

"Mother!" exclaimed Sophie, panic-stricken.

"Just so you can come back whenever you want," said Alexander. "Stay here all the time if it suits you," he went on.

"I'd like to see you settled, first," said Mrs. Ware. "You won't need me for that."

Sophie looked from one to the other. Again it seemed as though they shared some secret set of expectations that she was not a party to. *Honeymoon, settle down*—soon they might use the word *homemaker*.

"How much money did you spend on that horse, Alexander?" Mrs. Ware asked abruptly.

He smiled.

"We'll have to talk about that, too," she said. "You spent everything you had, didn't you?"

"Everything I had on me," he admitted. "I didn't like that guy much."

Sophie was very touched by the energy with which he said this. Obviously she had everything all wrong.

Alexander had wanted to give her another horse, that was all.

". . . lawyer, and make a settlement," Mrs. Ware was saying. "Sophie can barely handle her own money, let alone—"

"What?"

"Well, you can't go on paying Alexander *wages,* dear," Mrs. Ware pointed out.

"My God, I'd completely forgotten about that!" Sophie laughed. Alexander looked down at the empty glass in front of him.

"It isn't funny, Sophie. We'll have to make a fair arrangement. You're so scatterbrained, I—"

"You and Dad had a joint account, didn't you?" This conversation was becoming completely unreal to Sophie.

Alexander took her hand unexpectedly under the table.

"Better let me talk this over with Sophia, Mrs. Ware. She didn't have time to think about it yet."

"Yes, but there are things you'll have to buy right away," said Mrs. Ware. "At least Sophie should give you—"

"I don't want her to give me anything," he said mildly. "Poppa'll come through with something for a suit, I guess. I don't have one that fits."

Sophie squeezed his hand.

"Yes, but—"

"It's *okay,* Mother!"

His hand returned the pressure faintly.

"I don't know—you two!" Mrs. Ware inspected them irritably, sitting side by side. "You're not a bit practical, Sophie, and Alexander is hardly any better when it comes to this! You've only got a few weeks, and you're refusing to think about anything important! Marriage isn't all love and kisses, Sophie. You don't even have an engagement ring."

"Well, I've got a horse, anyway!" said Sophie, suddenly snorting with laughter. Alexander banged the back of her hand gently against his knee.

"All right, then. Here." Mrs. Ware took off her big diamond slowly, her eyes bright.

"Mother! What are you doing? Dad gave you that!"

"I'm giving it to Alexander, Sophie," said Mrs. Ware formally. "This is not up to you."

Alexander stretched out his hand and she put the ring in his palm, closing his fingers over it. Mrs. Ware sat for a moment, smiling and in tears. "Now," she said, "if you're going to drive him home, I'll go to bed."

"What do you expect him to do with that?" cried Sophie. "Pawn it?" She was nearly in tears herself.

Alexander lifted her left hand onto the table and separated her palm from his own. Mrs. Ware stood watching as he slid the ring onto Sophie's finger carefully, his head bent over their hands.

"Well!" said Mrs. Ware, drawing in her breath on a little high laugh.

"Thank you, Mrs. Ware," said Alexander, still looking at the ring.

"My name is Vera," said Mrs. Ware briskly. "Take him home now, Sophie. The poor man is exhausted—by your shenanigans, as well as everything else he has to do!" She went out of the room quickly.

Sophie rested her forehead on her other hand, now gazing at the ring too, in sadness and bewilderment. Her mother seemed to be giving up everything—the farm, her house, now even this ring. The property side of the exchange, such a joke to Sophie, was as important to her mother as it was to Alexander. Sophie swallowed a sob of her own.

"Better take me home like she says, Sophia," Alexander suggested gently. "I'm goin' to start on that fence first thing."

Tuesday was another scorching day. It was not yet July, but the dust was already blowing across the prairies, a rusty brown haze hanging over the land.

"Alexander is still working on that fence," said Mrs. Ware, looking with a pretense of carelessness at the ring on Sophie's hand.

The ring was also on Sophie's mind. What if she lost it? Or worse, what if somebody noticed she was wearing it? She had taken it off several times, then quickly and nervously put it back on.

"You'd better take him some lemonade," said Mrs. Ware. "It's terrible weather for putting in a fence. Are you listening to me, Sophie?"

"Yes, Mother."

"Sometimes I wonder whether you have any idea what it is to marry a farmer," said Mrs. Ware grimly. "You don't seem to be thinking about it."

"Where's the lemonade, then?"

"You'll have to make it. There are some lemons in the cooler. Not too much sugar."

"Do you do this often?"

"I did it for forty years," said Mrs. Ware.

"You did?" Sophie was startled.

"Your father liked water with vinegar in it. We couldn't always afford lemons in those days."

Sophie squeezed the lemons into a thermos, reflecting on this. Her father had been the only heroic male figure in her experience, despite the fact that he was short and balding. He had been slow-spoken, without any of Alexander's occasional flamboyance—just a steady, affectionate, humorous personality. He and her mother had been happily married for more than ten years before Sophie was born. She had always attributed their happiness to these qualities in him. But perhaps these things had to be developed in common with someone else. So far, what had characterized her relationship with Alexander was a kind of one-sided patience and restraint on his part, at which, she realized, she had been laughing in a cruel way from time to time.

She went out with the thermos clinking in her hand and walked across the pasture, noting the horses standing side by side, motionless, as usual. Rosi whickered at her, but did not move to follow as he usually would have. The mare cropped a mouthful of grass just under his front feet.

She spotted Alexander from a distance. He had his shirt off and was driving a post with gigantic lunging movements, the sledgehammer coming down in his clasped hands from over his head.

"That looks awfully hard," said Sophie, coming up behind him. He turned around, leaning the hammer up against the post neatly. She put the cool thermos in his hand.

"You've done a lot," she went on, surveying the line of posts with a certain awe. Her father had originally put this fence in, probably with the same sledgehammer.

Alexander wiped the sweat off his forehead with his palm, leaving a dark smear behind.

"Lemonade?" he asked with a smile. Like Mrs. Ware, he glanced at her ring.

"That's what Mother usually gives you, isn't it?" she said, looking at him curiously.

"Let's go into the shade," he suggested. "I'm about done with this for today."

"I bet you are! How long have you been at it?" She followed him down along the ditch to the windbreak.

"Only about an hour this afternoon. I worked on it this morning before it got real hot," he replied.

"You shouldn't do it in the afternoon at all," she suggested.

Alexander lay down on his arm in the shade and drank out of the thermos, sighing with the relief of the cool liquid pouring down his dusty throat.

"That's good," he said simply.

Sophie sat down, smoothing her school dress over her

knees. She turned her head and watched Alexander again, drinking in cautious, thirsty sips. The lemonade was too cold, she realized. The ice had been a mistake.

After a moment he lay down all the way, putting one hand contentedly under his head. He was magnificent, not like Sophie's father at all: like some huge, beautiful wild animal. His lips shone red and wet in the midst of his grimy face.

"The only thing you haven't got on this place is a real good place to swim," he said. "Even Poppa used to jump in the river when he finished doin' something like that."

"Did you always want to be a farmer, Alexander?" she asked. "My father used to say you had to be born to it."

"There's something to that," he replied. He closed his eyes. "I never thought about it till I came back here. It made me mad to see what Rudi was doin' with them fields of yours." He opened his eyes again.

"Alexander," she said hurriedly. "I don't—you know, I really like your family. I've got some things against Rudi, all right, but your mother and father are—"

"Yeah. Momma and Poppa," he said. "That's what they are."

"And Marfa, too. I like Marfa."

"Marfa's okay," said Alexander with faint irritation. "She's got to stop messin' around, though. That guy likes her and he likes her kids, but she doesn't give him much of a chance."

"I noticed that," said Sophie guardedly.

"I guess you didn't know what you were gettin' into, goin' over there," said Alexander, frowning. He rolled over and reached for a cigarette out of the pocket of his shirt, which was lying in a heap on the ground.

"Well, not really," admitted Sophie, somewhat incensed by his assumptions about her. After all, she had once had a sex life, before she met him.

"I thought Marfa was goin' to pull off some stunt like

that," he went on. "That guy who was her husband has a lot to answer for in hell, if you ask me."

"I really am old enough to look after myself," snapped Sophie. She regretted this immediately and lay down on her arm, looking into his face.

"Well, anyway, it would have been different if you had been there," she said, and smiled at him tentatively.

"You can bet it would have!" said Alexander. He looked back at her, his expression beginning to relax.

A cicada shrilled in the poplar tree above their heads. All around them the hot wind blew ceaselessly, carrying the black topsoil from Saskatchewan across Alberta; but they were quite sheltered in the ditch below the windbreak.

"Jesus, I wish I could get clean," said Alexander.

"You can come home and have a shower," said Sophie, preparing to sit up energetically.

"No! Wait. Let's not go yet," he said, rolling over on his side to face her and stretching out his hand in a hovering gesture above her waist. "It's nice here, talkin' to you like this."

"Oh." Sophie lay down somewhat self-consciously. Alexander drew back his hand. The sweat had come out over his forehead again in thick, glistening drops.

"I'm sweatin' like a pig," he said apologetically, wiping his face and adding a few new smears.

Sophie felt that she had clarified the things that were on his mind now, or at least she had clarified them as well as she could. She had an immediate, almost reciprocal desire to tease him. But seeing the look of peaceful contentment on his face, she resisted this; certain resolutions made quite recently served to forbid it. She was coming to see his simplicity in a new light; not as something lacking in him, but as a real, positive quality.

He cleared his throat.

"Have you been thinkin' about what Vera was sayin' last night?" he asked.

"About–?" asked Sophie vaguely. She propped herself up on her elbow and leaned forward slightly. The way they were lying, face to face, it would be very easy to kiss him. She wondered what would happen then.

"About makin' a settlement." He sighed.

Surely kissing did not fall into the category of teasing. She leaned up on the whole length of her arm and bent over him, putting her hand on his hot bare shoulder.

"You don't have to give me anything, Sophia," he said, raising his face obediently to look up at her with his strange, cloudy eyes.

"But I want to," said Sophie, thinking about this kiss that was coming. "In fact, I want to give you everything!"

His eyes began to darken in a highly satisfactory way. She watched, fascinated, as they became quite black. Sophie made her lips into a playful O and touched them to his. This was still not teasing, because—

Alexander's body came down firm and hard and hot on top of her, so heavy that she could not breathe, his head blotting out the sun. He was kissing her explicitly, sexually, as she had always wanted him to do. Sophie struggled a little, trying to express variation, trying to laugh. She had wanted this so much, and yet now it seemed it was not quite what she wanted.

The kiss became even harder and more demanding, then, at last, softer, as she ceased trying to do anything but respond.

Alexander raised his head momentarily and Sophie gave a small cry of desire. He rolled a little to one side, reaching up under her skirt, his hand hot on her belly as he found the waistband of her pants. At the same time he began to kiss his way down her neck to the bodice of her dress. She was already soaked with sweat, his and hers.

Sophie wrenched one of her arms out from under her back, where it had somehow become mislaid when he fell upon her, and reached up to help him with her buttons.

She was now responding totally; however quickly he wanted it, she wanted it just as quickly.

He seemed to sense some of this, for his gestures became slower and more restrained. At last he raised his head.

Sophie took his face between her hands, looking into his passionate eyes, at his reddened mouth.

"I love you, Alexander."

He withdrew his searching hand from under her skirt and pulled together the soaking, crumpled cloth across her bosom. Then he looked down at her steadily, thoughtfully, with eyes that were no longer so dark.

Sophie drew his head down gently, feeling a little nervous that she had said this. They kissed each other without any of the burning haste of a few moments past.

Alexander rolled away. Desperately, Sophie caught his arm and held it across her breasts, curling herself into his chest. He clasped her cooperatively and she cuddled against him. Her cheek felt hot against the wet hair of his body. She was now regretting bitterly that she had said anything.

"If only it weren't for this thing about money," he said abstractedly.

"What money?" Sophie asked. She rested her mouth against his nipple, fighting a losing battle with herself to hold still.

"I didn't know there was so much money until your mother told me the other day," he said. "And now there's *this,* too."

"What do you mean, *this*?" Sophie demanded, offended.

"You sayin' you love me. It kind of complicates things."

"I'm sure it does," snapped Sophie, prying away his arms. He did not seem entirely willing to let go of her, all the same, she noticed.

"Yeah. How can you decide anything when it's like that?"

"Oh, I'm sure we'll manage," said Sophie, preparing to stand up. "I suppose love is just one of the things that has to be negotiated in a deal like this."

"I guess so," said Alexander. Sophie ungraciously allowed him to help her to her feet. "I guess maybe you're right," he repeated, and she noticed with fury that his eyes were once again a distant, cloudy gray.

16

The Negotiating Table

Alexander did the chores after supper while Sophie fed and watered the horses. There was a high storm gathering distantly. The wind rode over the land, driving the dust before it, and tiny, menacing clouds could be seen in the east.

Sophie perched on the corral fence. The horses were restive. Rocinante persistently nudged Ring until both were huddled near Sophie by the gate. He wanted to go in.

"Is it going to rain?" asked Sophie as Alexander approached.

"I hope so. It's gettin' critical," he said.

"Rosi wants to go in."

"He wants to see what she looks like in the stall," said Alexander.

"So do I. I'm tired of watching them stand around like statues."

"You haven't tried ridin' her yet, have you?" Alexander asked as he went to get the bridles. "She's tricksier than he is."

"You're so tactful, Alexander," said Sophie bitterly.

"Want to take your mother over to my place tonight?" They began to lead the horses into the barn.

"I suppose you've already asked her."

"Yeah, I did. She said to ask you."

"Are they expecting her?"

"You don't need to worry about that. Momma's been expectin' her for weeks."

Sophie let Ring into the stall after Rocinante. He immediately pushed her against the wall and bit her.

"Alexander! He's hurting her!"

"Well, he thinks it's his place," said Alexander.

"But you said he wanted her to come in."

"Yeah, but he didn't know if he'd really like it."

"Can't you make him stop?"

"He'll stop as soon as we leave," said Alexander, propelling her out of the barn ahead of him.

"How do you know?"

"I just know." Alexander laughed.

Mrs. Ware sat expectantly between them in the farm truck, jouncing along the section road that led to the uplands. Sophie had not seen her wearing a hat for years. It was one of the hats Dad had liked, a blue straw with a snap brim. Sophie could still see them, circa 1959, on their way to church in the morning, her mother in a long soft wool coat and this hat tipped over one eye, her 'fifties permed hair and her bright red lipstick. Dad wore a porkpie tweed hat and a leather jacket with chestnut buttons.

"Does your mother still make her own preserves?" Mother was questioning Alexander excitedly.

"Yeah," said Alexander. "Poppa does a lot of that, too. He used to can fish."

"Can fish!" exclaimed Sophie and Mrs. Ware together.

"Whitefish," he said. "It's probably illegal. He had a net in the river."

Sophie felt that Alexander was teasing her mother.

"He didn't," she said flatly.

"Sure he did. Momma made him stop."

"You were poor," said Mrs. Ware. "But once upon a time we were all poor," she added cheerfully. "Your mother belonged to the Women's Institute after the war. I think I met her."

"Well, I guess Momma'll remember that."

"She was a beautiful girl," said Mother. "That was before you were born, Alexander."

"You must have been good-lookin' yourself, Vera," Alexander remarked.

"How can you tell?" asked Mrs. Ware flirtatiously.

"By your daughter."

"You're a sweet boy, Alexander," said Mother. Sophie was infuriated.

They drove up the long, rutted driveway. Mother was looking out the front with interest. The various evidences of Poppa's enthusiasms caught her eye one by one: the junkyard on the front lawn, the rabbit pens, the equipment for making molded plastic canoes, the steam engine, and finally, racing toward them across the pasture, the flock of geese.

"Here we are," warned Alexander.

Poppa was already standing on the steps of the back porch.

Alexander ran to fend off the geese. Meanwhile, Poppa moved forward and saluted Mrs. Ware by kissing her hand. Momma appeared in the doorway, watching this with disapproval. Mother was blushing.

Sophie stood apart, shuddering with embarrassment as Mrs. Ware, like Queen Elizabeth visiting a remote tribal kingdom, moved on up the steps to greet Momma. Poppa got to Sophie simultaneously with Alexander, and they stood over her like a couple of farmyard roosters as Poppa attempted to draw her hand to his lips.

To Sophie's horror, Mother had already broached with Momma the subject of how they were all poor once.

"Don't mind Mother," Sophie muttered, disengaging her hand from Mr. Bresnyachuk's with a clever twist. "She's just—"

"She is wise woman," said Poppa, now dividing his attention judiciously between Mother at the top of the steps and Sophie at the bottom. "This is very smart woman, you understand, Sasha?"

"I'm kind of fond of her myself," said Alexander, glancing upward. He had Sophie firmly by the arm, but she was used to this now. It was merely competition.

"We go in!" said Poppa, with a grandiose shepherding gesture of his whole body. "We have one, two, maybe three vodkas, eh, Sophia? Then talk! Is too soon to talk now!"

Momma had already swept Mother away when they attained the kitchen, presumably to see the supplies in the pantry. Sophie allowed herself to be pressed into an immediate drink. She and Poppa and a reluctant Alexander were having another when the mothers returned.

"You will have a drink with us?" demanded Poppa.

"Of course," said Mother sweetly.

"Mrs. Ware would like some sherry," said Momma quickly. She really could speak ordinary English when she chose to. It added to her aura of terror. Sophie tried to imagine what they had been saying to each other in the pantry.

"It's sweet wine, Poppa," said Alexander.

Momma produced a full unopened bottle for Poppa to see.

"Is okay," he said, sniffing dubiously. "So, now we drink something new!"

He poured out half a tumbler for Mrs. Ware, then a tiny bit for himself and Momma. He put vodka in both Alexander and Sophie's glasses, winking covertly at Sophie.

Mother sipped, sitting down graciously on the divan Alexander had slept on the night of the party.

"Good!" shouted Poppa hugely. "Now—where is ham, pickles, fat bacon, three kinds sausage? Veronika will get!"

"So—my little Sasha is marrying your girl," said Momma, sitting beside Mother and also sipping. "Is very good boy, you know?" She was letting up a little on the gentility of her language.

"Sasha," murmured Mother, evidently fascinated by the nickname.

Feeling the kick of the raw vodka in her empty stomach, Sophie got up.

"I could get the food," she offered.

Momma nodded. Sophie went into the pantry and found rye bread, pickles, ham, and sausage, all generously laid out. The fish she left behind. She wanted to avoid any further confrontation with her mother over the illegal fish question.

When she returned to the kitchen, plates in hand, Poppa and Alexander were evidently having a drinking contest, standing up, glasses raised, glittering eyes fixed upon each other. The bottle of vodka was nearly half gone already. Sophie confiscated it and put it on the sink drain.

"That's enough," she told Alexander.

Momma suspended chatting with Mrs. Ware to give her a sharp glance of approbation. Poppa had fallen upon the ham and sausage with enthusiasm.

"I grew up in this country," said Momma. "I am going to high school. Then—after the war—along comes this one." She made a dismissive gesture in Poppa's direction. "So I married immigrant," she said scornfully.

"Well, we're all immigrants," said Mrs. Ware merrily.

Sophie squirmed. "My husband's family came from Scotland, while my own—" In a moment she was going to tell them how she was related to the Duke of Argyle.

"My girl is finishing high school, too," said Mrs. Bresnyachuk. "With boys is more difficult. My Sasha—"

"Oh, do you really think so?" interjected Mrs. Ware interestedly. "Sophie was quite—"

"Sasha is electrical mechanic. Also plumber, furnace man, refrigerator fixer, and mudman."

"Mudman?" asked Sophie in an undertone, her eyes on Alexander.

"That was what I did on the rigs," he said. "I'll tell you about it sometime."

"This boy is very smart," said Poppa insincerely, exhibiting Alexander to Mrs. Ware with a clasping arm around his shoulders.

"He's a very good farmer," agreed Mrs. Ware. She held out her empty glass unexpectedly to Poppa. Alexander, seeking a means of escape, ducked away as Poppa went for the sherry bottle.

"He must have learned it all from you, Mr. Bresnyachuk," Mother went on.

"Yes! All from me!" said Poppa enthusiastically.

Sophie was trying to figure out which of them was playing the falser part in this exchange when the conversation took a new turn.

"Sasha will be a good father, too," said Momma in an intimate tone. "Is loving children."

"Well, of course, Sophie was an only—" began Mrs. Ware chattily.

"Do you love children, Alexander?" interrupted Sophie in a loud, clear voice. The level of embarrassment seemed to warrant a frontal attack.

"Yes, I do, Sophia," he replied over the head of Poppa, who had turned around to regard her adoringly.

"How many do you think we'll have?" asked Sophie in the same stentorian tones.

"At least six!" answered Alexander, shooting an amused glance at the two mothers on the divan, who were both listening openmouthed.

Sophie felt another one of those fatal blushes striking her. It seemed to move upward from the knees. She cast her eyes at the kitchen clock in desperation, but it was only half a minute to nine.

"Is lovely girl," said Mrs. Bresnyachuk to Mother. They both admired Sophie's blush for a long moment.

"Now we talk," said Poppa, sitting down in a businesslike way at the table. "Eat," he advised Mother, passing the bread.

"Watch this," said Alexander, reaching Sophie through a sea of salt water. He dragged her into a chair at the table, taking the one beside her and murmuring, "Don't get mad, Sophia."

"Yes, we must talk," said Mother, straightening her hat. "I've been trying to convince Alexander—"

"Is no good talkin' to Sasha," said Poppa pityingly. "Old people talk—is only way."

Momma stood up, ignoring Poppa, and motioned Mrs. Ware to the table. "Better to have talk now," she said quietly.

"I've told them that," agreed Mrs. Ware. "But Alexander says—and Sophie won't even discuss it!"

"Is good," said Momma. She gave Sophie a stern smile.

"Very simple!" said Poppa. "Split fifty-fifty!" He tilted his hand about forty-five degrees off the horizontal either way, then looked around to include everyone in a triumphant, flashing smile.

"I think that Sophie should make a settlement," said Mrs. Ware firmly. "But fifty-fifty is too much."

"Mother!" shouted Sophie.

"Just watch, Sophia," murmured Alexander.

"It's much more difficult than you think," said Mrs. Ware, friendly, hesitant, preparing to plunge into details.

"Yes. Difficult," agreed Poppa. "Hard. You see, Sasha?"

"Is a question of control, naturally," said Momma competently, still ignoring Poppa.

"Well, it won't be easy to *divide* everything," said Mrs. Ware. "We can't dissolve the trust fund, for one thing. And then there's the value of the land itself, royalty money, and the profit from harvest if there is any." She looked about engagingly.

"Trust fund is how much?" asked Mrs. Bresnyachuk.

"It's a lot of money, Momma," said Alexander, now himself unable to resist interposing.

"Is not your matter, Sasha," said Momma severely. "Let old people talk."

"Well, that money is Sophie's," said Mrs. Ware. "And, of course, I derive an income. Now, what I was thinking of suggesting was—"

"I'm not asking you to give me anything," said Alexander, looking at Mrs. Ware. "You know that."

"I was going to suggest," Mrs. Ware went on, paying no more attention to interruption now than Momma was doing, "that we fix a lump sum on Alexander out of the trust so that he can get started properly."

"Good," said Momma. "So now is a question of land."

"Not the land."

"Land. Then you tell how much is settlement."

"I'm afraid that's impossible," said Mrs. Ware calmly.

"Mother! That's not—"

Alexander seized Sophie's hand, pulling it under the table. She wondered how he could put up with this.

"Your girl doesn't want land," said Momma, concentrated. "She was tryin' to sell."

"He can have a settlement. We'll decide how much," said Mrs. Ware. "That's all."

"This is ridiculous, Mother!" cried Sophie, tearing herself away from Alexander's restraint. "Who do you think you are? A matchmaker? This isn't *Fiddler on the Roof*! Alexander and I can settle this ourselves!"

A battery of eyes was fixed on Sophie at once.

"Settle how?" inquired Momma.

"We'll share," said Sophie foolishly. The naïveté of the word struck her immediately. She had no idea what she meant by it. Alexander took her hand again.

"This is nothing," said Momma dismissively.

"Is good idea!" cried Poppa simultaneously. "Another drink? What do you say, Momma?"

"Mrs. Ware, you will have more sweet wine? I have some too," said Momma magnanimously.

"Very good," she went on a moment later, sipping decorously. "We are now down to land, fifty-fifty, and trust fund settlement. Naturally, I will agree with this offer."

"We could start him out with a quarter, I suppose," said Mother doubtfully. "That quarter over by the slough ought to be good for stock. But there wouldn't be as much in the settlement in that case."

"My son gets a quarter?" said Momma scornfully. "But he works all land. Money he could make as furnace man!"

"But not as a farmer," said Mrs. Ware. Sophie was amazed at how she was holding her liquor.

"This is not a good deal," said Momma. "To four quarters I could agree. My boy won't marry without land."

"I'm marryin' her anyway, Momma," said Alexander suddenly. He stood up, dropping Sophie's hand. "I love the girl. I'd marry her for nothing!"

There was a moment's pause.

To Sophie's horror, Mother began to smile, her lips dimpling firmly at the corners, a look of triumph in her eyes.

Momma was staring at Alexander in disgust.

"I love her," he repeated stubbornly.

"Another drink," said Poppa quickly. "Sasha, he knows nothing. Is all nonsense, he thinks."

"No more for me, thanks," said Mrs. Ware. She settled

back, quite calm again. "So there we are," she said. "A money settlement and one quarter."

"Sasha," said Momma sadly, shaking her head. She looked down at her hands on the table.

"I think you should agree to that, Momma. Mrs. Ware knows what she's talkin' about."

"Vera," corrected Mother.

"Veronika," said Momma, reintroducing herself immediately.

"I marry one time, too," said Poppa, still trying to save the situation. "And I am not interrupting my Momma!"

"This is modern, Poppa," said Momma resignedly. "Besides, I never see no Momma at all when I am marrying you!"

Alexander sat down again.

"Yes, this is the modern way," said Mrs. Ware thoughtfully. "What do *you* think, Sophie?"

"I think it's none of your business!" cried Sophie, pushing away Alexander's hand under the table angrily.

"It certainly is my business, young lady!" said Mother. "Your father worked hard and died young"—her voice broke—"on that land, and you're not going to throw it away. If I didn't think Alexander knew what he was doing, I wouldn't be here in the first place."

"Good," said Momma.

"Now, Momma," said Poppa, "you will tell what we are gonna give."

"How do I know?" cried Momma. "His will! He changes every week!" She waved her fingers impatiently.

"I'm gonna leave Sasha this farm," intoned Poppa. "To Luke and Rudi—half shares in the money."

"What about Marfa?" inquired Alexander ironically.

"To Marfa—nothing!" said Poppa.

"What money?" asked Momma, rolling her eyes.

"We will pay for wedding. Big wedding," said Poppa, gnashing his teeth. "Here."

"The bride's parents usually—" began Mrs. Ware.

"Wedding here," said Momma. "This we will do. Plus wedding ring, plus priest—everything."

"Sophie and I are Church of England," said Mrs. Ware.

"No priest?" said Momma, upset.

"Priest is nothing," said Poppa. "Big wedding. Everyone will come. My brother Alexei from Minnesota, even."

"A little wedding!" exclaimed Alexander. "By a judge. You're not goin' to put Sophia through—" He was standing again.

"Jesus, Momma!" said Poppa, also standing. "What are we gonna do? For Rudi we had a band, even. For Marfa the town council. And now this one wants to get married by a judge? Without a party?" He gestured at Alexander in despair.

"Let's have a drink," muttered Alexander.

Sophie went to get the vodka bottle.

"The wedding reception will be at our house," said Mrs. Ware firmly. "You can have a judge if you want, Alexander."

"Must be priest," said Momma.

"And a party," insisted Poppa. "Party here."

"Just remember, I love her, Momma," said Alexander.

"Okay, okay! You said this already. So you're gonna be married," said Mrs. Bresnyachuk wearily.

Sophie thrust the glass of vodka into Alexander's hand.

"Drink this," she said. "They're going to give the party."

Alexander was taking too many tricks with that card.

"Very well," said Mother, suddenly smiling sweetly at Alexander around Sophie's shoulder.

"All right," said Alexander.

"My Sasha," said Momma proudly.

"Is good?" asked Poppa.

"Is okay," agreed Momma.

"*Now* we drink!" said Poppa, seizing the vodka bottle from Sophie.

"No, now we go home," said Mother resolutely. "Take us home, please, Alexander."

"Sure," said Alexander. He cast a worried glance at Sophie's stony face.

Momma was pressing a jar of dill pickles on Mrs. Ware.

"Is dill and garlic," she said. "Very good for headache."

"Maybe you'll need it for tomorrow, then, Mother," said Sophie unsmilingly.

"Momma, give fish," ordered Poppa.

"No, no," said Mrs. Ware nervously.

"It's okay, Vera. It's Winnipeg goldeye, I think," said Alexander as Momma emerged from the pantry with a waxed-paper parcel.

There was a long silence as they drove home. Sophie stared out the window at the occluded sky, barely able to control tears of rage. She had not been expecting that. He could have warned her. He hadn't even been on her side. He had been on Mother's side.

"Alexander," said Mrs. Ware, "come in and have a cup of tea or something."

They went into the kitchen, and to Sophie's surprise, she got out the sherry bottle.

Alexander lounged uneasily against the kitchen door.

"That was one thing," said Mother. "Now here's another. What are you two going to do?"

Alexander laughed and came to sit down.

"Momma'll be asking me that, too," he said.

"Well, it's just good sense," said Mother.

Sophie turned away and put the kettle on for tea.

"I've been very frank with you, Alexander," continued Mrs. Ware. "You know what's involved, and if you're going to do the work here, I think you should get some of it."

"Maybe," said Alexander. "But Sophia isn't—"

"Oh yes," cried Sophie. "Ten percent of this and a quarter of that! Anyway, what is it to you, Mother?" She put her hands on her hips, just preventing herself from an angry stamp of the foot.

"I'll tell you, then, Sophie, shall I?" said Mrs. Ware sharply. "I married your father and worked here all my life, but that didn't make it mine. We didn't have a marriage agreement."

"But you had a joint account with Dad!" cried Sophie, stricken. "And he left you—"

"I don't know that a woman would settle for that nowadays, Sophie," said Mother with a dry smile. "As it happens, I was very well provided for. But that isn't the point."

The overfilled kettle boiled up on the stove. Sophie rushed to rescue it, her thoughts in turmoil.

"I think I'll take my tea to bed," said Mrs. Ware a few moments later. "I enjoyed meeting your parents, Alexander. Your mother is very proud of you—and so she should be," she added.

She left the room, teacup in hand. Sophie leaned over the sink, running cold water on her scalded wrist.

Behind her, Alexander sighed.

"So what are we goin' to do, Sophia?" he asked.

"I thought you had that all worked out! You and Mother!" Sophie turned around. "This is 'modern,' isn't it?"

"You don't have to give me anything," he said.

"We already heard that! 'I love the girl, Momma,' " mocked Sophie.

"I was tryin' to make it hard for her," he said gravely.

"And it's all part of the *deal*!" she cried. "I hated it!"

"So did I. But when you and I talk about it, we don't get anywhere. We just end up hurtin' each other's feelings."

Alexander was looking exhausted. The slump of his shoulders reminded her of the fenceposts. She suddenly saw the real meaning of his reiterated words, "You don't have to give me anything." It was she who had been hurting his feelings, not the other way around.

"See a lawyer on Monday?" he asked quietly.

"Okay. But I warn you, you're going to have to take a lot more than you bargained for!"

He smiled.

"I'm going to bed now, Alexander. I can't stand any more of this."

Sophie left the kitchen and went upstairs to her room. Mother's door was closed. She snatched up an ugly pair of pajamas and went into the bathroom. When she came out, the kitchen light was still on, but she proceeded determinedly to her bedroom and got into bed, turning out the light.

He could have explained. They could have talked about it, she thought resentfully. Then she remembered herself teasing him that afternoon: "I want to give you everything!" Of course, he didn't want her to give him anything. How could she have been so obtuse?

Her mother had tried to tell her, but she hadn't listened to that, either. So they finally had to let Momma do it in the old way: ancient and modern came together at last, squeezing out the joint bank balance and the family car, the pitiful private savings out of egg money or birthday presents. Mother and Momma both knew all about that, and they weren't going to let it happen to Alexander and Sophia.

Sophie began to cry quietly. Nothing could make up for this stupidity. She couldn't even explain that it was stupidity. Somewhere in his heart, Alexander was going to hold this against her forever. Especially the part where he said he loved her.

The kitchen light was switched off and quiet footsteps crossed the kitchen floor. Sophie lay rigid, listening for the snick of the back door lock, the sound of the truck starting in the yard. Instead she heard the distinctive creak of a stair tread. A moment later her bedroom door was opened stealthily and closed with equal stealth.

Alexander sat down on the edge of the bed. "You never drank your tea," he said.

Sophie sobbed aloud, sitting up with a jerk and a hiccup.

"Hey! You're spillin' it!" he whispered, putting one arm tightly about her back and groping with the other for the bedside table. He seemed to manage very well, for he started to kiss away the tears on her face a moment later.

"I'm a complete fool!" sobbed Sophie. "Alexander, will you ever—?"

Alexander pushed her back on the pillow and lay down full length on top of the blanket beside her, still kissing her comfortingly.

"You burned yourself," he said against her ear. "Does it hurt?"

"Yes! No! I don't care about that. If you'll only—"

Alexander had taken her wrist and was feeling the blister delicately. A moment later he put his lips against it.

"I was so mean!" said Sophie, becoming a little calmer.

"No, you weren't," he said softly. "You weren't mean at all, Sophia."

"Wasn't I?" she asked doubtfully.

"Just a little stubborn," he said, and she could tell that he was laughing to himself.

"Oh, Alexander! And all those other things—getting mad about the horses—" she said remorsefully.

Alexander seemed to be absorbed in an investigation of his own.

"What in hell have you got on?" he whispered, trying, not too successfully, to undo a button.

"Pajamas," she replied. "You do realize that my mother is in the next room?"

"She's probably asleep," murmured Alexander.

"I don't think so!" hissed Sophie.

Alexander groaned and put his head down on her

shoulder. Sophie stroked his rough hair and gently massaged his neck. They were again in one of those absurd teenaged predicaments.

A few moments later she realized that Alexander had gone to sleep, fully clothed on top of the blanket, his hand on her breast, still clutching the button of the pajama top.

17

I, Said the Fly

Sophie woke up very early. Alexander was gone. She raised her head and saw the imprint of a heavy body on the rucked-up blanket. She had not merely dreamed his being there. She rolled over to sleep again, luxuriously sniffing the Alexander smell of the pillow.

She got up as usual at seven-thirty to the sound of Mother preparing breakfast. Sophie peeked out her window into the yard. There was no sign of Alexander himself, but the truck had been moved. So he had gone home, then.

Feeling slightly self-conscious, she lingered on the stairs. Her incredible thickheadedness at the time of last night's bargaining was much on her mind. Not only had she hurt Alexander's feelings, something she was now optimistic he would forgive her for, but she had also insulted her mother, a slightly tougher nut to crack in the forgiveness line.

I must be the only unliberated woman left on the prairies, she reflected ruefully. The only farmer's wife in the history of the world who didn't want a marriage agreement.

Mother was frying bacon. Sophie went to give her an immediate, repentant kiss.

"Good morning," said Mrs. Ware in reserved tones.

"Please don't be angry, Mother," said Sophie, taking in the thin line of her mother's mouth. "I was an idiot about all that yesterday, but now I've seen the error of my ways."

Her mother turned the bacon carefully, saying nothing.

"I mean," said Sophie, fighting an uphill battle against sounding too cheerful, "we're going to do this the way you suggested."

"I know," said Mrs. Ware.

"You do?" said Sophie, surprised.

"Do you think I don't have ears, Sophie? I know that Alexander slept in your room last night." Mrs. Ware cracked an egg onto a plate, inspected it closely, and then decanted it into the frying pan.

Sophie was flummoxed. One could hardly deny this.

"And a good thing he did, too," Mrs. Ware went on severely, breaking another egg. "Someone has to knock some sense into you sometime, Sophie. If it weren't for Alexander, you'd probably go to your grave without knowing the elementary facts of life!"

Unable to think of any really good reply to this last remark, Sophie went out into the sunny dooryard to pat the dog.

Alexander approached from the corral. He had just put out the horses.

"It didn't rain after all," she said, smiling at him.

"No." He drew her farther away from the door, toward a clump of delphiniums just coming into bloom on the corner of the house. "I shouldn't have done that last night," he said quietly.

She perceived he was apologizing for something.

"That's all right," said Sophie happily. "I was pretty tired myself."

"Yeah, but I shouldn't have done that. I didn't want to influence you about that deal. And after what happened—"

Sophie saw that he was apologizing for something else.

"But nothing happened," she said, puzzled.

"Didn't I come into your bedroom?" he asked.

"Yes, and you lay down on the bed. But then you just went to sleep."

"Oh," said Alexander. He looked down at his feet, then at her again. "Nothing else?"

"Not with Mother next door," said Sophie, laughing. "I wouldn't let you, don't you remember?"

"I must have dreamed it," he said, smiling slowly.

"Oh, Alexander!" Sophie put her arms around his neck. "I hope it was good! Are you sure it was me, though? In the dream, I mean?"

"Oh yeah, it was you all right!" He continued to smile, holding her waist. The dog appeared beside them anxiously.

"Too bad I couldn't have really been there!"

"But you were," he said placidly.

"You must have woken up in your clothes," said Sophie. "You didn't take anything off."

"That's true." He looked surprised.

"Anyway, it was nice," she said. "Even if you were just asleep, as far as I was concerned."

"When I was sittin' down there in the kitchen, I decided—" He stooped to pat the dog, who was sniffing his trouser leg distrustfully.

"Decided what?"

"Decided I couldn't stand it if you were goin' to stay mad at me like that."

"I was horrible," said Sophie remorsefully. "I'm sorry, Alexander. You tried to explain, but I was too much of a pig to listen properly."

The dog began to edge between them, watching Sophie's expression attentively.

"Yeah, you're right," said Alexander, speaking to Argus. "You don't want me to touch her, do you? I kind of like this dog," he went on reflectively. "He's keepin' an eye on things."

"Sophie!" called Mother, leaning out the door. "Your breakfast is drying up on the plate."

"Just a minute, Mother," said Sophie, trying to hold Argus's collar and kiss Alexander at the same time.

"I'm sure Alexander would like some coffee," said Mother.

"Yes, I would, thank you, Vera," said Alexander politely. And Sophie saw her mother give him a look of real, rather shy affection as they went in.

Sophie went to see Annie again on Thursday. She debated taking some liquor, but decided against it. Friendship cannot be based upon false gifts. Anyway, Annie had her own supplies. Sophie preferred not to speculate too much about this.

Annie was baking, as it turned out. Tom, her old man, was coming home the following week. She was making pies, seventeen of them, all apple, the filling coming out of a gluey, waxed cardboard box marked RAISIN, with a heavy industrial cross stamped over it.

It was a domestic scene.

She had declined all help, and so Sophie was lying on the kitchen sofa, keeping her company and drinking a cup of tea. For the sofa itself she felt a serious if slightly strained affection. It was, after all, an object of some significance in Alexander's history.

Benedict Malone was doing his algebra homework at the kitchen table.

"Well, for Christ's sake, have a cookie, then!" Annie was saying to a small child at the door.

Covertly, Sophie looked at Benedict, trying to detect evidence of the rattlesnake whip in his physical makeup. He still looked like a skinny Indian kid to Sophie, a skinny Indian kid about five inches taller than most fourteen-year-old boys. In fact, despite his brown skin and his straight black hair, he had signs of Alexander all over him, like feathers emerging from a chick's fluff.

The child at the door burst into a torrent of tears, a bubble of snot welling forth from her nose. Benedict stood up with an Alexander-like stretch.

"Vicky doesn't like that kind, Ma," he said, and strolled toward the door.

"Well, it what we got," said Annie impatiently. "She pick them out—we were at the store."

"Yeah. She knows I like 'em," said Benedict-Alexander, taking two. "Come on, Vick, let's go over to Joshua's. He got a new foal."

"Finish your homework, Benedict?" Annie shouted after them.

"No." The sound came distantly on the breeze.

"Kids!" said Annie. She looked out the door after them thoughtfully.

"Is Vicky the youngest?"

"I sure hope so," said Annie, patting her angular stomach.

"How many do you have?"

"Three. I started late." Annie cast Sophie an oblique glance. "Thomas, then Vicky. Thomas, he the odd man out, I guess," she said.

"How do you mean?" Sophie wondered whether Annie

remembered the name of Thomas's kindergarten teacher.

Annie merely looked at her blankly for a moment and shrugged. She turned back to the counter and plucked a ball of pie dough from the bowl.

"When's your wedding?" she inquired. "You fix on a date yet?"

Recalling the setup at the Bresnyachuk bargaining table, Sophie began to describe this to Annie, self-consciously painting a very black picture of her own behavior. Annie seemed to be listening closely, but she did not laugh. Sophie wondered whether she was hurting Annie's feelings, too.

"You see what a fool I am," she concluded.

"But you don't know when, yet?"

"Soon, I hope." Sophie laughed. "We've got to get it over with."

"I was wonderin'," said Annie diffidently. "Can I come?"

Sophie shot bolt upright on the couch, kicking herself.

"Good heavens, Annie. Of course! We haven't invited anyone yet, that's all." But this did not seem adequate, suddenly. She saw that she had committed a crime, not merely a gaffe. "Are there witnesses at a court wedding?" she asked.

"I guess so. I never been to a court wedding," said Annie. "Tom and me got married in an R.C. church."

"You and Tom are married? Well—I guess everybody does it." Sophie changed this hastily. "Won't you be the witness for me, Annie?"

She was terrified at once that this gesture might smack of insincerity. She glanced at Annie's face. But to her relief, it reflected only genuine pleasure, nothing more.

"If Sasha don't mind," she said. "Who's goin' to be his?"

"I don't know. Maybe Marfa's boyfriend, if—" Sophie paused, thinking how odd this would be. Annie and the ghost of Benedict, blessing the union of Alexander and Sophia.

"I thought Marfa got married," said Annie.

"She did. Her husband died in some ghastly accident with a grader."

"It so long," said Annie softly.

It occurred to Sophie that she knew more about all of them now than any of them knew about each other. She was the repository of secrets, not just things that they didn't know, but things that they shouldn't know.

"I've had some talks with Marfa," she said cautiously. "About Benedict."

"I used to love Marfa," said Annie. "She so smart. As smart as Bennie."

"Benedict wouldn't let you see her, would he?" Sophie couldn't help saying this.

"No." Annie was remote, rolling out her dough. "But I could have—after."

"She told me about her—her love affair with Benedict."

"She kill Bennie's baby," said Annie, still distant.

Sophie knew what she thought about this. "He was very cruel to her," she said.

Annie carefully put the top crust on the last pie and wiped her floury hands on a cloth. Then she sat down at the table with a teacup, pushing Benedict's algebra book to one side.

"Bennie, he wasn't cruel," she said.

"I'm sorry, Annie. He's your brother, after all." Taking all three of them, Annie's loyalty was the only one that made sense, Sophie considered. It would be terrifying to have a sibling; he might commit the most awful crimes and one would have no choice but to forgive him.

"But he wasn't," Annie insisted. "He got hurt real bad."

"At the Stampede, maybe. But not by you. Not by Marfa. Not even by Alexander."

"Yes, he did. By me and Sasha first off, and then by Marfa. That one worse, Sophie. That one much worse."

Sophie was totally on Marfa's side in this. Much more on Marfa's side than Marfa was. But she could hardly argue with Annie. She remained silent.

"You know what those two are like," said Annie, turning her head to look at Sophie. "Sasha and Marfa?"

"Sort of larger than life?" asked Sophie. "That's what makes them so attractive."

"When you're with them, you got to see it their way," said Annie. "That why you think Bennie was cruel. Marfa tell you."

"Yes, but Alexander doesn't think he was. To Alexander he's a hero. But I think he was cruel to Alexander, too," said Sophie boldly. "And to you," she added.

"She couldn't leave him alone," said Annie. "She always after him when they were kids, too. But Benedict, he . . ." She went into a brown study, staring straight ahead of her.

Sophie had already heard about this. She considered that this was Benedict's fault, too.

"He lonely, Sophie. Real lonely. After Sasha take off, he got nothing."

"He had you," Sophie pointed out. Surely that had been the object of driving Alexander away, after all.

"You have your hand or your foot, Sophie? They not things you have. I'm like that to him." Annie shrugged. "For me, he more like my heart," she added.

"She said they just met at a rodeo."

"Yeah. She go square dancin' at the rodeo. With that little guy she used to sleep with. He's the principal of the school now. That's why I never go over there," said Annie with unconscious deadly accuracy. "She know Bennie was ridin'. She go on purpose."

"On purpose? To seduce him, you think?" asked Sophie.

"I guess she know what she know," said Annie, getting out a cigarette. "She always think she get him sometime. See, Bennie, he had a limit. He used to tell about it when we were kids. It like that in old times among us. The man, he always have a limit. Sometimes he sleep with his wife under the same blanket for ten years, and he don't do nothin'. Not like the way it is now. They don't have no kids till the man is ready, Sophie."

"Why did they do that?" asked Sophie, fascinated and horrified.

"The man got to be strong. Then he have the power. Then the baby have the power, too."

"The power?"

"When my baby cry, Bennie used to cover his nose, Sophie."

"My God!"

"He don't hurt him. But he can't cry. He goin' to have the power, you see."

"How—? That must have been an awful time for you, Annie."

"Yeah," Annie agreed. "But it worse for Benedict. You don't understand, Sophie."

"No, I don't!" said Sophie, suddenly losing all restraint. "When Marfa got pregnant, he treated her abominably! She told me. Much worse than Alexander treated you. He seems to have thought that he was getting his revenge on Alexander with Marfa. And that's disgusting!"

"He didn't get no revenge," said Annie quietly.

"Well, that's what she thinks! That's what he told her!" Thinking of Marfa's tears that night down by the pool in the stream, Sophie pursued her point recklessly. "This business about a limit, Annie! How could he talk about that when he hurt her so! And if he didn't want her to kill it, he shouldn't have told her that it was revenge!"

"He tell her that before she kill both of them," said Annie steadily. "She play with him, Sophie. She take away the power."

"The power!" cried Sophie. "What power? He was still a boy—like Alexander! He didn't have any power!"

"She never forgive him," Annie said.

"For what? For you and Alexander? I don't believe that!"

"No—for goin' with that whiteman. I told you. Marfa like me, Sophie. She was mad. Only I forgive him," said Annie slowly, "after I had my baby."

It was a new angle, one that had not occurred to Sophie before. She was already feeling somewhat ashamed of her outburst. She hated the myth of Benedict, but Annie was someone who had the right to love that myth.

"She torture him," Annie went on softly.

"I'm sorry, Annie," said Sophie unhappily. With a feeling of guilt, she realized that she was now avid to hear the rest of the story.

"You got nothin' to be sorry for. Marfa tell you." Annie shrugged.

"I think she loved him," said Sophie. "Well . . . I know she did."

"Sure, she love him. She want to have him—his power, everything! But she didn't want no half-breed baby!"

Sophie looked at her hands in her lap, aghast. Of course this was true. Her own point of view was suddenly swept aside to reveal an underlying reality—the reality Annie lived in. Annie, poor, maltreated, deserted, had had a half-breed baby, a child whom she and her extraordinary brother both deeply loved. Marfa could not have done that. Could she, Sophie, have done that?

"When she know she pregnant, she go for him with her hands. With her nails. Maybe she want to get rid of it right there."

"Was that when he said—that it was revenge?"

"All I know—he came home that night. He covered in blood, Sophie," said Annie through her teeth. "He got her mark all over him. There was even blood in his boots."

"Oh, Annie!" Sophie shuddered. But she knew she wanted to hear what had happened.

"He was takin' drugs," said Annie. "Maybe that save him. I don't know."

"What do you mean?"

"When she didn't have that baby," said Annie remotely, "nobody tell him nothing all winter. He was still ridin'—ridin' in the States. When he come back, he hear."

"Oh, about how she . . . fell off her horse?"

"That why he jump, Sophie," said Annie severely. "Me, I know. I was there."

"He jumped?" said Sophie stupidly.

"At the Stampede. That how he want to die. Because of that baby."

Sophie got up from the divan and took some pies out of the oven. She put four more in, and then went to the sink for a drink of water.

"I must be crazy, Annie. Why am I making you remember it all?" she said miserably. "Alexander doesn't know any of this."

"Maybe somebody got to know," said Annie. "Maybe you got to know so Sasha won't ever."

"Oh God! He must not ever know!" exclaimed Sophie, horrified. "The way he sees Marfa—he'd never forgive her."

"Don't let her tell him," said Annie neutrally.

"Yes. I suppose she wants to," said Sophie miserably. She remembered Marfa saying that she wanted to know what Alexander had told her. There was a great deal of truth in what Annie had said about the power; she saw that now. Marfa could deal Alexander a mortal hurt with this. "Do you forgive her, Annie?" asked Sophie.

"It not like that with us," said Annie.

"Indians, you mean?"

"No—women," said Annie.

"Oh."

But Sophie was doubtful about something else. How could she keep this from Alexander? She was now burdened with it. She put her hands over her eyes.

"There's lots of things like that, Sophie," said Annie,

looking at her queerly. "I never tell no one who was Thomas's father."

"Yes, but I'm going to *marry* Alexander."

"Thomas got Tom's name," said Annie. "But I never tell. Maybe Tom guesses. He never ask. And I'd lie if he did. There's always things like that."

"Yes. Oh yes," said Sophic, wringing her hands.

They sat in silence. The dry air outside was alive with a sound like the humming of telephone wires. It was the soft brushing of a million particles of dust striking against the side of the house. The relentless wind of the drought continued.

"After he got out of Foothills Hospital he go away." said Annie. "He go to the States—drivin' for Northern. Later on he was at Wounded Knee," she added, looking up.

"There was some fighting there or something? I don't remember what it was all about," said Sophie, still locked in her own thoughts of Marfa and Alexander.

"It was Indians."

"Wasn't it Sioux or something? You people are—"

"Yeah, but we're Indians."

Perhaps it was predictable that Benedict would become an Indian radical, Sophie reflected. It was the obvious outcome for his mystic worldview, his crippled, whiplash body. She remembered pictures from Wounded Knee—or was it Alcatraz? Something about genocide.

"This Reserve is rich now, isn't it?" she remarked. "After the oil and so on?"

"The government want to dam the river," said Annie neutrally.

"Oh yes, the Steamboat Valley irrigation thing." Who was it who had recently mentioned this? Her father used to say that a farmer's politics was irrigation. Now it was oil, irrigation, and Indians.

"It's our river."

"Maybe you'll get richer this way."

Annie did not reply. Sophie reflected that there was no point arguing about it with Annie, anyway. The West was already won. That had nothing to do with the silent, wounded bird that lived inside Annie. Benedict was a radical, so Annie was a radical; that was all there was to it. She wanted to know what had happened to Benedict.

"Did he ever come back?" she asked. Perhaps he was one of the hysterical, braided and hatted figures she had seen on TV, carrying banners at the First Ministers' Conferences.

"Yeah, he came back a couple of times."

Something had happened in Steamboat while she was in her last year of university. Sophie remembered it vaguely. She remembered arguing the Indian's point of view with her father, who had been pushing for irrigation since the thirties. The Indians owned the valley, and they held out for no dam.

It occurred to her almost as a comforting thought that Alexander was strongly for irrigation—another thing that separated him forever from Benedict.

"He didn't stay long," said Annie abruptly. "He was with a woman—a whiteman."

Naturally a white woman, a sort of groupie—one of those that hung around with native people, a cross between one of Annie's social workers and a prostitute. If the Indian people were politically serious, why couldn't they see that they were being patronized?

"I see her," said Annie. "She was a good woman for Benedict."

A masochist. Someone who swallowed Benedict's view of himself. Sophie still could not accept this—not the way Annie accepted it, or the way Alexander would.

"She was a rich girl. From somewhere in the States."

"What was her name?" asked Sophie absently. Probably it was a name like Ford, or possibly Pontiac.

"Mary," Annie replied.

Annie's mother now shuffled into the kitchen, carrying a tobacco can held out before her in both hands. She went straight to the stove, her swamp-turtle eyes hooded and unblinking, and poured herself a cup of tea from the pot, setting the tobacco can down carefully on the counter.

Annie got up with an exclamation of disgust and went into the bathroom with the can to dump it in the toilet. It was half full of tobacco juice and spit, Sophie surmised. The old woman carried it as though it were a piece of vital, life-sustaining equipment—like a hospital patient pushing an intravenous contraption down the corridor.

"Hello, Mrs. Malone," said Sophie politely.

Annie's mother turned her head slowly in Sophie's direction and gave her a long, introspective stare.

Annie returned and pushed the can at the old woman, saying, "Here!" Mrs. Malone sat down in a chair beside the table and fumbled in her caved-in bosom for a new plug of tobacco. Annie sat down as well, ignoring her mother completely.

"She was a real nice girl," Annie said, continuing where she had left off. "You know, she sort of like you, Sophie. She got red hair—real pretty."

Somewhat taken aback by this compliment, Sophie pursued her thoughts. Naturally, the radical Benedict would have a white woman who looked like a white woman. Slight, brown-skinned, non-WASP Marfa had not really made the grade. Sophie felt a slight empathetic surge for Marfa.

"She didn't know nothing about us. She thought we still eat buffalo meat."

The mother began to rock drearily back and forth in the creaking kitchen chair. Sophie was distracted. The way she rocked was like grief, her arms crooked as though for an absent child. Yet there was no expression on her face. Could she speak English?

"Bennie was ten, then."

"Haven't you seen him since?"

The mother shot Sophie an enigmatic glance of interest or hatred, impossible to tell which. Tobacco juice ran in the creases under her mouth.

"Bennie loved her," said Annie, ignoring the question. "But they didn't stay long."

"Does Bennie have a horse?" asked Sophie suddenly. This was a little on her mind after Robert's story.

"She gave him a pony."

Mary Edsel did have something in common with Sophie Ware, it seemed.

"I heard—somebody told me that he got into some trouble last fall," said Sophie nervously. "He stole a horse or something, didn't he?"

"Oh yeah," said Annie tolerantly. "Like Benedict and Sasha."

"Benedict!" said the mother on a rising note. This turned into a wail of anguish. The rocking intensified with her scream.

"Stop it, Ma!" shouted Annie, getting up from her chair.

"Bennie!" wailed Mrs. Malone, rocking furiously, her arms crossed on her breast, her head at an angle like a stroke victim.

"Shut up, Mama!" cried Annie.

Sophie became aware that there was someone else in the kitchen. There had been no sound, but the gaze of the old woman was fixed on something behind Sophie. She shifted around, her arms out, the hands hooking upwards in a gesture of supplication.

It was Benedict.

Annie also looked at her son, a quick, businesslike glance.

He took a reluctant step forward, farther into the kitchen.

"Want me to—?" he said, looking at Annie.

"No," said Annie shortly. She put both arms around her mother and pulled her upright with a gentleness that surprised Sophie. They made a slow, limping progress toward the hallway and the bedrooms beyond.

Benedict gazed after them for a moment, his head alert and his eyes intelligent. Then he looked at Sophie.

Sophie was rooted to her chair, embarrassed and horrified.

"Don't be scared," said Benedict. "She gets like that sometimes." He seemed to take Sophie's presence for granted; he knew she wasn't a social worker.

Annie came back into the room again and snatched up the tobacco can off the table with a violent gesture.

"Ma, can I have a pie?" asked Benedict hurriedly. "Vick and me—"

"Yes! Yes! Yes!" said Annie, leaving with the can.

"We're going to eat it in a place we got," said Benedict to Sophie. He looked carefully at the eight cooling pies and selected what Sophie had to agree was from all standpoints the best one. The screen door clicked behind him.

Annie came back into the kitchen. Sophie stood up.

"I'm sorry, Annie," she said. "I come here and remind you—and then your mother—"

"Don't go," said Annie, looking disappointed. "You don't have to go."

"But your mother—"

"It got nothing to do with you."

"Because we were talking about—?"

"Yeah. But that's okay. I like to talk about him."

Sophie sat down slowly. Annie checked the four cooking pies in the oven, then put more tea in both of their cups. She sat down, and Sophie saw that she was sincere. But it was with reluctance, not avidity, that Sophie asked the question that had been on her mind for some time.

"Annie," she said, "is Benedict dead?"

18

A Lovely Day

The school closing was at the end of the week.

As Sophie stood on the platform with the singing children, she thought how much more straightforward relations were with them than with grownups. There was no reflective action of the soul; being with children was as easy as swimming or eating. She derived some of her inner feeling that she was a good person from this, when she compared it with the self-consciousness and confused motivations of her dealings with adults.

She was looking regretfully at her kindergarten class now, running out onto the playground in all directions, when Alexander appeared beside her.

"You—here!"

"I came to see the school closin'," he said, smiling. He was wearing his good clothes again, the same he had worn to the restaurant.

"Well, well," said Madeleine, coming up to them and winding herself sinuously, as it seemed to Sophie, about Alexander's legs. "So this is the man, is it?"

Sophie introduced them quickly, glancing at Alexander to see whether he minded Madeleine. To her surprise, he was looking amused.

"He's so big! You don't look so big from a distance," Madeleine was saying to him with a histrionic shudder.

"I guess not," agreed Alexander.

"Sophie doesn't tell her friends anything," said Madeleine, squirming confidentially closer. "We haven't had a real old-fashioned talk for months. So when—?"

"Cut it out, Madeleine!" exclaimed Sophie. Madeleine was an outspoken feminist and was playing an elaborate practical joke. It did not make it any easier that Alexander was unfazed by this.

"I just wanted to know when the wedding is," said Madeleine, pretending to be hurt.

Alexander looked calmly at Sophie.

"July the fifth," she said promptly. Five was just a number, after all.

"You better invite your friends to the reception, Sophia," said Alexander. "Poppa's inviting all of his."

"Oh? It's at your *father's* place?"

A parent engaged Sophie's attention at this point, and she was led off across the playground as Madeleine continued, "She was *afraid* we'd give her a *shower* if she told the date in advance. Never mind, Sophie!" she shouted as Sophie receded reluctantly, looking over her shoulder. "I'll get you a pair of dishtowels and a matching tea cozy someday when you really need them!"

Alexander was looking pleased, if a little bewildered, as Madeleine turned coyly back to him.

A few minutes later he found Sophie again, cleaning out her desk in the empty classroom.

"Is this what you were doin' all day?" he asked, looking around at the art displays in surprise.

"Yes. It's only kindergarten," said Sophie hastily. "Don't you remember?"

"What's this?"

"Macaroni art." Sophie went over to stand beside him. "You see? This is a house, and a horse in the field—" She pointed.

"And stars in the sky," said Alexander, looking at it.

"You do see!" Sophie was delighted.

"I told that woman to come," said Alexander. "Haven't you asked anyone?"

"No, I—" said Sophie at a loss. The idea that she might invite anyone to this affair was a new one; it had only occurred to her recently.

"Maybe we better ask that guy you were goin' around with, too."

"No!" she said, panic-stricken.

"Why not?" he asked. "I know this'll be pretty awful, Sophie. It has to be, if Poppa's in on it, but—"

"It isn't because of that," said Sophie, trapped.

"Well, come on. Let's invite him, then. And who else?"

"Oh God, Alexander!" Sophie dropped into a tiny chair and put her head in her hands. Surely telling the date had been enough.

"Sophia," he said, crouching beside her. "What's the matter? Didn't you want me to come to the school closin'?"

"Oh no. It isn't that," said Sophie, groaning. "I did want you to. It's just—"

"Sophie, darling!" Robert hung in the doorway. "Embracing amid the rubble of last year's hopes?"

Sophie sprang up, and Alexander turned around slowly.

"I've come to offer my services as a bridesmaid," said Robert. "Madeleine mentioned a date just now. I see no reason why you shouldn't have two," he added.

"Yes, we were just talking about that," she said brightly. "Won't you come to the reception? It's going to be at the Bresnyachuks' house."

"Not even a small place as an altar boy? I know all about weddings. I'm a Uke myself, as I have to keep reminding you, apparently." He began intoning something that sounded to Sophie like a Black Mass.

Alexander grinned. "That's why we're havin' a judge," he said.

"Oh, it's to be a civil ceremony? Too bad. Pay fifteen dollars. Now kiss the bride! How like you, Sophie dear."

"Yes, and you're too late," said Sophie, suddenly thinking of something that lightened her heart. "I've already got a bridesmaid."

"Oh? Who?"

"Annie Malone."

"Annie Malone?" Robert looked at her in astonishment. "Why, who in the world might that be?" he asked a moment later. "Someone I don't know?"

"No, you don't know her," said Sophie serenely. "She's a friend of mine."

"Yes, I see. She must be," said Robert. He began to fade toward the doorway. An expression that Sophie had never seen before, a combination of ironic amusement and something like sadness, was crossing his face.

"We'll be expecting you, then," said Sophie.

"Oh, I'll be there all right, never fear!"

Sophie laughed. She knew she could not really hurt Robert. She had added a tiny bit to his knowledge of the world, that was all.

"You really asked Annie?" said Alexander, after he had disappeared.

"Of course I did, Alexander. She wants to come. And to the reception too," said Sophie calmly. "Don't be nervous," she added. "This is going to be a very good wedding!"

Sophie sang:

"Lavender's blue, dilly dilly,
Lavender's green,
When I am king, dilly dilly,
You shall be queen!"

Alexander was putting out a cigarette in the ashtray on the dashboard of Sophie's car, and glancing at him she saw with pleasure that the expression in his eyes was an expression of lust, pure and unmixed. Men liked women who could sing, she had noticed this before.

They were going to Marfa's house for supper. Alexander had brought along a case of beer.

Marfa greeted them with her usual detachment. There was no sign of Tim, but Sven was lounging in a garden chair, reading a newspaper. A joint hung loosely from his lips.

Alexander immediately went on an exploration tour of the farmyard with the children.

"Nice of you to come," Marfa told Sophie privately. "That was kind of a horror show last week, wasn't it?"

"Well, it's okay, anyway," said Sophie, unwilling to admit how horrible it had been. Talking to Marfa was dangerous.

"Sasha jumped right down my throat over the phone. He's getting eccentric in his old age. What did he say to you?"

"He thought I was testing him."

"And you weren't?" said Marfa cynically. "As I remember it—"

"Well, you remember wrong," said Sophie. "Tim lent me his bed for about two hours. That was all."

"You needn't think I told Sasha the whole story!"

"Tim was very nice about it," went on Sophie determinedly. "We talked a little—before he took off."

"Oh, you did? About what?" Marfa was abrupt.

"About how neither of us can ride a horse!" said Sophie, suddenly bursting into a laugh. "Forget it, Marfa!"

Marfa looked into her lemonade glass thoughtfully.

"Did he say where he was going, by the way?" she asked.

"No. But I got the impression he was coming back. What are you going to do about Sven?" Sophie said pointedly.

"Who? Oh yeah."

Sophie was embarrassed.

"Don't worry about it, Sophie," said Marfa. "You know—you and Sasha—" She tipped back her head to look at the pellucid sky. "Let's go for a swim," she said after a moment. "I guess Sasha will drag you away after supper."

They crossed the pasture where Alexander and the children were playing tag with the ponies, Alexander racing on foot. The air was soft and cool under the poplars. It was a relief just to be out of the continuous, hot, dry wind.

A few moments later there was a pounding of hoofs on the path and the children arrived, throwing off their clothing carelessly. Sophie had been floating in the shallows with Marfa, but withdrew discreetly to a deeper place. Marfa climbed out, refusing to be splashed, and went to lie on the grassy bank.

The children played in the water, as frisky as the ponies, showing off for Sophie, who began after a moment's thought to laugh and dive and splash with them. The water was cool and refreshing.

With a tremendous cleaving splash, Alexander dove into the pool from behind her and rose on the other side, blowing and shaking the water off his face and hair. Sophie, who had been defending herself against a water-fight attack from both children, was instantly deserted.

Treading water and occasionally resting a toe on the bottom, she watched the battle. Like a bear being assailed by bees, Alexander flipped them away, dove and sidestepped, throwing them back when they approached from the front, and crashing backwards when they grasped his neck from behind. There was a great deal of noise.

"Help!" shouted Alexander.

"Come on!" shrieked Emmie. "Duck Sasha!"

"Help! Help!"

Sophie approached cautiously, unsure whose part she was supposed to take. Emmie was clinging to Alexander's neck in a stranglehold, and Herbie, from the back, was trying to stuff his head down between their squirming bodies.

Sophie pulled Herbie back and was instantly engaged in a thrashing and kicking match. Alexander shed Emmie in a duck-dive.

"Herbie!" shouted Marfa from the bank. "Lay off! Leave Sophie alone!"

"It's okay," gasped Sophie, imitating Alexander by diving out of range.

"Do something about those damn ponies!" screamed Marfa.

The children scrambled out of the water and raced naked in the sunshine along the river's edge, chasing the skittish animals into the trees. Sophie rested against the opposite bank of the pool, holding on to a tree root with her arms above her head. From a similar vantage point about ten feet away, Alexander was looking over at her, smiling.

Marfa rose and strolled away up the path with an oblique wave, her clothes dangling from her other hand.

"You saved my life," said Alexander, submerging and then bobbing up again. "I can't float too good."

"Really?" Sophie pushed off with her feet and attained the center of the pool in a swanlike motion. She rolled over on her back, and then tilted her head comfortably onto the cushion of the water.

"Yeah," said Alexander, arriving beside her. "I don't float unless I swim." He pulled her down underwater with him and they kissed for a long time, their limbs intertwining, holding out till the last possible moment. He seemed to know when this moment arrived, for they shot to the surface just as Sophie was happily committing herself to eternity.

"See what I mean?" he said, preparing to do it again, but giving her a short rest while he treaded water for both of them.

"Sasha!" called Herbie.

"Uncle Sasha!" shouted Emmie.

"What is it?" Alexander continued to tread water, kissing Sophie on the surface now, and making her laugh in pure and happy amusement at his lack of self-consciousness.

"We can't catch the ponies!"

"How far did you chase them?" Alexander asked, still paying no attention, as the children dashed up.

"Miles!"

"They got into the woods!"

"Okay. Let's go find them," he said to Sophie, drawing her closer to shore and letting go of her to stand up.

"Maybe I—" Sophie crouched in the shallow water.

"Come on," he said. "It's nice. Real warm." He seized her hand.

They ran hand in hand along the bank together, splashing in and out of the water. The children darted ahead, leading into the flickering green light under the poplar trees.

"You don't mind—in bare feet?" asked Alexander solicitously. He slowed down a little.

"They're very tough."

"Well, mine aren't! You can ride home anyway."

The children came into sight up ahead with one captured pony. Herbie was on his back. The pony rolled his eyes comically and stamped at the sight of the wild-haired apparitions plunging out of the bush toward him.

"Give him to Sophia," Alexander directed. "You guys have feet like slabs of firewood."

Herbie jumped down cooperatively, and Alexander

swung Sophie up onto the pony's back as easily as he might have done with either child. The pony whinnied, but Alexander took the bridle.

"The other one'll come now," he said. "Just listen."

Sophie sat upright on the pony's back, giving him a reassuring gentle pressure with her knees, and smoothed back her wet hair. Like the others, the pony was listening alertly.

A moment later the other pony emerged from the woods on their right and the children flung themselves astride him with much the same careless technique they had used on Alexander in the water.

"There you go," said Alexander, handing Sophie the bridle and giving the pony a gentle thump on his rounded backside. Sophie careered off after the children, hanging on at first through sheer surface tension, but later, as she came to realize, through the cooperative skill of the pony, who was obviously wondering why she was so gentle.

"Want to come play in the field, Sophie?" shouted Herbie over his shoulder.

The pony paid no attention to any attempts to stop him by the river, and a short while later Sophie was playing tag with the others, nude, breathless, and utterly taken out of herself by the joy of the thing.

It was a game without any rules. They galloped toward each other, the ponies dodging at the last moment to avoid collision. Sophie was no longer timid; her animal was demonstrating that he knew his business. She threw herself into a long, satisfactory chase, ending up at the fence, where she tagged them and suddenly fell off.

Somewhat winded, but not at all scared, she sat up. The pony lingered a few feet away, apparently checking to make sure she was all right. The children were off on another wild tack in the direction of the house.

She caught the pony easily and mounted him by the first staple of the fence. Then, without much effort or forethought, they began to amble down the slope of the field together, enjoying the sun and the drying wind of the afternoon on their heated skins.

Alexander appeared on the path at the edge of the scrub, coming up from the river. He was wearing his trousers and carefully carrying all of Sophie's clothes. The pony spotted him and broke into a gentle canter, allowing Sophie to bring him stylishly to a halt around Alexander's back.

"He's a pretty little thing, isn't he?" said Alexander, patting him on the withers and helping Sophie down. "Have a good time?"

"Very," said Sophie, clinging to him with a sigh of pleasure.

"Them kids—" he began, as she put her arms around his neck. He bent his head obligingly and touched his forehead to hers. "—are comin' again!"

Sophie laughed.

"They want the pony," she said. She withdrew her dress from the top of the bundle on the ground at her feet and pulled it down over her head without haste.

"No shoes and stockings," she said. "Never again—all summer!" She tied them up securely with her underthings in his shirt.

The children came pounding down the field.

"I feel like lettin' him go," said Alexander, indicating the little horse, who was showing signs of restiveness. "They're too rough."

"What about the other one—poor thing!"

"Hey, you guys!" shouted Alexander. He caught hold of a flying bridle and ran after them. Sophie followed placidly, carrying the bundle of clothes and watching Alexander demonstrate decent and humane treatment of horses to Emmie a few hundred feet uphill.

"Marfa just lets 'em run wild," he remarked, frowning, when she came up beside him. Emmie was trotting forward at a discreet pace after her brother, who had already disappeared over the brow of the hill.

"She doesn't really," said Sophie. "She looks after them.

That must have been what you were like when you were children, after all."

"Yeah. That's what I mean."

"So—they'll be riders and swimmers, and, well—free people!"

"Think so?" he asked, glancing at her acutely and smiling.

"Well, it's good," she said, taking his hand and feeling the shadow of self-consciousness creeping toward her. "You and Marfa turned out all right."

"I don't know about that," he said slowly. "It could have been better. I'd like our kids to grow up different. Like you."

"What! All six of them?"

"Yeah. Six," he replied, laughing at her expression.

"I was the only one," said Sophie. "I don't know what it's like to play like that."

"Well, you'll see," said Alexander, "soon enough."

They paused, standing on the brow of the hill and looking down into the little dip at Marfa's house. A dry wind came rippling up the grasses. Sven still slumped in the garden chair, a copy of *Rolling Stone* open on his knees. The children had disappeared into the house, leaving the ponies to munch on the sparse grass of the lawn.

"Who is that guy?" asked Alexander, turning around and looking Sophie full in the face, his nostrils unconsciously flaring. "Where's Tim?"

"Tim took off the night I was here," said Sophie uncomfortably. "Sven—well, I guess he just stayed on."

"I thought maybe he was the one who—"

"No, not him," said Sophie, looking unhappily into Alexander's eyes. "He was—you see, he and Marfa—"

"Jesus! Marfa!" exclaimed Alexander in disgust. He paused. "Was it Tim, then?" he asked softly.

"Well . . . yes. But nobody had told him that you and I . . ." Sophie said desperately. "And then he was awfully nice about it when I didn't want—when I wouldn't."

"I hate that kind of stuff," said Alexander, continuing to stare at her. "It's like suckin' blood. You get a woman like her, and after a while there's nothing left but bone."

"But it's just sex," Sophie protested. "I mean, people can't help—"

"Yeah. That's the point. If you start thinkin' it's just screwin', then sooner or later that's all it is. You don't feel anything or think about it. Pretty soon you don't even care whether you're doin' it!"

"So you would have minded a lot if I had—"

"I'd have gotten over it," he said shortly. "You're not like that, anyway."

"How do you know?" asked Sophie miserably. She looked up at him, her skirt whipping around her legs in the hot wind.

"I can feel you," he replied. "The way you are." His expression softened and he put his hands on her waist and drew her against him. "Can't you feel me?"

"Yes," whispered Sophie, feeling a queer, welling tenderness all through her body. The raw feelings of frustrated sexuality and desire had all been wrung out of her by the swimming and the sun and the riding, leaving this thrilling tenderness. She stared into his darkened eyes, knowing that he felt it too.

Then as though neither of them was able to bear this for long yet, they broke apart spontaneously and ran down the hill hand in hand.

Supper was rather hilarious. Having stated his opinion, Alexander seemed to hold nothing against Sven. Sven merely occupied a black hole in space, with his long, cadaverous body and his guitar. Sophie had always seen him this way. She wished Tim were there, regardless of what disparate forms of irrationality his presence might set up in Alexander and Marfa.

In the meantime, it gave her great pleasure to see Alexander arguing with his sister, a joint in his mouth and a beer bottle in his hand. They were both Bresnyachuks, there was no doubt about that.

Sophie helped Marfa with the dishes while Alexander prowled around outside with the children, who came back to report at intervals.

"Uncle Sasha says we got any nails? He's fixin' the chicken coop."

"We counted the ducks, and a coyote must have got one."

The sun rode down over the hillside and a serene and purple dusk spread over the land. Sophie went to sit in the living room and fell asleep to the quiet plucking of Sven's guitar.

She woke up in peace. There was no sound in the house.

She went into the kitchen, looking for someone, and heard a quiet murmur from the loft room above. Alexander was sitting on the floor between the children's beds, smoking a cigarette in the dark and telling them some tale. Sophie sat down, unseen, on the top step of the stairs to listen.

". . . time when Poppa caught Benedict Malone stealin' potatoes. Indians were real poor in those days—not like they are now—and they had to eat, see? Poppa used to lay in wait for 'em on the Reserve road, because the Reserve had a real high government fence and to get back they had to take that road. He was ridin' a good old mare of Momma's named Bella. Now Benedict, he only had a pony, and he knew he didn't stand a chance against Bella—"

"Was it a pony like Misha?"

"More like the other one."

"Pal."

"Yeah. Like him. Spotted like that, only more white. Anyway, when Benedict saw Poppa come roarin' out of the bush on Bella, he just turned and rode straight for that fence."

"Were you there, Uncle Sasha?" asked the sleepy voice of Emmie. "Where were you?"

"I was in the potato field," said Alexander with a guilty laugh. "I just gave Benedict a hand with the sack, gettin' it up on the pony. Anyway—"

"You were helpin' Benedict steal 'em?"

"Well, yeah, but I was the one who had to dig 'em too. Hey, you guys, do you want to hear this story or what?"

"Yes, please."

"Go on, Uncle Sasha."

"Well, Benedict ran right at that big fence, and the pony cleared it and come down on all four feet, too, still runnin'. Poppa was mad as hell, but Benedict had to drop the sack on our side, so he got them potatoes back anyway." Alexander laughed again. "Later on he sent me to pick up the sack and I put about half of 'em over. I figured Benedict would be back to measure the fence sometime."

"How high was it?"

"Benedict claimed it was six feet, but I don't think it could have been. It was a real high fence, though." Apparently something occurred to Alexander now. "Hey, don't you try that!" he exclaimed. "No jumpin'!"

"Why not?"

"I bet Pal could."

"Misha could, too."

"Nope. Neither of 'em could. An Indian pony, he's got something else in him. The Indians treat their horses real good and they feed 'em better than they feed their kids."

"What do they feed them?"

"Oh—mashed potatoes, I guess," replied Alexander, chuckling. "But you've got to practice jumpin' horses. You've got to teach 'em."

"I'm going to practice," said Emmie.

"You're not doin' anything of the kind! You learn how to ride first. Watch Sophia. She rides real well."

"She fell off," said Emmie.

Sophie felt her ears beginning to burn.

"That's nothing," said Alexander severely. "You watch how she treats a horse. She doesn't half kill it with kickin' and jumpin' up and down like you do. She can make 'em do real fancy things you don't even know about."

"Can she make 'em jump?"

"Yes, I can," said Sophie, feeling that this had gone far enough, and entering the room. "Or at least I could. I bet you can, too," she said to Alexander, sitting down on Herbie's bed in a little resentment against Emmie. "You could show them with Rosi."

"I want to see you do it, Sophie," said Emmie, making Sophie feel more kindly toward her at once.

"Yeah, well, you just wait till someone shows you how," said Alexander. "And meantime, stop ridin' that pony of yours like a rockin' horse." He sighed and stretched. "How about goin' to sleep, anyway?" He stood up, looming tall and strong over the beds in the darkness.

"Mashed potatoes!" said Sophie, snorting on a laugh. She kissed Herbie good night and went over to kiss Emmie. "I don't believe a word of that story!"

"Fried, too," said Alexander, as she preceded him downstairs.

"Where the hell is Marfa?" he whispered angrily when they had attained the kitchen.

"I don't know," said Sophie. "I went to sleep."

"See? She even leaves you to kiss her kids good night," he said, and Sophie felt the intimacy of this "you" with pleasure, as though she were someone he now knew better than his own sister.

He walked over to the door and flung it open, looking out onto the pasture. Sophie followed him and saw the studio light on in the barn.

"There," she said, pointing.

"That's Tim's room!" said Alexander in disgust.

"Alexander!" cried Sophie, clutching him with both hands.

"I'm not goin' anywhere, Sophia." He turned around.

"What do we do now? Leave the kids alone and go home without sayin' good-bye?"

"Let's just stay here for a while," said Sophie pacifically.

"You were asleep already."

"I'm not tired anymore," she said, yawning.

"No?" Alexander smiled at her suddenly. Sophie shut the door firmly and pushed him into a chair.

"Something you mustn't forget, Alexander Bresnyachuk, is that we're *us,*" she said severely. She sat down on his knees.

"Oh yeah?" He rested his cheek against her breast, and Sophie put her arms around his head. "I was thinkin' that all afternoon, ever since we left the school."

"Me too."

"If only we could already be married," said Alexander in a muffled voice.

"Skipping the wedding part, you mean?"

"Let's go and do it tomorrow," he said, rocking his forehead against her bosom.

"We haven't got a license. And Monday is Dominion Day," she reminded him. He slid his hand from her knee up under the hem of her dress.

"We could drive down to Great Falls and get a license in about half an hour," he told her, pushing the hem up a little further with his knuckles.

"Hey! Is this sex?" Sophie asked satirically, and bent to kiss his lips. "We could step out the door right now, or go over to the No-Tell Motel and check into room 121."

"Have you ever been there?"

"No."

"Well, I have. And I'm not goin' there with you!" Alexander stroked her smoothly from hip to knee.

Sophie felt a twinge of something, not jealousy exactly. Alexander's conception of her character did not include lovemaking in a sleazy motel. It was somehow limiting.

But he really knew very little about her, she cheered

herself. If there were things he was keeping from her, there were things she was keeping from him, as well. She was not a jealous person, although she had been jealous, whereas he was a very jealous person. This protectiveness was not all one-sided.

She relaxed under his stroking hand.

"My pants are in your shirt pocket," she remarked. "Let's not forget to take them out before your mother decides to do a wash."

"I guess it wouldn't really worry her," murmured Alexander. "She'd know they were yours."

"Do you know," Sophie said, leaning back in his arms, "that's what everyone here thinks. It is only you and I who are . . ." She closed her eyes and slipped down further, lying across his knees. Alexander bent over her attentively.

"Are what?" he asked after a moment.

"Don't stop," said Sophie.

"My!" said Marfa, coming in swiftly. "What is this? The honeymoon?"

19

I Saw Him Die

Sophie sat up, flushed and happy.

"Well, don't mind me!" Marfa went on brightly. "I can—"

"Go talk to your kids," growled Alexander, half-buried. "They were wonderin' where you went."

"No, they weren't," said Sophie quickly, rearranging herself. "Alexander told them a story and they went to sleep. We were just—"

"Goin' home," said Alexander.

"And you look it!" said Marfa. She gave a breathy sigh and sat down at the table, her eyes odd and bright. "Well—Sven's gone. Have a drink?" she asked.

Alexander and Sophie answered simultaneously:

"Nope."

"Okay."

They both laughed guiltily, and Sophie got down off his lap, straightening her scanty clothing further.

"Okay," said Alexander grudgingly.

Marfa got a bottle of rye out of the broom closet.

"Nobody ever looks in there but me," she explained, seeing Sophie's smile.

It would be rye, Sophie reflected. It was an important detail of Marfa's biography that she did not drink vodka except at her parents' home. The rejection of all things Bresnyachuk was part of the Bresnyachuk charm.

She looked at the two of them over the rim of her glass. It seemed to her somehow as though she had never lived, as though life were something she had read about in books. She had been swept along on the top of the counterculture wave of her generation, a wave that had rolled past these people—people who were pregnant at fifteen or eighteen, had seen the inside of room 121 of the No-Tell Motel, who hated or embraced promiscuity, both of them completely involved and demoniacally in charge of their lives. The safe middle-classness of her background had always been around Sophie like a warm blanket. What was a stint in an ashram, a rather safe tour of Europe in a Volkswagen bus, and a few years in an electronically monitored apartment house in the Grove, compared to this?

Marfa was saying rather sharply, "Well, he's gone now!"

Sophie looked at her with empathetic sadness. The liberated terms that she took for granted were not, after all, Marfa's terms at all. The orderly progression from experimentation to a more stable form of life had come, in Marfa's case, to chaos.

"Look, I don't care, Marfa," Alexander was saying. "I kind of like Tim, is all."

"That layabout was to the taste of Mr. Work Ethic, was he?"

"You never gave him a chance," said Alexander.

"Oh yeah? I'll tell you what, Sasha. I spent nine years

giving chances to a guy who couldn't keep his hands off the rubbing alcohol and the Lysol spray. He couldn't keep his hands off me, either, if you really want to know! Now I'm doing my own thing."

"Yeah, but Tim isn't that way," said Alexander, staring at her.

"No, he isn't." Marfa dropped her eyes to her hands, resting on the table. Then she looked up at him again. "But I wonder whether you know what I mean, Sasha. Did anyone ever beat you up?"

She stood up abruptly, her eyes dilating.

"I mean really beat you up," she said. "Not one of those tin-pot brawls you men get into. What I mean is when a man wants to kill a woman!"

Sophie shuddered. Alexander slowly made a fist.

"Not with the fists, Sasha! Not with the fists! With the feet! So he gets blood all over his beautiful lizardskin Western boots. But, oh yeah, I forgot! You remember somebody who fought with his feet, don't you?"

Alexander said nothing, his face a little pale, turned toward his sister.

Marfa's gaze now shifted to Sophie.

"In the ribs, in the shins—anywhere so you can't get up and go after him with your nails. How would you like that, Sophie? The only place he doesn't kick you is in the stomach, oh no! But Sasha doesn't know about that, does he? He doesn't know about it at all!"

"No, he doesn't," said Sophie breathlessly, putting her hand over Alexander's whitened knuckles.

"Yeah. He doesn't," said Marfa, sitting down suddenly. She rested her forehead on the back of her hand. "He never will, will he?" she said in irony.

"Jesus, Marfa, if I'd have been here—"

"Well, you weren't," she said briskly. "So that's that! Cheers!"

"Why'd you ever marry him, Marfa?" Alexander asked after a moment.

"To get away from Momma and Poppa. Why do you think?"

"Yeah, but even Poppa—" said Alexander, his hand slowly relaxing. "Poppa never beat a woman. He thought that guy was real no good. He should have—"

"Oh yes. Should have this, should have that!" said Marfa impatiently. "It's all over and gone, Sasha. What does it matter now?"

One could look at this story one way and one could look at it another. Sophie remembered the nausea she had felt at Annie's description of the scratch marks on Benedict's body. But it had been Marfa's blood on his boots. Who had driven whom to what? It possessed them, this story, and now it possessed her as well.

"You want to know what I really see in Tim?" Marfa was asking Alexander. "He's forbidden fruit. Poppa can't even hear the name. I kind of like that," she went on pleasantly.

"Yeah. Poppa and the way he thinks about Indians," said Alexander. He glanced at Sophie. "But he's goin' to have to put up with it at our wedding, because Sophia—"

"I suppose you were going to invite Tim, were you?" said Marfa sweetly.

"Yes, I was," replied Sophie. "In fact, I guess I already did," she added, blushing.

Alexander gave her an unequivocal glance of love.

"Maybe Tim could be the best man," he suggested. "I haven't got anybody else I can ask."

"The hell you say, Sasha!" said Marfa. "You know what Poppa would do."

"I'll tell you, Marfa, the time Poppa'd be best off meetin' Tim is at our weddin'."

"Are you kidding? Poppa hates Indians, in season and out!"

"He's got nothing to hold against Tim." Alexander looked at Marfa somberly. "The only reason Poppa—"

"Yeah. Benedict. And I guess you think that was all

because of you, don't you, Sasha?" The manic glitter had returned to Marfa's eyes. The woman was dangerous. She was too articulate. It probably really hurt her to keep a secret. Sophie saw that secret burning in her eyes, leaping up like a flame against a fireguard.

"You think time froze back here the moment you left home, don't you, Sasha?" Marfa was continuing. "Well, maybe a few things happened. Poor little Marfa got herself hitched up with a squarehead sonofabitch who used to beat her up. I guess you know that—now," she said, and again her gaze shifted alarmingly to Sophie. "But maybe a few other things happened to your innocent little sister—or didn't that ever occur to you?"

"Most people," said Sophie, launching herself cautiously, "have some experiences before they get married."

"Yes, and that's good, isn't it, Sophie!" cried Marfa with a sudden shriek of laughter. "I bet it was good for you, anyway!"

"Not altogether," said Sophie desperately. "I mean—you have to find out. But those early experiences can really hurt, too. When you're young, I mean." She realized how feeble this was.

Alexander put his arm protectively across the back of her chair. Sophie noticed this, touched by how he misunderstood.

"No one could ever call you a whore, Sophie!" cried Marfa with another wild laugh. "I guess that's what Sasha likes about you. He sure as hell hates it about me!"

She was riding high again. Nothing could stop her.

"I'm not goin' to listen to any more of this!" said Alexander, pushing back his chair violently. "I'm takin' Sophia home, Marfa! She doesn't have to sit here and let you go on at her like that!"

"No, no!" exclaimed Sophie. If they were going to quarrel about her, it was almost as bad as the other thing they might quarrel about.

"Well, Jesus!" said Alexander, getting up and walking over to the sink.

"Don't be mad, Alexander," Sophie said anxiously. "Marfa and I like each other. It's just a way of talking."

She glanced at Marfa. To her surprise, there were tears in the corners of Marfa's eyes.

"I do like you, Sophie," she said.

"Well, I like you a lot, so that's all right," said Sophie with real sincerity. She jumped up and went over to Alexander. "You see?" she said, putting a hand on his chest.

"Have another drink, Sasha," said Marfa, pouring some rye into their glasses.

Sophie laughed. It was Poppa's basic technique.

"Don't you know you're my favorite brother?" Marfa went on. "Now that I think of it, that isn't saying much, is it?" she asked herself. "Still . . ."

They were great quarrelers, but they were also great peacemakers, this family.

Alexander accepted the drink.

"I've only got one sister," he remarked.

Yes, he only had one sister, Sophie reflected. She wasn't going to have him throwing this sister away. Marfa wanted to tell him something for which he would not forgive her.

"Larger than life" hardly described them. They could tear each other apart. But it wasn't going to happen. So far, she had been able to prevent it. Sophie began to relax again.

"You know, it was nice to see Sophie out there chasing the kids this afternoon," said Marfa warmly. "I didn't know you could ride like that, Sophie."

"Them kids ride like a horse's nightmare," Alexander told her. "You better let Sophia show 'em how."

"She has a good seat," murmured Sophie. "Except when she falls off."

"Never mind," said Marfa. "You stayed on in between."

"Alexander has to teach Emmie and Herbie to jump now," said Sophie. "I think he got committed to that this evening."

"Yeah, well—maybe," said Alexander.

"Not maybe at all! You can't tell stories like that and not expect them to—"

"What stories?" asked Marfa.

"Well, first of all, it was about his criminal tendencies," said Sophie with a snort of laughter. "But he covered up for that pretty well, I thought. Then he got into how a pony could jump a six-foot fence—a nearly six-foot fence—"

"Oh yes, I know that story," said Marfa. "It was a six-foot fence."

"And then about how the horse ate mashed potatoes."

"Mashed with salt," said Marfa promptly. "I know it was a six-foot fence because I was there when he measured it."

"I never seen no one who could ride like Benedict before or since," said Alexander.

"You should have seen him in the rodeo, Sasha."

"You did?" asked Alexander.

Sophie perceived that she had made a fatal mistake. They were treading the edge of the volcano again.

Marfa merely nodded. But Sophie saw the flame in her eyes.

"I'd like to have seen it too," said Alexander. "Not that there's much ridin' in a rodeo," he added. "It's mostly just stayin' on."

"Or falling off," said Marfa sharply.

"Yeah. I heard he got hurt real bad."

"Oh, you heard about that, did you?" She was sitting up straight in her chair. "What else did you hear, Sasha?"

"They say maybe he didn't fall," said Alexander somberly.

Sophie thought of Alexander talking to Annie in the bar. The slight feeling of unreality she had had then returned. It seemed he didn't know anything at all.

Marfa wasn't going to leave it that way.

"Maybe he didn't," she was saying. "Maybe he didn't fall." Again she stood up. "I fell off a horse once myself," she said. "Did you hear about that too, Sasha?"

Sophie could hardly attend to what was going on. All of a sudden she was seized by a consuming rage, rage against the two of them, against them all. She hated Benedict, but most of all she hated their obsession with him. Whatever they told each other was lies and evasions. Marfa herself could only tell half the truth.

"It hurts like hell when you're pregnant!" she was screaming.

Alexander was staring into the mad face of his sister with horror. "Fallin' off?" he asked.

"Falling off! That's what I said, Sasha!"

Sophie was still grappling with her anger. She could not let them go on like this. But the anger paralyzed her.

Alexander stood up, looking bewildered, and then suddenly sad.

"Jesus, Marfa," he said. "I'm sorry."

"Stop being sorry!" cried Marfa. "This is not something for you to feel sorry about, Sasha! You have no right to feel sorry!"

Alexander still didn't understand. Marfa's idea of cosmic justice had not reached him. He was putting out his hands to touch Marfa, to comfort her.

In a moment Marfa was going to tell him all about it.

"Don't you know he's dead!" shouted Sophie. "Benedict is dead now! He committed suicide, and it doesn't have anything to do with you!"

It was like sheet lightning on a summer's day. She saw their white faces, heard the echo of her scream.

Alexander's arms were just about to close around Marfa, and she had her hands already raised to push him back. They stood there in tableau, staring at her.

"He hung himself. With his belt. In a prison. Where he was being held for trial. Don't you know this, Marfa?"

She knew, all right. But she was determined to bury it beneath the load of her own guilt.

"He killed somebody. He murdered a woman, Marfa. A woman—"

A woman a little like me. A fair-skinned, light-haired woman, a naïve woman, a woman who was good for him. A woman who trusted him enough to want to have a baby. But it wasn't your fault, don't you see, Marfa? For this you were not responsible. It was she whom he killed, not you.

Now nearly fainting, gasping in her hurry to say it all before they could interrupt her, she continued, "He beat her to death. He killed her with his boots. They found him with her. He even told them he did it. He was high on something—they say he was drunk, too. Maybe that was going to be his defense."

The screaming and pleading went on all night. They had been in a cheap hotel somewhere in Montana. The other boarders told how it sounded like they were making love—they made love that way. There were parts of this story one could never forget, no matter how hard one tried.

The noise of sobbing went on until morning. Benedict went to sleep then. Went to sleep on the bed beside her while she bled to death in the hemorrhage brought on by miscarriage. Could he really have slept, or was it evasion, drugged indifference to what he had done, now that she was too weak to cry out?

"Did he really care?" Sophie demanded loudly. Was that the motive for the suicide? One could question it.

"Maybe he jumped from a horse once," she asserted, looking into Marfa's darkened pupils. "Maybe he did that. And, oh yes, I do believe he wanted to die."

It had certainly been his hand that suspended the belt. But it was one thing to die for remorse, and quite another to die for fear of life in prison. Couldn't he foresee what even the other prisoners would think of his crime? Perhaps Benedict just knew when the end of the road had come for him, and chose to make that last flamboyant gesture for his audience.

"Masochism!" cried Sophie. "He fed on it! Sometimes it was *his* masochism. He was really able to take you in, wasn't he? But other times it was *your* masochism. He liked hurting people. He picked on people who let him. Like Mary, that woman of his—only that time he went too far."

But the real victim, Sophie felt, was Annie. Annie wasn't playing any roles. She was the real person in Benedict's life, the only one he couldn't make into a corrupted symbol of what was wrong with him. And she suffered for it right down to the line, right down to the miserable, sodden ceremony in the prison yard at Missoula, where the chaplain couldn't remember Benedict's tribe or the name of the woman he had killed. Annie was there, a lone hitchhiker from Canada, to watch them shovel her brother underground.

"I hate him!" cried Sophie. "I hate him for what he did to you all, but especially for what he did to Annie. You ought to hate him now too!"

Her outburst had been directed at Marfa. Now she watched as Marfa reached out with a shaking hand for the pack of cigarettes upon the table. Detached, almost emptied of emotion, although the tears still poured down her cheeks, she saw Marfa struggle to light a match, fumbling with the matchbook.

She could not look at Alexander now.

It was all that she had sworn she would never do. Even when she had bleakly contemplated the years of lies she would have to endure in her marriage, Sophie had never considered this as an alternative. It went against her grain, the closemouthed Canadian Scot in her. It was against her principles; people found their own paths around the hard truth. What she had against Robert was that he could never leave alone; he had always to know and to tell. But now she had done this herself.

Somehow she had become involved. At first she had

been merely a voyeur, a thrill-seeker in this legend that dominated them, that they had invented. She remembered how curiosity had led her on, curiosity that she pretended was jealousy or some other emotion. The tears gathered in her eyes as she realized what a fool she had been. These people were stronger than she was, a race of giants, yet she had just dealt them a mortal wound.

Yet she had not done it maliciously; it had been without thought of the consequences, an impulse. It had seemed somehow necessary just then to tell the truth at last, to save Alexander from Marfa's truth, which was, after all, another lie.

Clinging to this thought, she stood before them.

Marfa spoke. Her voice was light, dry. "Who told you?" she asked.

"Annie," said Sophie.

"Annie? Annie told you about Benedict?"

Sophie nodded.

"But you don't know her. You haven't seen her in years," Marfa said disbelievingly.

Alexander cleared his throat.

"Sophia's been seein' Annie," he said.

Marfa stared hard at Sophie for a moment. Surprised, Sophie met her eyes.

"You have, have you?" said Marfa. "I can hardly believe that."

"Annie's comin' to our wedding," said Alexander.

Sophie was touched by his gentle, stubborn intervention. Perhaps he could forgive her, then, for what she had told him?

"I suppose Sophie invited her," said Marfa sarcastically.

"Yeah, she did."

"Christ! Okay, she did. Did you?" asked Marfa directly.

"Yes," said Sophie, suddenly embarrassed.

"And she really talked to you about . . . all that?"

"Yes, she did."

They looked at each other in silence for a moment. Sophie was beginning to see why this was so important.

"Annie talks about him. She says she likes to," Sophie said. "She knows all about it. And Annie doesn't lie."

"Maybe she doesn't forgive," said Marfa.

Sophie laughed suddenly. She knew what the answer was.

"Did you ever ask her?" she said.

They were silent again. At last Marfa turned away. Sophie was feeling the awful misery of reaction. What could she say that would ever heal this wound?

Alexander said, "You remember when we built them sweat lodges, Mashenka?"

Marfa swung around aggressively, back toward him.

"Benedict, he had a dream," he went on. "You were supposed to have a dream, that was the idea. It was mostly about you."

"No, it wasn't!" Marfa exclaimed.

"Yes, it was." Alexander took a step forward, closing the distance between them. "There was an eagle in it. That was you. And a buffalo, that was me. Annie, she was a ground squirrel. We were all in it, but you were the eagle."

"Sasha, you fool! We were just kids!"

"Yeah, well, but he was an eagle too. Don't you see what I mean?"

Marfa burst into a bitter laugh that turned to tears.

"You and him were one of a kind. So what if he's dead, Marfa? He dreamed that dream," said Alexander.

Marfa let him put his arms around her now.

"There's no one like you, Sasha," she cried. "No one else would remember that!"

They were both ignoring Sophie utterly now. At last he said, "I never should have told you. Maybe that was what I did wrong."

"It wasn't your fault, Sasha!"

"Yeah, but we weren't supposed to tell the dream."

"That has nothing to do with it!" Marfa withdrew herself from his embrace. She sat down at the table again.

"It doesn't matter, Sasha," she said coolly, a moment later. "That's all over and gone. Benedict is dead now."

"Yeah." Alexander sat down in the chair beside Sophie. She saw that he was still in the grip of a strong emotion. Uncertain what it was, and in her misery, not caring, she sat still, listening to Marfa.

"That whole dream business was bullshit," Marfa said, now completely calm. "First of all, he read about it in a book. I bet you think his grandfather told him, Sasha."

"Well, he did."

"No, he didn't! His grandfather wasn't even alive when Benedict— Besides, I read the book myself."

"Well, we made them sweat lodges, anyway," said Alexander obstinately, "whatever you think."

"You didn't dream anything!" said Marfa triumphantly. "I don't think he did either."

Sophie could hardly believe her ears. Quarreling again? And over this? In the light of what she had told them, how could they? It was almost as though nothing had happened. Where did they get this monstrous energy?

A light footstep was heard outside on the gravel. An instant later the back door clicked open. It was Tim.

"Hullo, Sasha," he said, surprised. He looked around at them, slinging the rucksack off his shoulder. "And the bride!"

"You again," said Marfa.

"Oh yeah. I can't leave forever, you know," said Tim agreeably. He went over and gave Sophie a civilized kiss on the cheek.

"I guess you couldn't leave that crop in the garden," said Marfa.

"Or my old woman, maybe." Tim turned around. "Sven gone?" he asked.

"You don't hear that damn guitar of his, do you?"

"Good timing." Tim grinned.

"Let's go home," said Sophie piteously. "I want to go home, Alexander."

"Sure," said Alexander. Then he said, "The wedding is on the fifth, Tim."

"Then I'll be there, I guess," said Tim, glancing at Marfa.

Marfa raised her head, but to Sophie's amazement she said nothing to this, nothing at all.

Alexander drove home in silence. Sophie, too, said nothing, pursuing her thoughts. What had happened, then? What had she accomplished in her rashness? At first it had seemed as though it made a difference, that her cry of *I hate him!* had penetrated their absorption. But then they had turned to quarreling over whether Benedict had had a dream once.

Could she never be free of Benedict?

Alexander got out of the truck in the farmyard and, still without saying anything, led her down the line of granaries to the edge of the field. He lit a cigarette, looking out over the rows of cabbages, silvery in the moonlight. They stood apart.

Of course Marfa had already known. She chose to hide her eyes in her own story, which was terrible enough in its way. But Alexander—why had he made no protest? Surely he ought to have cried out against her that it could not have happened.

He was still silent.

"You knew," said Sophie at last. She spoke dully; she was very tired now. "You must have known all the time."

Alexander blew a plume of smoke out over the moonlit field.

"That was another thing I didn't see how to tell you," he said.

Sophie looked at him, astonished. "Tell *me*?" she said.

"Who told you?" she asked a moment later.

"I read it in a newspaper," he replied. "Some guy way

up on the Arctic islands was gettin' a hometown paper from Montana. It gave Benedict's name, said he came from Canada."

"You mean you just ran across it like that?"

"I read that newspaper through, over and over again. It told all about it. I guess it was a big thing for one of them little towns."

"So that was how you knew," said Sophie flatly. She could not understand him at all.

"After that I came back," continued Alexander.

"Because he was dead? Was that why you came back?"

"I got to thinking about all that happened," he said.

"About Annie?" Sophie asked cautiously.

"About her, yeah. But about all of it. That stuff Marfa was tellin' you about tonight, too."

"How did you know about that?" asked Sophie, startled. It seemed that her attempts to protect him from Marfa had been wasted too.

"It was in the dream," he said remotely.

"What?" Sophie was infuriated. "Alexander, don't you realize—? He hurt her! He abused her!"

"I know." He now turned around and grasped her by the shoulders, stamping his cigarette out underfoot. "You don't understand, Sophia. I know what he was like."

"You do?" Sophie was still quivering with the return of her intense emotion of the evening. She lifted her face up aggressively.

"He came at me," Alexander continued as though she had not spoken, "down by the bridge. I had nothing, Sophia, and he was usin' his boots. If he'd had a knife— It wasn't fightin' he was after, it was murder, like it was him or me. I never told no one but Marfa about that. I warned her."

He was still holding on to her shoulders.

"That was when I told her about the dream," he said.

The dream. Sophie looked at him perplexed. Benedict's dream had nothing to do with this.

"My dream," said Alexander. "I had a dream, too, that time—when we built them sweat lodges. It was about him. Now I think about it, I must have seen even then how he hated me. It wasn't just later, because of Annie gettin' pregnant. It was everything, all along."

Sophie realized that he was right about this, too. It astonished her that he knew.

"What was the dream like?" she asked.

"It was him killin' me," said Alexander. "When I woke up I couldn't believe he'd do that. But when he came at me down by the bridge, it was like I'd seen it before. I'd seen he could."

Sophie understood, now that she was finally hearing from Alexander what she had received in vicarious form from all the others. She was listening, spellbound and a little tense, but he showed no signs of breaking off his confession.

"But here's the thing I never told nobody at all, Sophia. I could have hurt him that time. I could have hurt him real bad. It was *me* that could have killed *him*, and he knew that. I was the one that run away, but he knew I wasn't runnin' because I was scared. I guess the only thing I could do for him after that was get on the other side of the world."

A nighthawk had begun to produce its shrill, eerie night cry out in the wheatfield beyond the cabbages. Her face still uptilted to Alexander's, Sophie felt his breath on her lips, heard the even tones of his voice, and realized that this was one of those moments of communion that come rarely in a lifetime, especially one like Alexander's. He was telling her. He was finally telling her.

"If only there was something I could have done!"

"It wasn't your fault, Alexander!" Sophie pressed herself a little closer, but he seemed reluctant to let her comfort him. "Nobody could have saved him."

Nobody could save him; it was the truth. Guilt was

such a puny thing in the face of the forces of nature and society. One could only try to shield people, to preserve them from the tiny piece of guilt or responsibility that they bore.

It had been so easy for her to be herself, she reflected, and so hard for Alexander to become Alexander or Marfa to become Marfa. This was the land of their imagination—it was Benedict's land, usurped by farmers. But whether he liked it or not, Alexander was on the side of the white man, not the Indian. He had always been stronger than Benedict in every way. That was his guilt.

"When I came back," Alexander was saying hesitantly, "the thing I couldn't figure out was why no one was talkin' about it. Nobody said anything."

"Not even Marfa," murmured Sophie.

"I guess she knew."

Sophie said, "She wanted to tell you something else."

"Yeah." He rested his chin against her temple and stared out into the darkness over the field. Sophie knew that she was on Marfa's side in this. But she saw that she would not have to argue with him about it.

Something else occurred to her now.

"And Annie?" she said. "You've never talked to Annie at all, have you, Alexander?"

"There was that time in the bar with you."

"But that was all?"

"Yeah." He cleared his throat. "What you were sayin' to Marfa about Annie tonight—see, I've been thinkin' ever since I came back how maybe I'd have to tell her."

Sophie raised her head and they looked into each other's eyes.

"Then you—you kind of made friends with her," he went on, "and I was thinkin' how I'd got to tell you."

Sophie trembled and he put his arms around her.

"But every time I got started talkin'," he said, "I didn't see how to go on."

"Annie knew. She knew all the time!"

"Yeah, but the best thing," he said slowly, "the best thing was she told you."

Sophie felt a warm flood of relief and happiness. It had been in her power to make some difference after all. She was in the story herself now, not its helpless audience. She had been Annie's messenger to Alexander.

And she was free of Benedict forever.

"Don't cry, Sophia. Oh, please don't cry. We just had to talk about it sometime."

20

The Drought Continues

Days passed in the listless heat. They were beginning to lose the crop. They worked like slaves in the garden now, not in hope of compensation for the dying wheatfields, but to allay the claustrophobic suffocation of the drought. The land was like a furnace.

Sophie had retired to herself somewhat. It was not only the imminence of her marriage and the oppression of the drought. There was something she had to do. She knew that only she could do it, but she was afraid, terribly afraid, that she could not do it well.

She had not seen Annie again. But Annie was expecting her to do this thing.

"Alexander," she said, approaching him one evening after supper. Alexander was testing the well. He was working over the pump.

"Water's still comin'," he said. "That's a good well."

"Alexander, have you ever met Benedict—your son Benedict?"

Alexander stood back from the wellhead, putting his hands in his pockets. "I've seen him," he replied guardedly.

A surge of jealousy shot through Sophie. His very reserve made her jealous. However, she was prepared for this.

"When did you see him?"

"I went to the school closin'," said Alexander. He still was not looking at her.

"Oh," said Sophie flatly. "So that was why you went to the school closing."

"Well, yeah. I was pickin' you up, too."

"And that other time you picked me up at school?" she said softly. "You waited in the parking lot. Was that to see him, too?"

"Yeah."

"I see," said Sophie. "I thought I'd go visit Annie tonight. I think you should come." She noticed the coldness in her voice uneasily.

Alexander looked up anxiously. "I've still got some things to do around here," he began.

But Sophie could not have this, either. Alexander wanted Benedict, and Benedict needed Alexander. That they might come together someday without her was a thought she could not endure.

"I think you ought to come," she repeated. "He's your son, Alexander. You see? I really don't mind." This was not entirely true. But everyone including Sophie herself was going to be made to believe it.

"Maybe I could come later."

"In that case, you can bring the beer."

Annie's truckdriver husband, Tom, was at home. He was rather nice, to Sophie's relief. He was a Cree fron Ontario, as it turned out, large and easily friendly, with a handsome pockmarked face. He paid a lot of attention to Thomas. Sophie liked him for this.

Tom and Annie were putting in a hot-water heater. They were installing it in a closet between the kitchen and bathroom, and Tom had been busy all day making alterations on the closet.

The fact that Annie did not already have hot running water seemed strange to Sophie. The Reserve had everything—a huge recreation complex, including an Olympic-size swimming pool—and yet the houses didn't have hot water. It was like stepping out of Canada into the United Arab Emirates.

Thomas was reading the directions for lighting the boiler. The closet was small and awkward; big Tom, with his truck driver's frame, could not squeeze inside. Sophie had her hands over her ears so that she wouldn't hear the explosion.

"Gimme another match, Dad," said Thomas. Sophie closed her eyes as well. "I can't see how this thing works."

"Got the valve on?"

"Yeah, but—"

"Well, for heaven's sake turn it off while you're thinking about it!" cried Sophie.

Thomas crawled out on a gust of gas.

"I think it got on upside down," he announced.

"That ain't possible unless we got the whole thing upside down."

Sophie cautiously took her hands off her ears. She now heard the distinctive rattle and squeak of the farm truck drawing to a halt outside. Benedict wasn't around, which seemed rather a pity, now that they came to it. He had disappeared earlier with Vicky. On the other hand, Alexander was going to be very busy with the hot-water heater for the next while, she could see that.

"Is that Sasha?" asked Annie, also listening.

"I think so." Sophie suddenly did not want to participate. Alexander could look after himself. She squatted down beside Thomas in the closet doorway. "Maybe I can—"

Tom and Annie were diverted. Alexander's footsteps came scrunching around the house to the back door. Sophie squeezed herself between the water heater and the wall.

"Hi, Tom! Hi, Sasha! Hi, Annie!" she said to herself.

"Hi, Sophie," said Thomas, looking puzzled.

"Hi, Thomas," said Sophie, grinning. She lowered herself on one elbow. The instructions were upside down, no doubt about it.

"Hello, Annie," she heard Alexander saying.

"Hello, Sasha. This is—"

"Hey!" shouted Sophie. "This thing is lit!"

"What?" said Thomas, trying to crawl in across her hip.

"You must have lit it, Thomas."

"How could I of? The directions is on upside down."

"Well, you did."

"Let's see."

"Don't touch it! Don't do anything!" Sophie squirmed backwards, pushing Thomas out ahead of her. "Thomas lit the hot-water heater," she explained to Alexander.

"Yeah, this is Thomas," said Annie, looking pleased.

"How can that little light heat all that water?" Thomas asked Sophie.

"That's the pilot light. You have to wait a little while for the—"

Pphut! said the closet.

Sophie jumped. "You see?" she said. She was much happier than the occasion warranted. It was just too bad it had been Thomas, not Benedict, who had been so clever.

"You brought that beer along to look at, or is it to drink?" Tom was saying pleasantly.

"Oh yeah. Well—"

Probably Benedict would show up on his pony. That would be the last straw. Or was there such a thing as the first straw?

". . . drivin' all month. So then I come home and I'm a plumber," Tom was explaining.

"Got it all hooked up?" Alexander was taking an interest. Sophie stole a glance at him. He was looking as calm as ever. He followed Tom out of the kitchen to see the pipes in the bathroom.

Annie gave Sophie a beer.

"Maybe Thomas will go to college," Sophie remarked.

"If he gets grade three," said Annie.

"I got grade three, Ma."

"Oh yeah. School's over, isn't it?" Annie spoke of this as of some remote event, like a moon landing.

"I guess Thomas and I must have noticed that," said Sophie.

". . . tape," said Tom, in the hall.

"I've got some tape in the truck, come to think of it." She heard Alexander coming their way again.

Sophie looked casually at the case of beer. They each had one, that made four; and four into twelve went three times. It was a hot night. Allowing fifteen minutes per beer, subtract five for the one they were already drinking, that made forty minutes left in this visit. If Benedict didn't show up, that was just too bad. Too *damn* bad, Sophie corrected herself.

Tom stopped to put his empty bottle in the cardboard beer carton on the table, and Sophie mentally subtracted another ten minutes from the total as Alexander approached the back door.

"I've got the water-pump pliers too, since I was workin' on the—" he was saying over his shoulder.

"Ma!" shouted Benedict, bursting in through the screen door with Vicky.

Sophie's heart gave a sick jolt and she averted her

eyes. So there they were, in each other's arms already. She looked up again, unable to bear not knowing what they were like together.

They were standing three feet apart, but they were looking at each other. There was no question that Benedict knew who he was looking at, too.

Vicky had gotten behind him and was clinging to one leg.

"For God's sake, Bennie—" Tom began uneasily. Sophie knew exactly how he felt.

"Are you . . . Sasha?" asked Benedict.

Alexander nodded.

Vicky whimpered and clutched Benedict fiercely from behind.

"Ouch!" said Benedict. "Hey, Vick, don't be scared!"

"Come here, Vicky," said Tom.

But Benedict had already turned around to detach her.

"There's nothing to be scared of," he explained. "It's just—Sasha." He looked over his shoulder at Alexander shyly as he knelt down beside the little girl.

"Vicky should be in bed," said Tom to Annie.

"Oh yeah," said Annie, with a faintly sarcastic smile.

"I'll take her," said Benedict quickly, as Vicky made a louder and more threatening noise. "Hey, Ma, we sold three tickets tonight, Vick and me."

"Tickets?"

"Tickets to the rodeo," said Benedict. "We're sellin' 'em," he added by way of explanation, picking Vicky up and carrying her in the direction of the hallway. Sophie saw how confidently Vicky's arms closed around his neck.

"Rodeo?" Annie looked over at Sophie with a shrug.

"Yes," said Sophie, clearing her throat. "I think there's a rodeo in the Grove. I saw the—"

"You got that tape on the back of the pickup?" Tom asked Alexander. Benedict had disappeared with Vicky.

"Tape?" said Alexander. "Oh yeah." He looked at

Sophie, then at Annie, then at Sophie again. "Maybe . . . I think I'll . . ." He made an uncharacteristically clumsy movement in the direction of the hall.

"I guess so," said Annie.

"Not a bad idea," said Sophie. "I'm going to get the tape." She went outside quickly.

Remembering Alexander with Marfa's children, she did not doubt that he was going to do just fine. He would probably break the ice with a Benedict story and follow that up with another Benedict story. Didn't anyone tell Sasha stories?

"Here's the tape," said Thomas, rummaging around on the back of the truck.

"Good," said Sophie. "Hey, Thomas, do you know what a mudman is?"

As the days went on, not thinking about her impending marriage became almost a full-time occupation for Sophie.

"I think I'll go to Victoria first," said Mrs. Ware, consulting a sheet of timetables. "Although real-estate prices are high on the Island, they say."

Sophie salted her breakfast eggs mutely.

"Are you listening, Sophie?"

"What? Oh yes. Vancouver Island. Very cool."

"High prices, I said," Mrs. Ware repeated impatiently. "Now, today I thought we'd start to really pack up this place. I've done a few little things, but—"

"Are you taking the furniture with you?" asked Sophie, hardly understanding what she was being told.

"No, but for a start, I'm emptying my bedroom and having it painted tomorrow, washing down the basement, and giving away all your father's clothes."

"Oh."

"Do you think Alexander would like to have his pocket watch from the Buffalo Jump Fire Volunteers, or shall I give it away, too?"

"Give it away? To Alexander?" said Sophie stupidly.

"I wouldn't be giving it away if I gave it to Alexander, would I? Thank heavens! Here he is. Talking to you is like talking to the wall. Alexander, would you like to have Sophie's father's pocket . . . ?"

Sophie followed her mother around in a fog, doing her share of the labor but taking no initiatives. When they consulted her on the color of the bedroom walls, she looked from one to the other, her eyes blank with terror.

"Yellow is a nice color," Alexander suggested helpfully.

"For a bedroom?" said Mrs. Warc doubtfully. "I was thinking of a nice pinky white or an oystershell—"

"Sophie goes good with yellow," he said. "Like that yellow dress she was wearin' to school."

"Well, it's going to be your bedroom!"

That evening, after Alexander had gone home, Mrs. Ware sat Sophie down for a good old-fashioned talk.

"I know it isn't the same nowadays, dear," she said, putting a tiny glass of sherry into Sophie's hand and leading the way to the front room. "When I was married . . ." She sighed, and Sophie sat up alertly on the sofa where they had both been impelled to go by some inner law of nature governing such conversations.

"Well . . . even then," Mother conceded, "you know, your father and I had kissed each other. Of course we didn't go much further than that."

"Oh yes, oh yes," whispered Sophie. "Of course." She thought with love of her father, hoping that he had really gone much further than that.

"Now all that has changed," said Mrs. Ware firmly. "I know that you've had . . . experiences . . . and . . ."

"Do you, Mother?" Sophie gave her a wide-eyed look and went back to the kitchen for the sherry bottle.

As she returned, she noticed in passing the absence of the Dresden shepherdess on the mantel. "Where's my shepherdess?" she demanded.

"I washed it," said Mrs. Ware. "Pay attention, dear. I'm trying to tell you something."

Trying desperately to pay no attention at all, Sophie overfilled her sherry glass, slopping sherry all over her fingers.

"I've been watching you, darling, and I think you're going into this because you feel you must marry someone, and of course you want to have children. Now, I'm not saying you're not fond of—"

"Alexander," said Sophie, supplying the name.

"But you see," said Mrs. Ware brightly, "he is really much more in love than you are."

"Who told you?" asked Sophie suspiciously.

"He said so himself in front of his mother and father the other night, which must have been very difficult for him. Now you, on the other hand, are acting quite often as though you didn't like him at all."

Sucking the drops of sherry off her fingers, Sophie stared at her mother. This interpretation had never occurred to her. It had seemed to Sophie that every wild action she had taken during the last month and a half must have revealed her hopelessly deep in the toils of love and desire.

"But I want you to know that this feeling of fondness you have for him now will increase until you do love him, if you work on it. Alexander will make a very good husband, even if that isn't apparent to you just yet."

"He will?" said Sophie vacantly. The china lamp with the two swans on it had disappeared, she noticed now.

"Yes, Sophie. And after you have a baby, *that* side of things will become less important to him, and Alexander will settle down. So you don't need to worry about it."

"My God!" said Sophie, darting a mental glance at this appalling vision. "But—you didn't have me until you were married to Dad for ten years!"

"Well, but it wasn't like that with us, Sophie!" said

Mrs. Ware, scandalized. "Your father and I were both very much in love!"

Again remembering her father tenderly, Sophie was immensely relieved to hear this.

"And now, another thing—"

"No! No other things!" shouted Sophie. "Please, Mother!" She sprang up and went to the door, suspending her flight in the doorway for a moment.

"Oh, very well," said Mrs. Ware crossly. "I know you young people nowadays think it's all so different, but—"

Sophie fled.

"But I can assure you, it's just the same!"

On her wedding morning, Sophie lay in bed as long as she could, the smell of fresh paint in her nostrils. When she opened her eyes, it was to an unfamiliar yellow. Her own room had been gutted, and Mrs. Ware had insisted on sleeping there. Looking around at the walls, Sophie realized that from now on it was to be like this: all that was known would be unknown, while this horrifying strangeness would gradually become ordinary.

She got up miserably and put on the dress she intended to be married in. It had been laid out the night before, a flimsy summer thing that languished foolishly across the chest at the end of the bed. The shoes she decided to forgo until the last minute. It was already an unbearably hot day.

Mrs. Ware was frying bacon in her dressing gown and did not seem anxious to talk. Sophie realized that these changes must be even worse for her, although she was unfairly disposed to make her mother the instigator of it all. She drank her juice and went out into the sunshine, feeling oppressed.

The horses regarded her gravely, motionless beside each other, only moving back a little as she approached.

Along the road, a puffing trail of dust signified the

arrival of Alexander in the truck. Sophie wanted at least to look picturesque in her gloom; she struck a pose by the fence. Then, as the truck turned up the driveway and attained the yard, she made a run for the far end of the barn, too undecided about which was her real attitude and which the pose to stick it out. The sight of Alexander at the wheel of the truck had sent a wave of embarrassed gladness from the pit of her stomach to her stupid brain.

"Sophia!" exclaimed Alexander, coming around the barn after her. "What's the matter? Are you scared?"

"Aren't you?" Sophie had taken refuge in the shadow of a grain dryer.

He did look a little haggard.

"I'm not scared of the wedding," he said. "It's Poppa's party that's makin' me nervous."

"But aren't you afraid of being married?"

"No." He gave her a slow smile. "I was lookin' forward to that."

He too was wearing his wedding clothes—the dark trousers of a suit, and a white shirt with the sleeves rolled up. A tie protruded from his breast pocket.

Sophie might have found this funny if she had not found it terrifying.

"Everything's going to be different," she said wildly. "It's already different!"

"But that's not bad. We're still goin' to be the same people."

"Oh no, we're not! We're not the same people at all—even though we think we are!"

"Well, I guess if we still think we're us, then we are still us," he replied, struggling with this a little. "We're us," he repeated softly. "Remember?"

"Yes," said Sophie, gulping. She allowed herself to be embraced, still in the shadow of the grain barn. It was very comforting to have him take her panic in hand like this.

She remembered that he was much more in love than she was.

"Didn't someone try to have a little talk with you last night?" she asked, tilting her head back to look at him. How could he be so calm when he was marrying a person he didn't love at all?

"Poppa kept me up all night drinkin'," he replied.

"Oh, I see. That's sort of the male equivalent of a little talk, I guess," said Sophie. She giggled suddenly, imagining Poppa on the subject of marriage.

"You're all excited, Sophia," said Alexander, kissing her smiling lips and smiling himself.

"Come on," he said a moment later. "I'm goin' to water them horses." He led her back to the paddock fence and leaned her against it firmly. The horses regarded this incuriously and backed a little farther away.

"What's wrong with them?" asked Sophie.

"Maybe they're shy about something."

"But they just stand there like that all the time," she protested. "They don't do anything."

Alexander balanced the bubbling hose on the lip of the trough and vaulted the gate. He advanced slowly, almost idly, on the horses, his hands in his pockets.

Ring whickered and backed into Rosi. He thrust her aside, almost as though he were telling her to get behind him, not taking his eyes off Alexander. Ring began to dance nervously on her little hooves, but still the stallion regarded the advancing man seriously.

"Be careful!" cried Sophie, catching herself in the impulse to shriek. She mounted the gate.

"It's okay," said Alexander. He stretched out his hand to Rosi, murmuring, "It's okay, isn't it?"

Rosi stepped forward, stretching his neck, his nostrils a little distended. This was too much for the mare, who whinnied wildly and fled. Rosi shuddered, still staring at Alexander, then wheeled and galloped after the mare. Sophie jumped into the paddock and ran up to Alexander.

"See? Look! Like I said!" he exclaimed. He seized her hand in excitement.

Rosi and Ring were galloping in tandem across the longest stretch of the field, their tails and manes streaming in the sunlight. When they reached the opposite fence, they wheeled in perfect accord and made off in the direction of the field farthest from the house, racing together, shoulder to shoulder.

"We shouldn't watch!" Sophie dragged on his hand. "We should go away and leave them."

"In a minute." Alexander was watching the loveplay of the horses keenly, a smile on his lips. "They don't care," he said, glancing at her sideways. "They just didn't see how to tell each other before."

Sophie felt a resurgence of that hot wave of feeling, and wondered as it overtook her whether she was going to faint.

"Jesus!" exclaimed Alexander in concern. "I forgot about that hose!" He whirled Sophie around and swept her before him back to the fence, lifting her up onto the gate, and went to deal with the water flowing freely over the edge of the trough.

"I knew I was goin' to get 'em dirty, but somehow I just couldn't put on anything else this morning," he remarked ruefully, looking down at the flecks of mud on his trousers after he had stopped the hose.

"Me too," said Sophie.

"Goin' to marry me in bare feet?" he inquired, jumping back over the gate and watching Sophie swing her legs up and around.

"Come and eat breakfast, you two!" called Mrs. Ware.

"I'm not sure I can eat anything, Vera," said Alexander, leading Sophie inside.

"Well, it's a good idea to try now. Lunch will be even worse," said Mrs. Ware cheerfully.

Sophie whimpered. They were getting married at one-thirty.

"And don't forget, you're going to be drinking at that reception."

"Yeah," said Alexander glumly.

"I think the weather's changing," said Mrs. Ware. "It's almost muggy. It might rain, do you know?"

"Maybe it'll be a short party," he said, looking at his plate, but making no move to pick up his knife and fork.

Sophie sipped her coffee, gagging slightly.

"What a pair!" said Mrs. Ware, laughing at them. "Both of you are all dressed up!" She began to butter a piece of toast calmly.

Mrs. Ware finished packing her luggage with Sophie's dutiful assistance. Meanwhile, Alexander moved in: a saddle, two suitcases, a northern sleeping bag, a box of tools. That, at least, seemed rather simple to Sophie. Probably it was everything he owned. She watched carefully, but he made no frightening innovations. The sleeping bag went in the attic, the tools and saddle in the barn, and the suitcases in the yellow bedroom.

He remained in there for some time, but when Sophie went to find him, he was not unpacking. He was making the bed.

She watched him from the doorway.

The room was completely empty of objects for personal use, aside from the two suitcases and Sophie's shoes. A pair of white curtains, hastily made out of an old sheet, blew in at the open window. The paint smell was going away.

This tidy, bachelorish action Alexander was engaging in struck Sophie as both touching and somehow ominous. She realized that sometime later that day, she was going to be brought to this room, to this very bed, and the primal act of human social affairs was to be enacted there. In the absence of an old Baba and a chorus of virgins and revelers to prepare the way, Alexander was simply making all ready for that scene.

Watching him, she was reminded that Alexander was a descendant of primitive Central European tribes that had made a two-thousand-year-old resistance to the invasion of cruel, slant-eyed Tartar barbarians from the East and cruel, pale-haired Teutonic barbarians from the West, preserving as an ancient form of sanctuary certain customs relating to the virginity of the marriage bed and the conservation of the wheatfields. Almost spellbound, Sophie felt that she was witnessing a rite.

Alexander now lay face downward on the fully made bed. For a horrified moment she thought he was praying, perhaps to a goddess of fertility, but then she realized that he was probably measuring its length. It was true that his shoe-clad feet stuck out over the end of the bed six inches or more.

Alexander rolled over, shifting up so that his shoulders rested on the pillow, and Sophie dodged behind the doorframe. When she looked again, he was staring at the ceiling.

She paused and he raised his head.

"I was just makin' the bed."

"It's too short for you," said Sophie, feeling her nerves jump.

"Come here."

She went over and sat down beside him, her eyes lowered, feeling that she looked like an unwilling virgin, but unable to do anything else.

"I'm scared as hell," said Alexander. "I was lyin' before."

Sophie felt her eyes slip sideways, flirtatiously, demurely. There was no normal way to deal with this, but that way.

"What if I died—like your Dad?" he said.

"Then I'd be a widow," said Sophie incredulously.

"At least you'd have the place," he went on. "But with all them kids—"

"Maybe I'd marry again. You'd marry again, wouldn't you, Alexander?" she said piteously.

"I don't know," he replied.

"Oh my God! What are we talking about!" cried Sophie. She threw herself down against him.

"I was only thinkin', Sophie," he said, and she felt his heart beating, warm and sure under her cheek.

"We'll be all right, Alexander," whispered Sophie, kissing him. "We won't die. We'll be fine."

"Sophie!" Mother could be heard approaching.

"I guess so," said Alexander, now clasping her and not letting go. "I guess it'll be all right," he repeated dubiously.

"Of course it will!" Sophie struggled to free herself. "I swear it."

"Oh, *there* you are," said Mother. She peered at them mischievously. "Alexander, that bed is much too short for you!"

"Well, I guess it's just an ordinary-length bed," he said in surprise, sitting up with Sophie in the curve of his arm.

"My husband used to complain too," said Mrs. Ware. "He always said his feet froze on cold nights."

Sophie thought of her short, dapper father. It seemed impossible that his feet could have protruded unless he and Mother were sleeping in very odd positions, crosswise or at the end of the bed. It startled her slightly to realize that she had probably been conceived in this very bed.

"Sophie," Mrs. Ware went on, "I can't get that suitcase of yours to close."

"I'll sit on it," said Sophie, jumping up. "It always closes when I sit on it."

"I'll sit on it!" exclaimed Alexander. "It'll close for me!" He also leaped up.

"No, you can't!" cried Sophie, beating him to the door. "You'll crush it!"

"Not the way I'm goin' to do it!" he shouted, bounding down the stairs.

"My goodness," said Mrs. Ware, following placidly. "It's just that the lock doesn't work."

"We'll fix it!"

Alexander went home for lunch. He was going to pick them up at one o'clock sharp to take them into Buffalo Jump.

Sophie nibbled on a sandwich. She knew she was hungry; she was, in fact, very hungry, but the thought of Alexander at home with Momma and Poppa, unable to eat, stayed her hand. He had not eaten any breakfast, she remembered this clearly now.

"The main thing is that Alexander can take care of you," said Mrs. Ware. "I could never had agreed to it otherwise."

"You could never have—?" Sophie put down her sandwich.

"No, I couldn't have. Now tell me about this Indian woman who is going to be your bridesmaid," said Mrs. Ware coldly.

"Well . . . she's an old friend of Alexander's," Sophie began cautiously, already prepared for this question. She had been expecting it for over a week.

"You know that she had a child by him, do you, Sophie?"

"Of course I do!" said Sophie hotly. "And that's why—"

"Well, thank God he didn't marry her, at least," said Mrs. Ware. "He might have become—I don't know what!"

"And what about her?" asked Sophie passionately. "What became of her?"

"Sometimes I think you're still a little girl, dear."

"You too?" cried Sophie. "You and the class of '69? And all the rest of those horrible, cruel, stupid— You don't care about what happened to Annie! All you care about is the most—" She got up and rushed to the window.

"I only care about you, Sophie," said Mrs. Ware, beginning to cry.

Sophie realized that she had overreacted. How could you expect your mother to understand things like this when you had spent most of your life trying to conceal from her all the important facts about yourself? Mother had wanted to ask her about Annie before, no doubt, but could not bring herself to do it. But the way she saw it, she couldn't let Sophie go to the altar without knowing.

"Oh, Mother!" She turned around, bursting into tears of contrition.

"Sophie, darling!"

They clutched each other, weeping.

"These things just happen to young men, Sophie! You mustn't think he ever loved her the way—"

"You weren't really thinking of it like the Buffalo Jump Ladies' Auxiliary! How could I ever—"

Alexander entered the kitchen warily.

Sophie slumped into a chair. Mrs. Ware blew her nose.

"Is that your dress?" he asked Sophie doubtfully after a moment.

"What's wrong with it?" Sophie summoned the emotional energy to be alarmed.

"I've already seen it," he replied. "You were wearin' it this morning."

"Good heavens!" exclaimed Mrs. Ware. "Something blue! Sophie, have you got something blue?"

They were both maniacs. Mrs. Ware was now rummaging through the knife and silverware drawers for something blue. She found a piece of blue ribbon at last, and Sophie thrust it down the front of her dress.

"Let's go," Sophie said. "Or better yet," she added, "why don't you two just go along and I'll see you later. At the reception, maybe."

21

Just Married

The Bresnyachuk parents were already at the courthouse. Sophie suffered herself to be kissed on all sides, and then, leaving her mother to an extension of the same treatment, fled to a sterile bathroom on the second floor to gaze dismally at herself in the mirror.

"Come on, Sophie," said Marfa, entering briskly. "Your turn's coming."

"It's bubonic plague," said Sophie. "I looked it up. I have all the symptoms."

"Shut up, Sophie." Marfa dragged her away from the mirror.

"What are you doing here, by the way?"

"You'd better be glad I came, kiddo. I brought the best man."

"Tim? Oh good."

"Yeah, well, let's wait till after the party and see what we think then," said Marfa. "Here, for Christ's sake, put on some lipstick or something!"

Sophie applied some of Marfa's lipstick and had time to see that it combined with her pallor to make her look like a Rotary Club clown.

"Hurry up!" said Marfa impatiently, as Sophie slowly and fumblingly began to remove it with a paper towel.

The door opened quietly and Annie stepped in, looking entirely unfamiliar in a blue pantsuit with a blue polyester tie blouse. She stood there in silence, lighting a cigarette and putting out the match with an expert twist of her wrist that went very strangely with her apparel.

"Annie!" said Sophie, realizing that her last hope was gone when she saw the pantsuit.

"Annie!" said Marfa.

"Yeah," said Annie. She tilted back her head and looked at Marfa with an expression that was no expression.

"Jesus! Annie!" said Marfa, in tears.

For a moment they both seemed to have forgotten Sophie altogether. She saw again that there was an underlying web of things to which she did not belong and could never belong, even though she had been born here as surely as they. The wild children, who had ridden and played together—they all knew each other as she knew none of them. The idea that she could bring these two together out of their estrangement was laughable. They had never really been apart.

A moment later they were both looking at her kindly.

"All ready?" asked Annie.

"Let's go," said Marfa. "Buck up, Sophie. It only takes a minute."

Sophie was now in a very weakened condition. Her only experience that compared remotely with this was crossing from India into Pakistan with half a gram of hashish done up in her hair. This was much worse.

* * *

"Sign here."

"Congratulations, Mr. and Mrs. Bresnyachuk."

"Mrs. Bresnyachuk?"

"Come on, Sophie!"

"Well, just this once."

"Hip, hip, hooray!"

"Don't cry, Mother."

"My Sasha."

"Now we will have a party!"

"Don't cry, Momma."

"Everybody is coming!" cried Poppa grandiosely, including Annie and Tom, Marfa and Tim under the sweep of his arm. "Alexander, we must invite judge."

"No, Poppa, he's—"

"I will invite judge. Take darling girl and go, my son. We will bring Mother later. Also judge."

Alexander suddenly seized Sophie's hand and ran with her, taking the stairs in flying leaps. On the outside steps he caught her up bodily and raced for the truck.

A moment later, Sophie saw what he meant by this. A shower of rice hit their faces. The truck, once a sober and dignified old pensioner, was decorated with every emblem of Ukrainian marriage art, vintage 1954. Plastic roses twined around the bumpers. Shoes and boots dripped from handles and knobs. The words JUST MARRIED were sprayed on the side doors in shaving cream.

Still carrying Sophie, Alexander dodged the spread arms of the genie, Rudolph, and thrust her headfirst in the driver's-side door.

"You were expecting that!" she cried reproachfully, as he took off with a squeal of tires. Then she slid over to her side and hung out the window to wave. It had been rather exciting, after all.

Rudolph was dancing in the street, waving his arms, and shouting distantly, "Kiss h—!" as Alexander veered around the corner.

"My goodness," she said a moment later, and looked over at him timidly.

"Next time we do this, we'll go to Great Falls," said Alexander, still driving very fast.

Sophie edged back across the seat toward him.

"Are they followin'?"

"I can't see anyone."

"Russians!"

"That was doing it *right,* I guess," said Sophie thoughtfully.

"I can't stop, Sophia. They'll be onto us, the whole pack of them!"

"What would they do then?"

Alexander turned onto a back road out of Buffalo Jump. He glanced in the rearview mirror, then slowed down.

"For one thing," he said, switching off the ignition and letting the truck drift along the roadside. "They'd stop us doin' *this.*"

"*This?* Here?"

"Oh my God! Here they come!"

Alexander started in second gear and the truck was wrenched into an unhappy third half a minute later. Sophie wriggled her shoulders back into the sleeves of her wedding dress and carefully folded Alexander's suit jacket.

Alexander grinned. "I was gettin' there," he said.

"Where?" Sophie craned her neck to see behind. The whole cavalcade was following, honking, hooting, waving and shouting. The truck was considerably slower than their cars. "Where?" she repeated.

"To that piece of ribbon."

"Oh!"

"I was thinkin' about it all the time we were gettin' married."

What was *I* thinking about? Sophie inquired sorrowfully of herself. She remembered standing there, that was about all. Then she thought of Annie's radiant face, Annie looking at Alexander as she signed for Sophie.

Sophie sang happily:

"He promised to buy her a
bunch of blue ribbons,
He promised to buy her a
bunch of blue ribbons,
To tie up her bonnie brown hair!"

"Yeah, I'm still thinkin' about it!" said Alexander.

"I like to think about you thinking about it, anyway," said Sophie, settling back comfortably and ignoring the noise behind them. "My God, we got married, didn't we?" she said suddenly.

"Yeah. It wasn't something I'd do every day, though."

"Nor with just anyone, I hope."

"Hey, look at them clouds," said Alexander, as they drove westward into the uplands. "Maybe it is goin' to rain, after all."

The clouds did look like rainclouds, but they were still piling up behind the mountains a long way away. They had seen this before—so many signs of rain and never a drop fell; all washed away on the western slopes or dissipated in the relentless wind blowing overhead. The heat seemed overwhelming, unendurable. A Chinook tension was in the air. It might rain. But it was an Armageddon year. It could just as well snow or hail; even an earthquake seemed a possibility.

They pulled up into the Bresnyachuk dooryard slightly in advance of their retinue, which had been lulled into apathy by their decorous progress up to the Steamboat Lake road. At that point, Alexander, with a sudden wild Russian cry, had put his foot on the gas.

The honking, rocking, yelling cars came up the driveway. The screen door slammed as Luke came out of the kitchen, carrying a loaded tray. Robert and Madeleine peeked around from the picnic table. A menacing flock of geese began to move in from the pasture as in a World War II film of the SS on parade.

"Jesus! Poppa brought the judge!" exclaimed Alexander, raising his head from Sophie's upturned face as the wave broke over them.

A sort of panoramic party now began, as a crowd of laughing, back-slapping, loving people lined up to kiss and shake hands. Sophie was developing calluses on both cheeks. Mother was kissing her, then Tim, then Tom, then Momma, then Rudi, then Marietta, then Alexander's Uncle Alexei from Minnesota. Then Alexander was kissing her again, and fragments of conversation floated disconnectedly past her ears.

"Yeah, is steam canner. Take fish, clean him up good, and . . ."

"Well, of course, during the Depression we were *all* . . ."

". . . know Annie? Well, I'm her old man. These are my kids here, Vicky, Thomas, and Benedict."

"Oh, I see. Emmie! Herbie! Come here, and you can play with . . ."

"Do my poor old eyes deceive me, or is this my maiden dream Marfa Bresnyachuk . . . ?"

". . . good crop this year. Where? Oh, over in Bitter Root with my old lady, there."

"No, I'm a judge, actually, but I do have a little acreage myself, out by . . ."

"Not a patch of mustard in them fields now, yet when I started workin' for her dad . . . !"

"You are teacher with Sophia? Here is my son Luke. Is very good boy . . ."

A sudden, squealing, high-pitched note sounded from down the driveway, and a kilted piper paraded into the yard playing "The Campbells Are Coming" for the benefit of the descendants of the Duke of Argyle. He strode three times around the picnic table, making the full circle of Poppa and Mother; Mother was blushing furiously. Poppa never did things by halves.

"Now we drink!" cried Poppa enthusiastically, pressing a glass of vodka on Mrs. Ware and another on the piper. "Holding the throat open! Not closing the throat!"

". . . saw you last at a rodeo, didn't I, darling? After that you dropped out of my . . ."

"Yeah. Thomas is kind of shy. Not like . . ."

". . . can imagine what them caterpillarth were like at the thchool. In the kidth pocketth and tho on . . ."

"So naturally I am leaving all land to nephew Alexander. Is too bad Minnesota is so far from . . ."

"I don't want you to push me on the swings, Herbie! You can push Vicky. I want Benedict to . . ."

"You see, Sophie's great-great-grandfather came from Auchinleck and was actually the third cousin of . . ."

"Yes, I suppose you might say that law or divinity is the destiny of us Scots. My own father . . ."

"Canadian literature, did you say? Or did you say *Ukrainian* . . . ?"

". . . have to read another novel about a woman finding herself, I swear I'll . . ."

"Oh dear, what can the matter be?
Oh dear, what can the matter be?"

"Oh, I'm thinkin' about it, all right!"

With another excruciating preliminary shriek of the pipes, the piper made off down the driveway, weaving slightly and playing "Blue Bonnets Over the Border" with a good deal of quaint old Russian charm.

It was some time later that Sophie, long detached from Alexander, saw that Poppa was making a speech from the picnic table. He was actually standing on it, among the pickles, fish, ham, sausage, fat bacon, pirogies, cabbage rolls, vodka, beer, and champagne, gesticulating with both arms and crying out for silence in the three Slavic and two Germanic languages he spoke.

"It cures my heart," shouted Poppa, "to see my son marry such darling girl—beauty, rich, granddaughter of count! Pardon English! I am fighting Nazis as underground resistance in Warsaw! To Sophia, the bride, she lives long and happy!"

"I'll drink to that!" murmured a small voice in Sophie's ear. "Why not, after all?"

"And to groom, who is son of mine: let him remember how parents are careful, tell him, 'Sasha, my boy, is done this way, education, work hard, wait for right girl, is all paying off!' To Sasha!"

"Sophie, darling, have I got to drink to that?" asked Robert plaintively, refilling his glass from Sophie's.

"Wait, Poppa!" Now Marfa also leaped on the table. Sophie could see the wild gaiety in her face. She took a step forward and then, relieved, saw Alexander making his way through the crowd around the table. Marfa laughed down into his worried face.

"To my favorite brother!" she cried mockingly. "I leave him everything in my will!"

"If it isn't that he's taller than I am," whispered Robert, "what is it, then?" He drank again and threw his plastic tumbler carelessly over his shoulder.

"And to my sister-in-law, Sophie, the happily-ever-after girl who just married him!"

Several people in the crowd now surged forward, all longing to jump up on the picnic table, but Alexander thrust them back with his long arms and jumped up himself.

"To Momma!" he said. "And to Vera, Sophia's mother! And to your will, Marfa! And now to no more toasts!"

"No, another," said Marfa. "To the past!"

"And to the future!" Alexander could not resist going on any more than Poppa, who already had his mouth open for another speech.

Sophie pressed her glass into Robert's hand and made her way over to the picnic table.

"Alexander," she said. "Get down."

On the other side of the table, Momma was addressing some similar remarks to Poppa.

"Is no reason to put foot in plate!" she expostulated.

"Or to break a perfectly good jar of pickles," said Sophie to Alexander.

"You were talkin' to that guy over there," said Alexander sheepishly, getting down. "So I—"

"Whom you invited to this party," replied Sophie severely. "And now, we'll take this bottle here, and Marfa, if she'll only get down, too, and—"

At this moment the darkened sky above them split open with a rending crack of thunder. A gust of wind came out of nowhere and bore everything—cups, hats, glasses, paper plates, guests, napkins, and geese—before it across the lawn.

Alexander and Sophie were left embracing in a kind of eddy behind the picnic table.

"Rain!" said Alexander, raising his head and gazing upward. "Rain, Sophia!"

"Rain!"

And it began to rain.